One M

LOIS WALDEN has worked as writer and lyricist with a variety of major artists and composers including Dionne Warwick, Jane Fonda, and Charles Fox. As founder of the star studded singing group The Sisters of Glory, she has performed at the Vatican for the Pope. She co-produced the group's critically-acclaimed album, *Good News in Hard Times*, for Warner Bros, as well as writing and co-producing her solo album, *Traveller*. She was the lyricist for *American Dreams Lost and Found*, based on the book by Studs Terkel. Her life and music have been profiled on the CBS shows *Good Morning America* and *Sunday Morning*. Ms Walden is currently writing her second work of fiction.

One More Stop

LOIS WALDEN

Arcadia Books Ltd
15–16 Nassau Street
London W1W 7AB

www.arcadiabooks.co.uk

First published in the United Kingdom by Bliss Books, an imprint of Arcadia Books 2010
Copyright © Lois Walden 2010

A catalogue record for this book is available from the British Library.

ISBN 978-1-906413-61-3

Typeset in Garamond by MacGuru Ltd
Printed and bound in Finland by WS Bookwell

Arcadia Books supports English PEN, the fellowship of writers who work together to promote
literature and its understanding. English PEN upholds writers' freedoms in Britain and around the
world, challenging political and cultural limits on free expression. To find out more, visit
www.englishpen.org or contact
English PEN, 6-8 Amwell Street, London EC1R 1UQ

Arcadia Books distributors are as follows:

in the UK and elsewhere in Europe:
Turnaround Publishers Services
Unit 3, Olympia Trading Estate
Coburg Road
London N22 6TZ

in the US and Canada:
Independent Publishers Group
814 N. Franklin Street
Chicago, IL 60610

in Australia:
Tower Books
PO Box 213
Brookvale, NSW 2100

in New Zealand:
Addenda
PO Box 78224
Grey Lynn
Auckland

in South Africa:
Jacana Media (Pty) Ltd
PO Box 291784,
Melville 2109
Johannesburg

Arcadia Books is the *Sunday Times* Small Publisher of the Year

For My Sister

Prologue

Imagine. My mother enters. Quick, run into her outstretched arms … She lifts me above her head. I am six, seven, eleven. Higher. Higher still. I am locked inside her gaze. Suddenly, she lets me down gently, places my right hand on her quivering shoulder, my left hand around her skinny waist. We glide like skaters on fresh ice; one two three, one two three, one two three. So old-fashioned … Beat changes. Lindy… and a one two one two three four, one two one two three four, and on and on … and …

Exhausted, we sit down.

… Our dance is over.

She reaches for a pack of Camels hidden inside her polyester, lime-green housecoat. How she loves polyester.

'You can't smoke in here,' say I.

'*Why not?*' asks she innocently.

'There are rules.'

'*Like dancing.*' She lights up a cigarette.

'Not good for you.'

My mother shakes her head in despair, looks at the beige walls, lifts up her right foot, rests it on her left thigh, like a child about to tie her shoe for the first time. She snuffs out the cigarette on the bottom of her pink and grey fuzzy mule, flicks the butt across the room. She stands. The unspoken. Who leads? Who follows? She leads. I follow. And so it goes ... Our eternal dance ...

I prefer the slow dance. This is not completely true. Depends ... Age, place, time. History... It is always about history.

Road Map

> *'Humpty Dumpty sat on a wall,*
> *Humpty Dumpty had a great fall; had ... a ... great ...*
> *fall ...'*
> 'Then what happens?'
> *'Never mind. It's only a nursery rhyme.'*

'03

When Stuart Manly, the education director for The Actors
Cooperative, told me that I would be teaching in a town called
Beatrice, Nebraska, I could hardly wait to get there. Beatrice
was my mother's name. She had died nearly twenty years ago.
Her life was her undoing. Her death was my undoing. Maybe
I would find her in the streets of the town that was named after
her. Maybe it was our time to finally say goodbye.

'Don't you ever forget about me, baby.'

'I won't. I promise. I won't.'

When you long for something too much, you can convince
yourself you will not survive another second unless it happens
right now. But the more desperate you are, the more it is a
bona fide guarantee that you'll have to wait.

Stuart Manly made it clear. It would be a long journey to
Beatrice: '... primarily a Midwestern tour. You'll be preceding

the company. And isn't *O Pioneers* the perfect play for that part of the country?' He does not wait for my response. 'You start out in Mississippi, fly to Chicago, then it's Iowa, on to Colorado, next stop is Nebraska, maybe Montana, maybe not.'

Maybe I don't want the job. 'Sounds great.'

'Loli, we here at The Actors Cooperative are interested in you because of your varied writing skills and your unique musical talent. We feel teenagers will understand their ancestral heritage through your cutting-edge teaching methods.'

He has no idea what I do. 'Thank you, Stuart.'

'One second, Ms Greene.' He puts me on hold. 'I'm back.'

Hate hold. 'You know I don't deal with text.'

'We know. *And* you prefer contemporary literature.'

'No. Not at all. My strength is working with teenagers, dealing with contemporary *themes* and *issues*, so that they can understand themselves better through process and self-exploration.'

'Of course.'

Hope I don't have to deal with him. 'I look forward to working with you, Stu.' I don't want this job. I don't want *any* job. But … gotta get away, away from Simone. Think about my future, our future. What future? Always liked the road. Best part of being a performer was … the road. Discover who you are; not in relation to anyone, anything. The road.

My plane lands in Memphis approximately seven hours and eleven minutes later than my estimated time of arrival. I am too pissed off to get myself depressed, but as I drag my ruined red bag off the conveyor belt, I ask myself out loud what the fuck am I doing here? I am here to teach – a fact that boggles my mind.

'Mine too, honey.'

The little Enterprise rentacar bus drives at a leisurely pace to the parking lot, which happens to be fifteen minutes, as the crow flies, from the baggage claim area. At least the sleek, blue, almost new, made for you, 2003 Esprit is waiting for me. I am given my instructions by a good ol' young Mississippi boy, who clearly played fullback for Ol' Miss. His neck is twice the size of my underused, oversized, top of the line, green Gymnastic Ball.

I begin the drive. The wind blows my spiffy Enterprise automobile from one lane to another. A truck speeds by, at no less than eighty miles an hour, splatters slush on my windshield. My wipers get stuck. The rear-window defogger ceases to function. I am unable to see out of my rear window. But I can't stop. I have to get somewhere. I have a destination.

I arrive in Oxford, Mississippi at eleven p.m. Why am I here? For the kids … For the kid in me. My classes begin tomorrow. At some unforgiveable hour, I will attempt to wave my travelling teaching wand at a schoolroom filled with tired, toxic teenagers; to tap into their imaginations. Teaching is something that I have to do, want to do for those tormented teens, for myself, and finally for her.

'Thank you.'

'You are more than welcome.'

'Anything is possible, honey, if you want it badly enough, and you do it well enough.'

To love is to be free, to live is to die, and to hope is to get through. Tomorrow is what we wait for. Today is all I have. Tomorrow I just might get my ass onto another jumbo jet plane and fly away forever. Don't need to wonder what that's about.

'Honey, it's not about anything.'

It's about you. It's always about you.

The storm has let up. I want to get the lay of the land tonight. Christ! Go straight. Now turn right. Continue on ... What's the name of this road? Who cares. Follow signs to town square. There it is – lovely little square. What's that sign say? 'Ajax Diner.' Go there tomorrow. I bet it's not as good as the Beechwood Diner? That was the best diner that ever existed. Ever.

Time to find my southern sleep zone. Cannot wait to get my feather pillow out of my bag. Love sleep. Hope the sheets are polyester. Love polyester. Reminds me of her.

So, I'm currently comfy and cozy in my cabin in the Mississippi woods. We are talking a very southern world. It's foreign; not Baghdad, no bombs, no need to panic. I will survive.

Gloria Gaynor! Remember her? Disco-era dance diva. Where was I then? Having some forbidden sexual encounter somewhere, which then led to another unfortunate sexual encounter somewhere else. I *won't* do that anymore. Too old. Old age is scary. Mourn all that dies.

'Don't get sentimental. Mustn't wallow in the wasteland called yesterday or dream about tomorrow.'

Glad you could make it.

'Where's the party, hon? Don't get home too late.'

M-I-S-S-I-S-S-I ... Just spelling it gives me that home cookin' calm: mashed this, corn bread that, southern black-eyed peas, the bees knees, and double dippin' if you please. Can't wait to eat at the Ajax Diner. It will have to wait until after tomorrow's class.

Morning. Next day. A note is slipped under my door. I read

it out loud. 'Snow day. No school.' Hooray! Still feels like it did when I was ten or eleven. Crawl back into bed and doze my way to dreamland between those polyester sheets. I looked forward to those days of lollygagging in synthetic luxury.

Look through the frosted windowpane. Hell! There is only one quarter of an inch of ice on the ground. So, what's happened to that Civil War spirit?

'Why isn't there any school?' I ask.

'We are just not as courageous as we use to be, darlin',' replies my sexy southern hostess, who owns the log cabin where I currently reside.

Speak for yourself. I'm down here in fraught-with-Faulkner territory, flyin' by the seat of my polyester panties. Memories – those marvellous madcap adolescent memories. Let's not go there. How many times can you whisper 'I love you'?

And again I whisper, 'I love you.'

'*I certainly hope so, darling. I love you too.*'

Phone rings. 'What if someone dies?' says a disembodied voice on the phone. 'Someone you love has left you all alone. Are you prepared financially for a sudden death in your family? We can help you through this trying transition. No interest, money back guaranteed.'

'I'm visiting, you asshole!' Hang up. Don't talk to me about death. Talk to me about life. What are the survival tools needed for living in this world? I am well aware of the innumerable tricks for getting out of it. My mother was my mentor.

First period class. It is seven forty-five a.m. Exhausted. Can anyone learn anything at this hour? Homeroom teacher is out sick with shingles. I can see why... Let me tell you about the kids with their full hearts and deep fears. Most of them have conveniently forgotten that they ever had an imagination. They wallow in the wild wanderings of the mind without giving the mind much thought. Most of them hunger for at least one moment in which they might control those uncontrollable desires that are controlling them. These are the teenage years in a nutshell.

Hey, you over there! I am well aware that you are in the middle of some mid-teen masturbatory exploration. And you over there with the oily skin! I know that your little vulva is vibrating. I know that young Jake's wanger has been wigglin' in a wringin' wet Spalding sweat sock. Tell me, baby boy …who is she? One of the Dixie Chicks? Norah Jones? Your mother?!

What if the girl is a guy? Poor Jake. You have ventured down the road to perdition. Mr and Mrs Boll Weevil are disappointed in you, Jake. They would much prefer the sock. You can't get in trouble jerking off in a sock. Out of sock you can get Aids. You can get that, young boy. You can get some kind of love, not their kind, but some kind. And, you can get free. No, Jake, you mustn't get free. Because if you do, you will leave the Weevil family behind while you are getting it in the behind.

'Jake, wake up! Say something.'

Yawn. 'I don't get this exercise.'

'How could you get it if you're sound asleep?' Or jerking off.

'I wasn't sleeping.'

'Fine. What don't you get about it?'

'I can't explain.'

'Try.'

'I don't want to.'

Help! Where is the homeroom teacher? 'What's the problem, Jake?'

'My little brother's got the flu. I think I got the flu. My head hurts.'

'You got a fever?' I walk over to Jake's desk. He cowers. Remember can't touch his forehead. Against school rules. 'Why don't you go to the principal's office. Have them call home. See if your mom can pick you up.'

He looks relieved. 'Okay.' He bends over, pulls up the back of his pants with his right hand, picks up his books with his left, rises from his seat, walks as if he had a ton of bricks in his pants, makes his way to the door. All eyes are on his exit. They too wish they had a fever. They are out of their minds with envy.

When I was their age, I was out of my mind. The apple doesn't fall far from the tree.

'The bough's breakin', baby.
Down will come baby cradle and all.'

I knew the bough was breakin'. She lived inside her tears. My heart still swims in her sorrow.

As the door slams, I shout. 'Look at the ceiling, look at the lights, look at the walls, look at the floor! Sense that every single thing that you see is alive! Do you hear what I'm saying?! Alive! As alive as you and I are! Sense the breathing floor beneath your feet, the living walls surrounding you. We are a part of a phenomenal world where everything is alive, interconnected, and anything is possible. Imagine that right here, in this *living* classroom, burns a golden fire.' Perplexed. They look perplexed. 'Now turn that raging fire into pure gold. Place that pure gold inside your heart. Inhabit your heart. Become your heart; a breathing, living creation filled with pure love, pure gold. What have we got here? What is that called? Anybody?'

Some girl in the back of the room has the balls to answer: 'Crazy.'

'No! … Alchemy! I have always loved the art of science, the science of art, the transformation of something into something other than what it was believed to have been.' This alchemical notion, at this particular moment in that particular high school leads me into my next topic … potent space. Let me see if I can explain it to them; the *it* being potent space …

As I fix my gaze upon a room full of shiny, terminally toxic, teenage faces, some black some white, I hear in my head the willful silent challenge from each and every one of them. 'Who the fuck are you? Prove it. Whatever it is, prove it.'

'When you move in relation to that which moves you, that which moves through you, are you moving it or is it moving you?' … Glazed looks, more acne and no response until …

After class, Lydia approaches. She breathes hideous packaged egg-beater breath on my violet meditation beaded necklace. The beads fog up before her eyes. She looks frightened. Finally, she speaks. 'I am an avid reader and an avid Christian. I believe that your potent space diatribe borders on the demonic.'

I am taken aback. 'Can you explain?'

'Well, it just doesn't seem Christian. It appears to be somewhat, no, extremely metaphysical without any inherent faith-based ideas in the explanation.'

It starts at home with the parents. Parents go stupid, filters down to the kids. Soon you have second-generation soul sludge. It's a form of practical prejudice. Works for everyone at home … Hopeless situation for the rest of us.

'Metaphysics is not demonic or anti-Christian, Lydia. Look, why don't you give it a chance. See how you feel by the end of the week. Then, we can continue our discussion. I look forward to it.'

Lydia never returns. Her family prays for my soul's retrieval. They are not the first to pray for my soul. They will not be the last.

Seated at a window booth in the Ajax Diner, on the town square, looking across the square at the Oxford courthouse, at its newly painted pillars, downing my third piece of corn bread I think about Lydia as I remember my time of demons. Oh Lydia, Lydia, you do not have the faintest idea about demons, do you? I know demons … I knew Judas. His hands touched my body.

In 1983, after my mother's untimely death, my Judas incarnate appeared as one Lothar Bovar. He posed as a healer. I fell under his spell, fell into my holy hell, heart first into his world of sin and shame.

I was in from Los Angeles visiting my sister Dina in New York. It was a dark, wet, wintry day when I strolled into his West End Avenue apartment. The living room floor was tiled in shiny black and white vinyl squares, like a chessboard. The pawn enters. Me. Old queen moves with clarity and absolute cunning toward victory over the pawn's soul … Trance time in Tormentville!

There he stood, all four-feet six-inches of him. He was a short man. His silver hair was slicked back like a postmodern teaspoon: fair skin, thin lips, and eyes such a deep-sea blue that I wanted to dive right into them. The blue surrounded the blackest dilated pupils you could possibly imagine. The whites glistened, you know, over easy, no butter, no oil, no blood vessels … no humanity.

'Welcome, Loli.'

'Hello'

'Are you feeling sad?'

(pause) 'Yes.'

'Having trouble sleeping at night?'

(deep breath) 'Yes.'

'Nervous?'

(heart pounds) 'Yes.'

'Confused?'

(how does he ... is he reading my mind?) 'Yes.'

'How long have you felt like this?'

'A long time I guess.' How 'bout my whole fuckin' life?!

'A very long time. Correct?'

'Yes.'

He squints. 'I can see your black pain. It surrounds you. Terrible ... Terrible ... I see it, sucking all of your energy ... killing you. My poor child. I have rarely seen ... oh no, I have never seen anything like it.' He cradles his face in his hands, makes a high-pitched whimpering sound. I freeze in *my* psychic sludge. Sweat pours from his noble brow. 'Will you let me help you, Loli?'

(Bite lower lip. Draw blood, swallow hard, lips parched, lips make sound.)

'Say yes.'

'Yes.'

'Good.'

She whispers, *'Yes.'*

'Now, Loli, let me place my fingers on your neck.' He places hot fingers on jugulars. Hell hath landed in a blaze throughout my body. I erupt like Vesuvius. 'Good. That's very good. Now say the word ... music.'

'What?!'

'I can't hear you, Loli … The demons can't be released until you say the word … Please … don't be afraid … Say the word music and you will get free.'

I say, 'Music.'

His fingers shake, rattle and roll as my head shimmies like a newly charged vibrator. He lurches backwards, nearly falls on the shiny vinyl floor. He moans.

(moanin') 'Loli.' (moanin' again) 'Loli.' (moanin' low) 'Loli.' He smiles his satanic Pepsodent smile. 'We have succeeded. For the moment, you are free of the demons.'

'I am?' Then why do I feel like shit?

'Yes, you are.' Silence. He stares right through me. I shiver. He cocks his head like a dog having its first idea. 'Come back next week. In the meantime, if you feel the demons return, feel free to call me at this number.' He hands me a black and white checkered vinyl refrigerator magnet card. 'Place the phone on your neck and say the word "music" out loud three times. I will be able to release them over the phone. Now don't forget to call. If I'm in session, just wait by the phone. I'll get back to you right away. Are you clear on the procedure?'

'Absolutely.' Place phone on neck, say the word music three times, and let demons be demons. Look, Ma, I'm free …

'My ass, you are, little girl … You'll never be free. You're my little girl.'

After Oxford, Mississippi, I wend my way via United, coach class, last row, no oxygen, to Chicago. I am one stop closer to teaching in my mother's town … Beatrice.

'Patience is a virtue.'

Lovely advice from the departed.

O'Hare airport is to flying what Forest Lawn is to dying …

large and lonely except for the bodies. It is snowing again … We land two and one half hours later than our ETA. After sitting in between a four-hundred-and-fifty pound computer suiter playing Nintendo and a seventeen-year-old Hispanic transvestite listening to syncopated salsa, I can't wait to deplane. I sprint to baggage, like Jim Thorpe in his heyday, wait forty-five minutes until my ruined, red, torn bag arrives.

The bellman ushers me up into my brown room. Brown couch, brown rug, brown curtains, brown bedspread, brown bureau, and drip … drip … brown tap water.

'I can't do this room!'

'Is something wrong, miss?'

'It's brown. The entire room is brown. I'll die in here. Don't you have any other color room in this hotel?'

'The hotel is being renovated. Some of our new rooms are beige.'

'Are there any beige rooms available?'

'Oh no, miss, the renovation won't be completed until next fall.'

I tip the doorman, bolt out the door. On Rush Street I spot a massive Marriott Hotel. I roll my bag right *into* the revolving door. With all of his brute strength, the doorman stops the door so that my bag and I squeeze neatly between the glass panels. He maneuvers the door. It moves. I move with it. He is not impressed with me or my rolling.

I'm in the lobby … a successful transition. Next stop front desk! 'How much is a … look, just give me a room whatever it costs.' Ryan (his name tag pinned neatly over his Marriott pocket) is more than Midwesternly courteous.

I drag myself into the mirrored Marriott elevator, stumble toward the room. The plastic key slides right into the slot. The room is four by four, the size of my sister Dina's SUV, which is parked in her Park Avenue garage. I sit down on the edge of the miniature bed, pick up the phone to chat with young Ryan.

'I need more space. I'm a yogi. I can't even stand in mountain pose in this room.'

I make one more stop at the front desk. Young Ryan hands me the new holographic plastic key for room 711. 'Thank you.'

My new upgraded room is adjacent to the elevator. I can do yoga, I can lie down on the floor, but I can't hear myself think.

I reappear at the front desk. Ryan acts as if he truly cares about the noise problem.

He hands me the key to room 1956. He promises that I will be exceedingly happy…1956 …

The year of my birth. The gala event, I am told by my sister Dina, went something like this. Granny was sleeping in the easy chair in the living room. At six a.m. my sister appeared, bewildered. She awakened Granny, asked her why her mother and father weren't in the bedroom.

'Your mother, *thank God*, is at the hospital. Your father is with her. You have a brand new baby sister. Isn't that just wonderful?' No reply… 'Her name is Loli. You just wait and see. It's all going to be different.'

My sister went back to bed, possibly suspecting that her position as the focus of absolute adoration was in jeopardy.

Ryan ushers me into my birthday room. He opens the door and very slowly strolls with me around the ten by ten space. I listen for noise. A hum … It's the florescent light in the bathroom. I'll close the door at night. This is turning out to be a good day after all.

I hand Ryan a five-dollar bill. He refuses. Instead, he stands there, sinks his hands deep into his pockets. He gazes longingly into my eyes. Don't tell me … Here it comes …

'May I come back later? After my shift is over.'

Does he want to help me unpack? 'Why?' He moves closer. Should have slept in the elevator.

'I thought …'

'Ryan, I'm old enough to be your mother.'

'So?'

Wonder what it would be like with this pretty windy city boy who hardly knows he is a man? Probably like not worth it at all. 'I … I'm sorry, but …' Think fast … much faster than this. 'I'm married.'

'You're not wearing a ring.'

Why not just fuck him. A front desk clerk at a Marriott Hotel?! You've got to draw the line somewhere.

'Look, Ryan, I'm exhausted.'

'I love my mother.'

'I loved mine too but … but …' Stand perfectly still. Wait for the next move. He looks down at the floor, rocks from side to side. He's waiting. I could let him fondle my breasts? Not tonight.

I open the door. He looks so forlorn. Men are such boys, such babies. Maybe that's why we love them. As he exits, my clitoris quivers at the thought of what might have been.

I unpack, shower, get into bed, and masturbate. I imagine young Ryan writhing underneath me, pounding his organ into my private property. Imagination is a wonderful thing.

… The next day: another school day on the road.

'Come on boys and girls.

Everybody sing along with the Mouseketeers

M- i- c- k- e- y- m- o- u- s- e.'

Welcome to the Walt Disney school or duck and cover in Chicago.

(Don't forget about the five-year-olds.)

The road is an unpredictable place, especially when you are working for a bankrupt theatre company. I am almost always met with unexpected surprises: six a.m. wake-up call (always difficult for a nocturnal menopausal woman); seven a.m. shower (after a brief visit to my yoga mat and an even briefer visit to my mindful meditation); seven forty a.m. leave hotel (green tea in hand), eight a.m. arrive school …

Nobody is at school … absolutely nobody. How is that possible? *How?* Why, it's the road. I walk around the Mickey Mouse school compound three times, sit on a stone-cold, almost-shovelled school stoop, stare at my bold red tightly woven Nikes. They are still with me. That is a comfort. They are soaked. That is not a comfort.

I yell to an obese, elderly woman trying to shovel her car out of a snow bank. 'Miss, oh miss! Why no school?' She shovels with a vengeance. Pays no attention to me. 'Miss!'

She stops. Catches her breath. 'Holiday, holiday, Poloski Polish day!' She mutters, 'Idiot.' Continues the dig out, as if I weren't there.

Not a Polish holiday? Another Stuart Manly travel blunder. I want to go home so badly.

My father always said that I was a quitter. Damn him! I'll show that bastard a thing or two.

'Oh baby, your father loves you so much. He only wants the best for you. Why can't you try to understand? He had nothing when he was growing up. Poor like dirt. You have so much, so much. He works so hard for all of us. Tell him that you're sorry. Please, for me.'

All right, I will return. Just for you, Pop.

'What about me?'

You too.

'Thank you, honey. That's my baby girl.'

The following morning, there I am, administering in a thirty-minute duck and cover drill; K through 12. After much ado, the five-year-olds with their teeny hands on their tiny little heads face the wall. They look like multicolored marshmallows with arms. They look frightened, as if the drill is a reality.

Back when I was their age, during any drill, I was convinced that my mother could protect me from anything. Even though she didn't make my breakfast, fill my lunch box, or send me off to school. She was a p.m. kind of mom. Night-time was our time together. We both loved the moon. During my early years, I believed that she hung the moon.

My third day in Mouseketeerville. I am having a nervous breakdown teaching eighth graders. This is not my chosen grade. I remember specifically telling Stuart Manly: 'Stuart, I don't do eighth grade. I do tenth, eleventh and twelth.' ... As a last-ditch effort to reach the unreachable eighth graders, I decide to risk my life. I will teach the interview technique ... but how? Engage ... Encourage ... Energize.

'Let's form a circle.' Could they move any slower? 'We don't have a lot of time.' After ten minutes, they have formed the perfect circle. I pull up a chair, squeeze myself between two sleepy boys; eyes closed, foreheads on desks. I turn to the cherub on my right. 'What's your name?'

He turns his sleepy head in my direction. 'Me?'

'You.'

'Phillip.'

'Nice to meet you, Phillip.'

Phil is stunned by my tactics. Lifts head, looks into my eyes, replies, 'Nice meeting you too.' Forehead returns to desk.

Begin. 'Sometimes, when I'm stuck … working on a particular character in a script, I'll interview the character as if he or she were a total stranger. Are you with me?' Heads nod. 'Good. What happens can be absolutely fantastic.' I am fired up here. Think I'll stand. 'So, what we're going to do in this class is pair up and interview each other … Ask questions … probe … listen to what your partner has to say. Write it down. Let one question stimulate the next question. Think of yourself as a cub reporter who's trying to uncover something that you genuinely want to know about your classmate … your friend … even your enemy.' Phil's up! Paper in hand. Unbelieveable. He's writing. Way to go, Phil … 'There is always something we *don't* know about a person. We think we know each other so well. But, people are full of surprises.' Damn! Do I have to answer a question now? 'Yes.'

Shy girl with braces, pigtails and a zillion freckles asks, 'What if we don't want to do the exercise?'

Never fails. 'In my class, you don't have to do anything you don't want to do. But you might want to try this exercise … You can have a lot of fun working with each other. Honest.'

'Maybe I'll try.' She smiles. Her braces glisten.

'Great … Be sensitive. If your partner doesn't want to answer the question, move on to another question. And remember, you want the truth. The truth is what matters … Let's go … Pick your partner, write down your questions, five minutes each interview. And most important of all, have a good time.' Look at them move. Yes! They get it!!!

During the final interview exercise, Sophia is without a partner. I volunteer.

The Interview

'Name?'

'Sophia'

'Age?'

'12'

'What event has changed your life?'

'9/11 … I lost two cousins. I realized that life is fragile.' She turns away, wipes her eyes. So young. She's so young. 'I'm sorry.'

'Don't be … What do you love to do?'

She looks at me as if no one has ever asked her a question before. 'Write poetry. Read.' She thinks for an extended moment. 'I love to observe the world around me.'

'Tell me about your family?'

'My mother's a single mom. My father lives in Verona, Italy. I don't speak to him. My mom's a lawyer. I have one brother. He's older. I don't like him much. Men are stupid. Women have all the power.'

This girl is twelve? 'What's your worst trait?'

'I don't forgive. Oh yeah, and I have a short temper.'

'Do you like school?'

'It's fine. But, people are jealous of me because I'm a good student. I'm different from most of the kids.'

'What is the number one question you ask yourself?'

'What am I doing here? Why did my cousins die?'

'What if anything do you believe in?'

'I'm a devout Christian. Christ.'

Uh oh, another literate born-again.

'I believe God is with me always.'

Time's up!

Sophia readies her pencil. She begins to grill me. 'Are you gay?'

'What?!'

'Are you gay?'

I am speechless. Ultimately, I do speak. 'Why do you ask?' Why am I embarrassed by the answer? Why is this truth so hard?

'Well, you're not wearing a wedding ring.'

She is twelve after all. Maybe I should introduce her to Ryan. Together, they could wile away the hours, scoping out each and every fourth-finger left hand, only to discover that everyone is either gay or catting around ... 'Next question please.'

'Do you live with someone?'

'Yes.' Where the hell is Simone. Never calls. Why don't I call her? Don't know what to say? *I miss you* would be a nice opener.

'Are you faithful?'

Why didn't I ask her if she's fucking anyone? 'I am now.'

'What does that mean?'

It means that I'm lying. 'I'm not.'

'Why?'

'It's a long story.'

'Tell me about it.'

'I can't.'

'Why not?'

'Look, I don't want you to think that everyone's fooling around, that love doesn't exist, that there's absolutely no future in commitment or ...'

'I don't think that.'

'Maybe I do. And that's my problem not yours. You don't need to know why I fuck around. I'm sorry. I didn't mean to say the f word.'

'I say it.'

'Do you do it?'

She sighs. 'I'm interviewing you, right?'

'Absolutely. You're in charge.'

Crack Up

'84

Spring of '84. Lothar left New York ... quickly. Started a fire with a sage wand in his West End Avenue apartment. The Board threw him out. He moved to Los Angeles, where I lived. Took complete control of my life. Whenever I felt depressed, I would pick up the phone, dial his number (now committed to memory), place the earpiece against my neck, and say, 'Music.' I could hear him doing something or another on the other end of the line. For all I knew, he might have been masturbating. But more likely, he was making the sign of the holy cross or sending energetic plasma through the phone into my neck.

During this period, my dear friend Tanya kept an overprotective eye on me. She was a major player in the 'Music' cult. Her specialty was apparition observation. She could identify whether ghosts were floating, flying, or caught between the astral planes. She also identified when I needed to place a demon-releasing phone call. That girl was crazy as a loon trapped beneath a frozen lake. How could she not be? She, like myself and all of his followers, were surviving on the nutritious egg-whites-and-sugar diet.

'How's your blood sugar, hon?' she would regularly ask me.

Word came through Tanya that it was time to enter the next

phase of commitment. Lothar was to inform us of our new and even greater responsibilities in the war against evil. We were summoned to a rococo mansion in the Hollywood Hills.

Thirty some zombies seated on yellow and blue tie-dyed furniture, three huge unbathed Afghan dogs lying on top of each other at the foot of a winding staircase, enough lavender verbena incense to smoke out any terrorist group, and a full moon ... Wasn't it a full moon when my mother died?

It was my turn to go upstairs. There he sat on a pink naugahyde throne, looking more like Beelzebub than ever. His sinister, sunken, blue-eyed gaze made me feel like a helpless animal on the way to slaughter.

He whispered, 'How are you, Loli?'

'Not so good.'

'No? I thought we were doing so well.'

'It's not working. I'm scared, I cry all the time, I can't sleep, and the egg whites aren't enough anymore. I've been eating real food.'

'You have? I'm terribly disappointed.'

'I had some nova two days ago. I'm so hungry.'

'No, Loli, the demons are hungry.'

He sidled up alongside of me. His hot breath penetrated through my crawling skin. He pressed his bony fingers deep into my jugular. I wanted to throw up. Silence ... All of a sudden, he yanked my hair. My head ached. I was in the maniac's clutches. Somehow, he managed to get me in a half, no, this was a full nelson, I could no longer breathe.

'Stop it! Stop it! You're killing me!!!'

'I'm killing them. Now you will be released forever!'

I writhed, undulated, slid sideways off the pink throne. The madman dove over the throne, pounced on top of me. I was totally entangled in his grip. My heart raced. It felt like the Kentucky Derby at the finish line … *'And the winner … by a neck … is …'*

Somehow I got free, lunged for the door, opened it, slammed it in his face, grabbed onto the banister, stumbled down the stairs, fell headfirst onto the living-room floor, sobbing.

Finally, I took a deep breath, pulling myself up, tripping over the tie-dyed furniture. I was still alive. I looked around the room. The zombies had not moved. I heard a strange piercing sound in the kitchen. Tanya was blending another egg-white-and-sugar special. I shouted, 'HE'S CRAZY! He tried to kill me! WHAT IS THE MATTER WITH YOU PEOPLE? Don't you get it?! HE'S A FRAUD!'

Tanya entered, egg-white sin fizz in hand, three Afghans by her side. She strolled over to the front door, opened it with mindful conviction.

'Get out! You are not welcome here. Your polluted ego is in control of you. You are no longer protected by the light of the group's energy. You're on your own, hon.'

I wept my way toward my car. I looked back … No! Mustn't do that. The lights faded in the rococo house. I tripped, fell, picked myself up, opened the car door, parked my ass in my moonlit silver BMW convertible. Took off. Demons followed me. Demons sang a hideous Gregorian chant in my ear.

'You will die,
You will die.'

I drove down one dark canyon road and up another. Some force greater than myself guided me home. The raging demons screamed louder:

'You will die!
You will die!

You will die!'

I ran into the house, opened the refrigerator door, grabbed all the eggs, dumped them one by one down the garbage disposal until they swirled out of this world. I shoved a piece of nova deep into my throat, opened cupboards, found a two-year-old jar of Planters peanuts, flipped open the lid, chug-a-lugged the rancid nuts as fast as I could.

In the bedroom ... The demons. Gray slime slid along the hardwood hall floors. Smoke filled the air. Voices screamed: *'You will die ... you will die ... you will die'*... I am dying. I wanted to die.

Door slammed ... mind split. I reached for the Valium in the medicine chest ... five ... ten ... fifteen milligrams. Is this how my mother felt? Is this how she died? I sat in a hot bathtub filled with lavender bath salts. I sweated, screamed, sobbed until completely empty, crawled into bed. Shaking. At four a.m. I reached for the telephone to call my old psychiatrist, Dr Guttman. The answering service picked up.

'Hello, this is Dr Guttman's exchange.'

'Where is he?'

'Doctor Guttman will be away until August 29th.'

It was August 2nd. 'My name's Loli Greene. I need to speak to him right away! Please?'

'I'm sorry, but Dr Guttman left strict instructions. He is not to be disturbed, unless it is an absolute emergency.'

'Is suicide enough of an emergency? Is it?! I swear on my ... I swear to God I will kill myself if you don't get him on the phone. I mean it!'

Pause. 'Hold please.' Centuries went by...

'Loli?'

'Dr Guttman?'

'Loli, it is four a.m. in California. What seems to be the problem?'

'I'm losing my ... The demons ... If I take too much Valium, I'll die like my mother did ... Please. Please come back now. Please.'

'Now listen to me, Loli. Calm down. Listen to me. I can't come back, but I can call up one of my colleagues, Dr Dot. He will get you through this crisis. Just calm down. Breathe. Take another five milligrams of Valium, a hot lavender bath ...'

'I already did that.'

'Do it again. Go to the medicine cabinet, take a Valium, run the bath, and breathe.'

'They're after me.'

'Nothing is after you. You are going to be fine. Hang up the phone so that I can call Dr Dot. Remember, breathe and bathe.'

'Breathe and bathe.'

'You'll be fine. I promise. I'll see you in September. Until then, I think it would be wise if you saw Dr Dot on an every-day basis.'

'Are you sure that his office will remember to call?'

'I'm positive. Now hang up, Loli. Good night.'

'Good night, Dr Guttman.' Click.

The one and only reason August *is* a wicked month is that all of the finest psychiatrists in America gather on Cape Cod. They play Frisbee and frolic near the water's edge while psychotic patients spend thirty-one days anxiously awaiting their return. On August 1st at 12:01 a.m. Eastern Daylight Savings Time, a severe and sudden agitation develops in the astral planes, because millions of helpless, hopeless Americans cannot deal with their psychiatric withdrawal. Nothing can be done about this, unless one is willing to throw oneself, one's angst, and all of one's hysteria into the psychiatric arms of an inept stranger.

Dr Dot was my inept stranger. For the longest twenty-nine days of our lives, we were thrown together, while Dr Guttman rode the waves on old Cape Cod.

Drive at Your Own Risk

'03

Because I was so eager to get myself to Beatrice, I was thwarted by Cedar Falls, twin town to Waterloo (telling name), Iowa. The twin towns were located in the middle of a middle state in the middle of nowhere. I was beginning to feel and look like my red rolling bag.

By March of 2003, NASDAQ has lost approximately seventy-eight per cent of its market value. The S&P 500 has lost forty-nine per cent of its net worth. I am interested in these financial facts because, unfortunately, I am my father's daughter. He was a stockbroker. There had been cutbacks, shutdowns, kickbacks for the rich, and all kinds of costly shenanigans. The arts are not a priority with our present administration.

No, this is the 'not one child will be left behind' administration. No child will be left behind but not one theater, music, art, or dance program will be left alive. The young adult will have the thrill of struggling through 'How to take a test'. He might never understand the content of the test, but he will learn the tricks to passing it, so he can forge ahead, making his community and country proud when he enlists in the marines and learns about life and death while fighting for his country under fire. He will never learn about the likes of Picasso, Eugene O'Neill, Sarah Bernhardt, Nijinsky, Copeland, Bach or even Pink Floyd. He will learn math and science. He will add, but art will be subtracted from his life …

Because of the situation in schools around the country, I have a job. Because of the massive budget cuts at the already bankrupt theater company is why, on March 3rd at seven p.m. I ended up at the Pennysaver Motel. Behind the dilapidated desk sat Becky (name tag pinned over her Pennysaver pocket), a rotund perky person, eating a bag of pork rinds and drinking a Pepsi Light. Slowly she turned:

'Hi. You must be Loli Greene?'

'How'd you know that?'

'It's mostly hunters and truckers stay here. You're the only girl to walk through that door in days … 'cept me. Name's Becky.'

'Hi Becky.' I notice the many deer heads on the wall, one of which is missing an eye. Can't stop staring at the eye hole.

'Bullet went right through its eye.' I cringe. 'Amazing huh? We gotta great jacuzzi. You're gonna love it. Sign right here. You're in room sixty-nine. Don't you just love that number?' I am speechless. 'You have to carry your bags down those stairs. It's real quiet down there.'

Apprehensively, I look at the red metal stairwell. 'It's below ground level?'

'Oh yeah. It's underground. Stuart Manly said you wanted a quiet room for meditating. I do TM every day. You're right near the jacuzzi. Might be a couple of truckers in there tonight.'

Thank you, Stuart. 'My bag's in the car.'

'Park right in front of the office. Those are the basement stairs.' She points at the stairwell.

I drag *the* red bag downstairs. At the end of the basement corridor, I see a whale-like flotilla. Two drunken, tattooed truckers romping in the bubbles.

'Come on in, honey.'

'This is great for all that ails you.'

'Thanks guys, but I've got a date with a bed.' Better get into the room pronto.

'It's only seven thirty. Don't you wanna party? Come on, hon. It's party time.'

Flashbacks to Tanya and Lothar. Hon! I don't like that word.

I am now underground in my Pennysaver suite. There is a miniature casement window above my bed right below the beige ceiling. I climb up onto my bed, look out of my window … Oh. A bulldozer. Construction site. Good night. Where is the Valium?

'Sweet dreams, dear.'

Bulldozing begins at seven thirty the next morning. Fortunately, I am on my way out the door. I enter the hallowed halls of education. The walls are cracked, floors strewn with school debris: bottles, cans, candy wrappers. Smells like a urinal. Beechwood High didn't look like this. Great place. Great town. Almost perfect. Almost. I look for, but can't find the principal's office. Open a door, stumble into a pitch-black auditorium. It might as well be a morgue; not an ounce of life or art in this crypt.

Reach for a crumpled piece of paper in my pocket. Room sixty-nine. Laugh at the numbers, find the room, enter. I see teenagers seated at desks too small for their bodies, teenagers with sad eyes that look up to me for some assurance that this hour will be worthwhile. Here is a room full of poor, deprived children, the children whose parents collect unemployment checks, welfare checks, disability checks. There are no checks and balances in the lives of these abandoned faces … These kids don't have a prayer. All they can hope for is one day to get out of town.

'Write about or write to someone who has influenced you.'
Vacant stares. 'Someone who has been a pioneer, an influence, who has changed your life. Tell them what you want them to know about you. What do you want to say to them? What do you *need* to tell them?' Give them time … more time. Christ. Most of them look so old. Weary. Without future.

'Time's up! Okay. Who wants to start?'

A beautiful black girl in the front row stands tall. She looks so alive, so grown up, like a whole grown person. Escape! Get out now. Leave this town before it kills your spirit.

'Harriet Tubman.'

'If you don't mind, could you tell the rest of class who she is.'

'She was a runaway slave who became a conductor on the Underground Railroad during the Civil War. She helped other slaves get free.'

A voice from the back of the room. 'She was the first real freedom fighter.'

'Adolf Hitler!' The blond male mall rat stands up. 'I like Hitler. That dude is my hero because he almost got rid of all those dirty Jews. Harriet Tubman didn't do anything compared to Adolf Hitler,' says the blond mall rat. Peals of laughter in the schoolroom.

Don't tell him that you are a Jewish, gay, liberal woman from the east coast. They are looking at me. They know everything about me. Where does all this hatred come from? Parents. Somewhere at home is a soul-sucking, right-wing fascist …

'Honey. It's okay. Believe me. Everything is just fine.'

No, it's not! 'Since the beginning of time,' I say … That beautiful black girl in the front row, she understands forgiveness. That wee young boy in the third row, who looks like he wants to say something, I bet he loves his father and mother, they love him, even though they are destitute, and he's on the school lunch program. I bet he understands forgiveness.

'There's no mill here no more. But we stay 'cause it's home,' says the wee boy.

What railroad are you gonna jump on to get away from here? Let me take you away from your suffering. Please. There is a place, a divine place. We can get there together ... She sits front row center. Looks through me. I feel her inside me. Again.

Later that afternoon, I walk 4.8 miles through a snow-covered wheat field in Cedar Falls, Iowa. The field and I can't wait for spring. I scream to the future and to the past. 'Please forgive me, even if I can't forgive myself.'

Later that evening, in my underground mole motel room, I pick up the cracked black telephone, dial forty-three digits so that I might have the privilege of getting an outside line. I place the receiver to my ear (not my neck) and await my sister Dina's lovely voice on the other end of man's vast web of telecommunication.

It is now eight fifteen p.m. in New York City. She will be readying herself for sleep. I have at least fifteen minutes before her curfew is in effect. Hopefully, we will have an adult, sisterly conversation.

Sound of phone dropping on floor. She picks it up. 'Ouch. Hello.'

'You all right?'

'Where are you?'

'Cedar Falls, Iowa.'

'Where's that?'

'Somewhere in the middle of the country.'

'Why are you there?'

'Why are *you* there?'

'I live here.'

'I know that. But, why are any of us anywhere?'

'You sound depressed.'

'What's new?'

'Ralph has shingles.'

'Oh shit. How's he doing?'

'He read in some science book somewhere that if it develops near the eye, the cornea can be affected and blindness might occur.'

'Is it near his eyes?'

'No, it's right under his ribs in the front down near his belly button.'

'Then why's he worried?'

'It's Ralph.'

'Right. How's business.'

'He's got shingles. That's how's business.'

'I thought it's from chicken pox?'

'It is. But he's nervous. Doesn't help things.'

'How are you?'

'Let's see. Sara, your niece, is sleeping with a forty-two-year-old pre-med student recently returned from germ-filled darkest Africa after serving in the Peace Corps. He will be fifty when he becomes a resident. And boy does he have big plans. He hopes to specialize in environmental pediatric medicine back in his hometown of Topeka, Kansas. By the time he hits sixty, if he's still standing and she's off Prozac, they want to adopt a couple of wonderful Bosnian children.'

'At last, a doctor in the family.'

'He's too old to be a doctor. And, at the age of twenty-seven, she, your niece, has decided to go back to school and finally get her diploma … in photojournalism … which she's never studied. You are so fortunate that you never had children. I wish I were gay.'

Simone must have given her that idea. Got to call her. When does she leave for Zurich? 'How's my nephew?'

'Charlie, your nephew, has recently informed his father and his mother that he has all intentions of moving to Shanghai. American food no longer agrees with his newly acquired Asian palate and his yen for Asian studies.' I try to get a word in edgewise. 'He has also informed his parents that Asian women have more body and luster to their hair. American hair is not turning him on anymore. But Asian hair turns him on a great deal. I'm so glad he spent a year abroad.'

'Prell.'

'Prell? The shampoo?' She yawns. 'Didn't I use Prell? I have terrible hair. You have the great hair. You got our mother's hair and nails.'

'That's not all I got. I'm quitting.'

'No, you're not. You love those little cherubs in Indiana.'

'Iowa! I had a Nazi in my eleventh-grade class today.'

'How do you know he was a Nazi?'

'He stood up and told the class that Hitler was his hero.'

'He didn't know what he was talking about. He lives in Iowa.'

'What does that mean?'

'I'm trying to cheer you up. When everything feels like it's falling apart, someone has to …'

I hear my mother's voice. *'Sat on a wall*
Had a great fall

cannot put … cannot put …
together … again
together … again.'

'I am depressed.'

Dina pauses: 'Look, my friend Ruby, the part-time pilates teacher in my office, gave me the name of a therapist. Her name is Mary Michelin.'

'Like the tire?'

'What tire?'

'The one on your Mercedes.'

'Oh. (She laughs). Like the tire. She's your kind of therapist – a present-lives regressionist.'

'That's ridiculous. Past lives maybe. Present lives is not possible.'

'Mary Michelin believes that the present life is the only life, and in it are all of our past lives. She takes her patients back to their childhood by downloading or offloading or devolving back with some Jungian Kabbalistic techniques. Sounds interesting, doesn't it?' I yawn. 'She works with a lot of artists. You should see her when you get back from … where are you again?'

'Iowa. But I'm going to Nebraska next.'

'Where's that?'

'Does it matter?'

'Yes. I like to know where you are.'

'You wouldn't believe where I am.'

'You're in Iowa. I was listening.'

'Good night.'

'Good night.'

'Send my love to the kids. Tell Ralph not to worry about going blind. I read in my nutritional healing book that a secondary infection brought on by shingles can cause death if the bacteria isn't treated. Let him worry about that.'

'I can't tell him that. He'll believe it.'

'It's true.'

'I better go make sure that he's all right. Give me your number. I'll call you from the office.'

'You can't reach me. There's no switchboard.'

'Where have they got you this time?'

'The Pennysaver Motel.' We howl as we hang up. I do love my sister.

'Your sister loves you almost as much as you know who. Go to sleep, my angel.'

Road Kill

'84

'Look, Dr Dot ... it's very hard for me to be here with you. No, don't speak. Please don't say anything until I'm through talking. I guess Dr Guttman told you a little about me. I'll tell you what I can, but I'm afraid to tell you everything. I don't know if I should tell you about the demons? They're everywhere. I can't fight them. I abandoned the work. The group isn't protecting me anymore. You probably think I'm crazy? I can't stand it, I'm always hungry. I have a pit, this pit right here in my stomach. Can't fill it up. I need to eat, but when I eat, I feel like I'm going to throw up. I hear voices. Since she died, I hear voices. They're louder now. How do I know you're not a demon? No, don't say anything. I'm not ready to hear your voice. One more voice will put me over the edge. I left my mother ... my mother's house last year. My sister left too. My father went to work. Bastard. My mother drank a bottle of Drano. Ate up her stomach. How could I leave? She told me that she didn't want to be a burden anymore. Didn't want to spend my father's money. Never saw her again. My father sees ghosts in the bedroom, where they used to sleep. Ghosts everywhere ... I hope he dies soon. I'm not protected anymore. Christ, I'm shaking. No, don't come any closer. I'll just sit here and shake. I like to rock back and forth.'

'Rock-a-bye, baby'

'We all left her.'

'Down will come baby.'

'I tried to save her … Her best friend Mrs B. found her in the tub … Are you a real doctor? It's August. Why are you here? Why am I here?'

He speaks. 'How can I help you, Loli?'

'Kleenex, please.' He hands me the box of Kleenex. 'Are you really a psychiatrist?'

'Yes, I am.'

'Can you help me?'

'I hope so.'

'You look like my father. I hate him.'

'He loves you, honey.'

'She says he loves me.'

'Who says he loves you?'

'My mother.'

'I'm sure he does. Loli, do you live alone?' I nod yes. 'Is there anyone who might come and stay with you? Is there anyone you trust?'

I nod yes again. 'My sister Dina. But she's very busy with my nephew. He's sick. That's why she couldn't stay … with my mother. I could have … stayed. I could have saved her.'

'Loli, no one can save anyone, unless they want to be saved.'

'I'm tired.'

'Go home. Get some sleep. Do you work?'

'Not since my mother died.'

'Call your sister. Tell her you need her. I'm sure that she'll understand.'

'Can I call you?'

'Absolutely. My exchange can reach me any time night or day … Please call your sister.'

'I will. I'm sorry if I'm … I'm just sorry … Thank you. Bye.'
Three blind mice!
Three blind mice!
See how they run!'
Dina and I ran … So did Pop.
'Goes the …'
We all ran.

Night Blindness

'Twinkle twinkle little star how I wonder what you are ... Have I told you about the moon and the stars? Well, everyone in the world tells the moon their biggest secrets. The moon is the world's best secret keeper. But the moon is so so busy with the tides and the rest of its work on earth, that it has to create millions of stars to help it guard everyone's important secrets. If you tell a secret to anyone but the moon, all of the stars will die because of the moon's disappointment. One by one their light will fade from the night sky. And the moon will be too busy to take care of you and me and the rest of the people on earth.' I remember. She pointed to the glistening sky. Then, she lit a cigarette. I blew out the match.

Dot's office ... a.m.

'84

After reading Dr Dot an exceedingly long dream entry from my journal, I peek up to see if he is still awake; to my surprise, he is. *'Then I ask her, "Where's my aqua scarf?" The bitch steward-ess doesn't remember. My favorite scarf. My mother gave it to me years ago ... disappeared. Why does everything you love, everything disappears. Damn her.'* ... Sad or angry? Sad. I think about the song 'Cry me a River'. *'I cried ... a river ... over you.'*

He hands me the Kleenex. This is becoming our intimate routine and it's only our second meeting. 'I still don't trust you. I need you but I don't trust you … I don't know what to eat … The demons … I can't talk anymore. You talk.'

'Loli, your mother took her life. Believe me there is nothing more painful or difficult. But we can deal with it.'

'She's not dead. She's right here in my belly, in my heart, in my head, in my crotch. I'm going to get sick. Wastebasket please. Now!' Dr Dot holds the bucket. *Rock-a-bye baby on the tree …*'

'SHUT HER UP.' I puke one more time for good luck. We stare at each other. I wipe my mouth on my sleeve. Station break … 'My sister arrives tomorrow. Can I come later in the day?'

'I have a four p.m. cancellation.'

'Bad time. Fucks up my whole day. I was gonna try… I'll try to write in the morning. Hate the mornings.'

'Is that time all right for you?'

Mockingly. 'Is that time all right for you? I'm sorry. I don't mean to be sarcastic. Look, I don't know what I'd do without you. But I really hate needing you. Really hate it.'

'Down will come baby cradle and all …'

'It's fine, Loli. Four o'clock. I'll see you then.'

I get up to leave. I turn around. 'She was so beautiful.'

'Who?'

'My mother.'

'I'm sure she was.'

Memories Lane

Next Day

I drive around LAX at least four times. On the fifth police whistle around, there she is with her steamer trunk. Copious tears, uncontrollable sobbing. Here stands Dina, my older sister. She has come to watch over me.

She gets into my BMW convertible, rolls down her window, looks at me as if I am the me she has always known and loved, comments on my thinness, points to the circles under my eyes, and finally tells me how glad she is to have traveled to western shores. She talks about the family, the weather, the palm trees, my nephew's rash, my brother-in-law's pinkeye, my niece's asthma. 'She's just like you. If she doesn't want to do something, she simply can't breathe.' I don't respond ... She wouldn't hear me anyway ... My niece and nephew will spend the week with my father and his new housekeeper Patty. 'It will do him good. He needs his grandchildren around him.'

She walks into the house, puts her trunk in the guest room, checks out the closet space, hangs up her travel clothes, puts on her sweats, L.L.Bean slippers, calls home, marches into the kitchen, opens the almost empty refrigerator, finds some organic cranberry juice, drinks, puckers, gulps, then rummages through the empty cupboards. 'No Pepperidge Farm Milano cookies?' She asks.

'Old Mother Hubbard
Went to the cupboard,
To fetch her poor ...'

'Shut up!' I shout. Dina looks confused. 'Nursery rhymes. Mother ... talks to me ... in ... nursery rhymes.'

Dina shuts the cupboard door. 'Our mother never knew a nursery rhyme.'

'... all the time. Rhymes ... Old rhymes ... *Mother Goose*. Makes me crazy. After my ... break ... there were demons and voices ... and nursery rhymes.'

'Good juice.'

'Why did it have to happen?'

'Loli, you have to get on with your life. Write, work with kids, do something. She would have wanted you to. She was your biggest fan.'

Pause. 'It was my fault.'

'It wasn't your fault!'

'I should have brought her out here to live with me. She didn't need shock therapy. He just wanted to get her out of the house. He didn't want to see her lying on the kitchen floor again. Got tired stepping over her body on his way upstairs to wash away his sins.'

'Loli. Stop it.'

I become hysterical. 'She never would ... no one ... was ... there. Where ... were ... we ... I ... knew ... I knew ...'

Dina smacks me. I am stunned, but I do stop crying long enough to sit down on the kitchen floor. Dina sits with me. 'I had to. Sorry. I read about it in a ...'

'It's o ... kay ... Helped.'

'I think about her every day, you know. But I won't let her ruin my life. I have a family. You have me, your millions of friends, and your work. You have to work.'

'The pink dress. I can see her pink chemise. Her legs. She had great legs. Didn't she?'

Dina smiles. Her eyes light up like the night sky. 'I loved watching the two of you in the living room. Jitterbug. Lindy. Dancing. Always in sync. She had great rhythm, and you. That's something you were born with. Her Glenn Miller records, your rock 'n' roll – you were meant for each other.'

'Why would she …?'

Dina says, 'She didn't want to go through it anymore.'

'Go through what?' My chest aches.

Dina places her hand on my heart. 'I don't know.'

'Foxtrot, lindy, jitterbug. She taught me the box step. She taught me how to dance.'

'Come on,' says Dina. 'Get up. Let's lindy.' We get up. Off we go. Dancing fools. Loli and Dina together again. And a one two one and two, and a one two one and two. Repeat that again. And again. Slide the arm down her shoulder, over her arm. Grab her hand. Style … we got style. Swirl her round and round. Put my other arm around her waist. She puts her arm around mine. Index fingers in the air. Shoulders up and down … Mouths open … breathing hard. Holler … Hollering …

'Don't stop!' Keep it going. Listen to that big band playin'. Now it's Elvis. I can hear him singin' 'Blue Suede Shoes.' Music from my mother's generation … my sister's generation, and finally The Beatles sing 'She Loves You' from my time. Sisters dance to the sounds of the musical ghosts that made us, and my mother, who we were, who we are. 'Don't stop! Keep it up … Fast … Faster! Faster!'

My mother sings. *'Here we go round the mulberry bush.'*

I scream. 'Mulberry bush!' Dina stops. I keep on dancing, spinning around again and again. I grab her. She pulls away. Turns toward the kitchen sink. Her shoulders shake. I turn her toward me. She is sobbing. My older sister sheds her snakeskin on my kitchen floor. Together we cry our hearts out.

I sob. 'I miss her so much.'

'So do I.'

'Is it ever gonna go away?' I ask.

'Maybe not. Maybe ... some day.'

'Please say it will.' We hold on fast. This is family. This is what I need to survive.

For the next ten days, Dina and I walk the canyon roads, hit the beaches, play in the sand. We don't have pails or shovels. We do have each other.

I make my daily visit to Dr Dot. My hysteria is abated. I begin to eat solid foods, drink liquids, sleep through most of the nights.

It was raining that day of my mother's death. I was in Dina's kitchen. She'd cut herself. I ran to get a Band-Aid. The phone rang. When I came back Dina sat me down. 'She's dead. Mrs B. found her in the bathtub.'

I choke. 'Mommy?'

Dina cries, 'I better call Ralph.'

'Where's Pop?'

'On his way home.'

'What about the kids?'

She organizes the rest of the day's activities. 'Ralph'll take care of them.' We'll take the car to Beechwood.

'Do we need to do anything? Shouldn't we do something!?'

'I have to change the Band-Aid. Wait here. I'll call Ralph.'

'I don't want to be alone ... Can I come with you?'

'Sure.' She grabs my hand. Runs around her nine-room apartment looking for a Band-Aid.

'Why couldn't I …?'

'You couldn't have done anything about it.' Opens the kitchen drawer. 'You were her favorite, you know.' Hands me a Band-Aid. 'She was so happy you came home.'

'I wasn't home. I was here, with you.'

'She was waiting for the right time.'

'She didn't know what she was doing.' I wrap the Band-Aid round her finger.

'She didn't want to live. You can't make someone live.'

'You can try.'

'We did try. It was her choice. Her death.'

'I can't go … home.'

'We have to. Pop will be waiting. He needs us.' She grabs the car keys off the kitchen table.

'What do we tell people?'

'She died. We tell them that she died. That's all.'

Now in LA we try to solve the mystery. What made her so unhappy? Why couldn't anyone help her? We have no answers. In asking the questions, we see how little we knew about her struggle.

Where does mental illness come from? Who do you blame? Who do you forgive? How do you forgive yourself? I blamed my father and me. Dina blamed my mother and the doctors. I think my mother blamed herself for something hidden from those of us who loved her most. She left no note, no will, no goodbye.

Dina was in touch with the next-door neighbor, Mrs B., who had found my mother in the bathtub. Dina knew the gory details. I didn't want to know them. Finding my mother had a terrible impact on Mrs B. Every day she mourned her best friend's death. Her husband, a traveling salesman, got fed up with her grief, found himself a younger woman. Mrs B. took to the sauce.

'Needles and pins, needles and pins,
When a man marries his trouble begins.'

'I bet that's true.'

Dr Dot asks, 'What's true?'

'They never should have gotten married. She was smart, educated, sophisticated, had lots of friends, but never thought she was good enough for him. He never graduated from high school, never knew how to behave, had no friends, hated her father and *he* thought he was the cat's meow. He worked for her father. That's how they met. Her father supported them … for a long time. He hated taking money from him. Proud prick. Screwed around. And she still loved him. Why do people get married?'

'Many reasons.'

'Name … never mind. Here's another question. If two people make each other miserable, why on earth would they stay together?'

My sister had the answer. Night time … 'They loved each other. He adored her. Did you ever notice how he looked at her?'

'Are you dreaming? He didn't love her. He was dismissive, cold, never had anything nice to say about any of her friends, especially Mrs B. Why on earth did they stay together?'

Dina thinks out loud. 'They had a … a kind of love. History. They never knew life without each other.' Dina stares at our silhouettes on the wall. 'Shadows. That's it. They were each other's shadow.'

For a moment, I feel wild, like the old days. 'Come on. Let's get high.' Roll it tight. Hand it off to my favorite straight-as-a-nail person. Deep inhale. Don't let the paranoia seep into my brain.

'Three blind mice ...'

'Come on. Let's get out of here. Go to Ralph's.'

'Ralph's in New York.'

'Ralph's supermarket. Put your loafers on. We're going shopping.'

Down the hill. Talkin'... Talkin'... Talkin'. Into the Food Emporium. The fluorescent lights blaze, the cash registers chime. Grab a cart. Great night for the Greene girls. In the candy section. I spot our favorite: Lindt dark chocolate with hazelnuts. Slide off my left clog. She slides off her right shoe. I reach for two chocolate bars. Place one bar in her shoe, the other in mine. Slide our feet neatly back in place. Nuts crack under foot as we hobble down the paper goods aisle, grab some Scott double-ply toilet paper. Ready to leave the scene of the crime.

Checkout line. The cashier rings up the toilet paper. The store manager walks up to the cashier, whispers something in her ear. My sister pokes me hard with her elbow. The manager smiles at us. We smile back. My heart races. The nuts crack in my clogs. My sister is close to handing over the chocolate bars. I give her the dirtiest look of her short-lived crime-ridden life. The manager walks back to his cubbyhole. We bag the toilet paper and run for the door.

Jump into the BMW, take the chocolate bars out from inside our shoes, eat the stolen goods. We beat the system.

Drive up Laurel Canyon; Joni Mitchell's on the radio. Dina grabs my hand. 'Promise me something.' I savor the yummy luscious chocolate. Turn up the volume. Sing along with Joni.

Dina grabs my arm. 'Promise me that if I'm not here and things get bad, if you're afraid …'

'If ifs and ands were pots and pans …'

'… that you will find me. You will call me. You won't do anything foolish.' She does love me. It's not a substitute for a mother but …

'I'm right here, baby. You'll always be my baby.'

'I promise.' Dina changes the station. The Ronnettes sing 'Be My Baby'. I turn it off … Dina stares at me. My mother continues jabbering. I take a deep breath, relax into the madness … turn the radio back on … *'Be my be my baby … My one and only baby.'*

My sister knows that something other than the song is playing in my head, but she can't hear it.

'Whistle, daughter, whistle;
Whistle for a pound.'
'I cannot whistle, mammy,
I cannot make a sound.'

'She adored you.'

I change the station. 'I know.'

Denver: The Blizzard of '03

(Snow Tires)

Four p.m. March 17th, 2003 ... My plane arrives at Denver International Airport. I have a spur-of-the-moment teaching assignment wedged in between Iowa (Huskers) and Nebraska (Buckeyes). Another detour in my Beatrice plans.

My plane stops 200 feet from the United gate. We are *forbidden* to deplane. The baggage handlers have evacuated the area, because of one solitary bolt of lightning some ten miles due south of the airport. We're talking one good union. An hour and a half later the lightning has passed us by. We are set free from United's airplane bondage. The busy little baggage handlers are back on the job, doing as little as possible.

Fortunately, my ruined bag arrives posthaste. I head on over to the Enterprise van ... As usual, the rental vehicles are parked in the next state. That would be Wyoming. I figure that I have some serious nap time in store. I take full advantage of the altitude and quickly pass out. In my reverie, I hear fellow Enterprise van passengers' voices.

'Three feet. A damn blizzard.'

'That much? I heard two.'

'Glad I'm not driving behind a semi any time soon. Not up those hills.'

'If we droplift you up the mountain, you can ski back to Denver. For sure you'll beat the traffic.'

'Beat my wife anyway.'

'What do you beat her with?' Gales of laughter awaken the rest of me.

'What blizzard?' I say.

'Don't you watch the weather channel?'

'I …'

He interrupts. 'We're about to have the biggest blizzard since '03, 1903. It's a good thing you're picking up your car now. Not gonna be a car on the lot for days. Oh wow, look. It's started. Do you ski?' Before I can answer, he's onto the next question. 'Where you from?'

I am so tired. 'New York.'

'I have a friend in Park Slope. His name is Steve Goodman. You ever run across him?' He's not gonna stop, is he? 'He's a great guy. Makes antique furniture.'

'How do you make antique furniture?' I ask.

'Think he uses a bellows. Blows dust on his mother's old tables and chairs. She's senile. Doesn't sit at the dinner table anymore. Eats in her room. He makes a lot of money off her furniture.'

Snow falls … Blankets of white powder puffs fill the sky as my vehicle and I pull up to the Sheraton Hotel. I check in, go to my room, unpack, organize my toiletries, open the curtains, plug in my air purifier and pick up the telephone.

Saul Rudman, my personal Peter Pan, a flamboyant gay motel owner in Wyoming, keeps a loft in Denver. I'm hoping that we can connect. His machine tells me that he will be out of town until Friday. So, I swim 200 laps in the bacteria-laden, over-chlorinated, ninety-degree, ten-foot, kiddy pool.

Out my window is a wall of white. I'm thinkin': 'It's Colorado. They know how to deal with snow.'

I eat a lemon zest Luna protein bar for dinner. I meditate, file my nails, loofah my dry skin, try to call Simone to congratulate her on having had an impact on my niece. Of course, Simone is not home. Read Susan Weed's *Menopausal Years*. Women have so much more to deal with than men. As if I didn't already know that one.

Then I sit in the hotel lounge surrounded by some honest-to-goodness cowboys. We watch television. Mad King George wages war on Iraq: The famous weapons of mass destruction, protect the world from the Axis of Evil.

I return to my room. I cry for mankind. I lay me down to sleep on my own feather pillow.

'*Now I lay me down …*'

'Go away. Please.'

At six thirty a.m. it is a veritable white Christmas, even though Bing Crosby is dead. At seven thirty a.m. the phone rings.

'Hi. It's Bobbi.'

Who the hell is calling me at this hour? Oh! I fumble for my school folder, the teacher. 'Hi. How are you?'

'I've been shoveling. Got to get a handle on this blizzard. They say it's going to last for at least seventy-two hours. Turn on the Weather Channel. Won't be any school today.' She continues her monologue. 'My kids were really looking forward to working with you. I told them that you were going to jam their computers. Told them they would have to use their imagination. Kids just don't dream anymore, do they?'

'Some do.'

'My daughter does. She's an actress. She's back east. Lives

in Park Slope. Lives with an antique-furniture maker named Steve.'

'Goodman?'

'No. Feingold.' Pause.

'Sorry that we're not going to meet today. Bend your knees.'

'What?'

'Your back. Shoveling. Bend your knees.'

'I always do. How's your room?' Before I can answer she shouts, 'Bruno! Get in here! Damn dog. Call you tomorrow.'

For three consecutive mornings, Bobbi does not call. Phones are dead, cable's out, Denver is completely shut down. No external distractions. An array of internal disturbances.

I dine on undetectable, inedible hotel rations for a record-breaking seventy-two hours. I finish off my last lemon zest bar, steal apples from the front desk, and convince myself that as long as I eat the bristles on my toothbrush I will have enough fiber in my diet to survive. I read whatever's in the hotel's lending library; no comment.

Finally, on Friday, the snow stops. Bobbi calls. 'You won't believe it!'

'What?'

'No school.'

'Why?!'

'They're afraid the roof might cave in. It's flat.'

'Hope you and the kids get to see the show next week.'

'We will, if I can get the parents to sign the waivers. Most of them don't read English.'

'They don't?'

'No. This is an English as a second language class. Almost all of the parents don't speak it at all.' Thank God for the blizzard. 'Are you busy tonight?'

'Yeah. My friend Saul Rudman's in town.'

'Saul? From Wyoming?'

'Saul from Wyoming.'

'I went to one of his Halloween parties. Tell Saul, Bobbi, the dominatrix, says hi.'

'Sure will.' Another missed opportunity.

'Come back soon.' Click.

At eight p.m. Saul Rudman, the dearest man I know, picks me up in his Cadillac SUV. I pole vault up, over, and down into the passenger seat. We hug, howl and get high. We drive through a snowy Denver, pull up in front of a trendy nouveau restaurant.

Saul orders a gin martini. I order a vodka martini. They are cowboy drinks, bigger than the state of Texas. Saul downs his in a blink of an eye. I take one sip of my martini and spit it out. I hate gin. Saul grabs my glass, downs my drink, orders another. I get my first. He drinks his third. He regales me with stories about his audience with the most famous back specialist in the world; who is, of course, located in Santa Monica, California. Dr Painfree has Saul on a cutting-edge medical protocol. Yes, Saul is on the muscle-relaxant, raw-juice diet. The boy hasn't eaten solids for three days.

His eyes cross. He sways like an American flag on a windy night.

I shout. 'SAUL, CAN YOU HEAR ME!?'

'What? What'd you say?'

I slap my hands in front of his face and talk deaf talk to him. 'CAN … YOU … HEAR … ME?!'

'I better break my juice fast.' With his right hand, Saul reaches for a piece of bread. It drops onto the floor. With his left hand, he places something into his mouth. 'Bite, crunch, crack, yech.'

'Saul, what the hell are you eating?'

He spits out little pieces of plastic and wire into his right hand. 'My hearing aid. My two thousand dollar hearing aid.' Saul has one more Martini for the road. I take a cab back to my hotel.

Late the next morning I hear from Saul. 'I am so sorry.'

'Don't be. How'd you get home?'

'I hitched a ride.'

'Are you crazy?'

'No. He's in the kitchen making me coffee.'

'I can't believe … Guys. Can't keep it in their pants.'

'You're just jealous.'

'I probably am.'

'Did I make a fool of myself last night?'

'Absolutely.'

'Don't tell anyone.'

'Who am I gonna tell? Do you even remember last night?'

'Not really.'

'In memory nothing is foolish. Experiences make us who we are.'

'Did you make that up?'

'No. Got that one from my dear dead mother.'

'She must have been something.'

'When she was, she was quite something.'

'*When she was good*
She was very very good …'

'I suggest that you stop taking muscle relaxants. Meditate instead.'

'I will. I'll call and tell you when I'm coming to New York … How's Simone?'

'Rough patch.'

'Therapy. You need to get yourself back in therapy.'

'She doesn't believe in it.'

'I'm talking about you not her … Oh fantastic. Eggs Benedict and coffee.'

'Love you.'

'I love you too.'

'How fortunate for me,' I reply.

Saul shouts, 'What'd you say?'

'I SAID GET A CHEAPER HEARING AID!'

Rear End

The rear end of any extraordinary adventure is much more sensational than the front end. On a rollercoaster, when you are seated in the last car, you experience a giddy near-death feeling. As you dive down and your gastric juices rise up into your esophagus, believe me, the people up front are not having half the good time that you are having in the rear. On the rear end of the blizzard of '03, I felt as if I had been somewhere unimaginable. I had that near-death feeling. I had scaled Mount Everest. I was ready for my next death-defying experience ...

I have a three-hour delay, before the long-awaited trip to Lincoln, Nebraska, where I would then rent an Avis (no Enterprise available) in order to reach the town of Beatrice. With time to kill (strange expression), I flip open my Verizon cellphone, push the button. I call Dina. It is eight p.m. in New York. She might be having her pre-bedtime wine spritzer. Maybe she is flossing, or Sonicaring her teeth. Whatever she is doing, I need to tell the tale ... ring ... ring ...

'Hello.'

'It's me.'

'Oh hi. Where are you?' She sounds fatigued.

'Denver International Airport.'

'Do you really teach, or are you perpetually traveling from one place to another without ever setting foot in a classroom?'

'Not nice.'

'The wine went to my head.'

'Don't you want to know about the blizzard?'
'What blizzard?'
'The biggest blizzard in one hundred years.'
'Was there a lot of snow?'
'For an intelligent woman, you are ridiculous.'
'I've been busy.' Dina sighs.
'Who is it this time?' Dead silence
'Pop.'
Up and down the City Road,
In and out the Eagle,
That's the way the money goes,
Pop goes the weasel!'
'Is he still alive?'
'Loli, he's your father.'

'No! He's *your* father. He is merely the sperm donor who fertilized the weird egg that hatched *me* into this cognitive world.'

'Twenty years! How long can you blame him for her death? It wasn't his fault that she was crazy. Haven't you figured that one out in therapy yet? Even I know that, and I haven't been in therapy since I was eleven. Why meditate? Why do yoga? Why do any of it, if you can't forgive?'

'When did you get to be Miss Love, Peace, and Harmony? I know. He never meant anybody any harm ... tried everything ... couldn't understand ... sent her to the best doctors.'

'It's a matter of maybe a few months.'

'Good! Call me when he's gone.' Click. That mother son of a philandering lousy prick! What am I supposed to do about it? Love the bastard!? Never. For all I care, he can rot in his blue boxer shorts with his shriveled-up dick in his hand.

'He loves you, baby.'

'Would you shut up already!' I look around. A few normal

people, and there are only a handful, are shocked by my outburst. I redial 212 et cetera …

'Yes.' She is cold as stone.

'I'm sorry.'

'So am I. The timing couldn't be worse. Ralph's been kicked upstairs into the research department. Your nephew is, in fact, moving to Shanghai. Your lovely niece is depressed because her new love, Methuselah, has an obsessive compulsive disorder that manifests in either sleepwalking, bedwetting, or midnight jogging in Central Park. Not only is he old, he is certifiable. Why did I ever get married? Why did I have children?'

'I love your kids. Wish they were mine … What's wrong with him?'

She sighs again. 'Cancer. Everywhere. They say that he's been sick for a very long time. There's no point in chemo …' She cries quietly. 'I am so tired. And work is so stressful. My boss Richard, that asshole, just took himself on a junket to Zurich. The museum is bankrupt and he's writing off a ski holiday in the Alps.'

'He's no fool. I'm coming home next week. Oh! I forgot to tell you about my next stop.'

'I can't imagine.'

'Beatrice, Nebraska. Bee as in honey, a as in have, trice as in tryst without the final t. Is that amazing?'

'Dad's convinced that Mom's come for him. She's in the bedroom.'

'I hope she's not getting ready to reincarnate; another nervous breakdown waiting to happen. We will have to get high when I come home. I'll be back for a week before they send me to Montana.'

'You're flying into New York then flying back to Montana?'

'Don't … The travel plans are mind-altering.'

'How's Simone?'

'I guess she's fine. Haven't heard from her.'

'Where is she?'

'Marbleizing wealthy kitchen walls in Zurich. Sucking up to some famous art dealer in Geneva. Then she'll visit her demented mother in Normandy: "The salt air … the rocks … the dead soldiers … so much history."'

'Do you miss her?'

'Sometimes. Mornings. Mostly, I miss the sex.'

'Ralph won't leave me alone. I pretend that it's great. He needs that right now.'

'Your family is lucky to have you. I include myself. You are so good.'

'When she was good.'

'Would you shut up!'

'What?'

'Mom's back. The nursery rhymes.' Let's keep it light. 'How's that possible, if she's in Dad's bedroom?'

'Are you … all right?' Dina's voice falters.

'Sure. Great to have her back again.'

'Did you call Mary Michelin yet?'

'I will.'

'You should.'

'I know.' Deep inhales on both ends of the phone.

'Mrs B. is in the hospital. Diabetes.'

'What other good news do you have?'

'She's going blind.'

'That's good news?'

'Remember how beautiful she was?'

'Most beautiful legs I ever saw, those luminous hazel eyes. I can't believe she's going blind. Old age is frightening. My plane is boarding. I'll call you from Beatrice.'

'Say hi to Mom for me.'

'Very funny.'

It was his time to die. Twenty years had passed. I still blamed him for my mother's death. Everyone in Beechwood knew that he was a fool-around. Had a wondering eye. Couldn't keep it in his pants. Loved the ladies.

We were more than less estranged. After she died, I never went home for the holidays. Refused to meet his lady friends. The final straw was when he hit on my lover Simone. He could not, would not understand that I had ventured into Sappho territory.

Before my mother died, I had shared my secret with her. She sent me to her shrink, who in turn, asked me to give it up for Mom's sake. 'Young lady, I am most certain that your sexual dalliances are merely a phase.'

After my mother died I wrote a letter to my father. Told him that I was gay. Wanted to save him from the embarrassment of making a bigger fool of himself than he already was. He disowned me. That was my relationship with 'Pop'. You always hate that which reminds you of yourself. My meandering was a mere mimicking of his philandering.

During her sane years, she appeared to adore him: '*We should all be proud of his accomplishments.*' I heard that line innumerable times. My sister swore that Pop loved Mom 'til her dying day. My theory was the following:

Peter, Peter, pumpkin eater,

Had a wife and couldn't keep her.

As a child, growing up in the Bronx, Pop was dirt poor.

Shared a bedroom with his younger brother and sister. Mother threw white sheets over the furniture in the summer. Took them off in the fall. Father worked in a garage. They all shared the same bathroom. As far as I was concerned, the only thing Pop worshipped was money ... And monkeys. He loved his good-luck monkey collection.

He was alone now, padding around (my mother padding after him) in that white house with a million windows and two million green shutters. Patty, the housekeeper, cleaned the house, kept him company, laughed at his jokes, while she stole him blind. Since my mother's death, my father's life meant nothing to me. I had no idea that he would be part of the story. Life is full of surprises.

My mother was back in their bedroom. And, she was talking to me ... again. These were uncharted waters without a skipper on deck.

Molly Malone

(New Directions)

I remember, as a young child, I would sit on the pink piano bench, gazing at my mother's fingertips as they traveled over the black and white keys of our Baldwin acrosonic piano. She played a lyrical Irish folk song over and over again. The first few lines go something like this ...

In Dublin's fair city
'Sing my pretty baby.'
Where the girls are so pretty
I first set my eyes on sweet Molly Malone.

From the air, Nebraska looks like a dark brown on light brown farmers' chessboard. In this country, in fact, it is the crop growers and grain givers who feed us and keep us alive. They are a dying breed. Their children cannot wait to get away from the cow dung and the prairie mentality.

When you arrive in Nebraska, you sense the dying-off of the farmer and his glory times. Archer Daniels Midland, the giant agricultural corporation, is no replacement for the real thing.

Before I arrived, all I knew about Nebraska was that Willa Cather, a gifted and prolific writer, grew up there. I know she eventually worked elsewhere; even though she apparently loved Nebraska, she couldn't wait to get the hell away. Yet Warren Buffet, a very successful businessman, has remained in Nebraska for most of his life. What attracts one person repels another. What is acceptable to some is rejected by many. It is both challenging and difficult to be in the minority, especially when the majority rules or shall I say makes the rules.

Midflight I untie my blue silk scarf. I lift it from around my neck, lay it on my lap, fold it into perfect quarters, unzip my knapsack, place it inside the sack, and zip it safely away.

The plane is three hours late. It is pouring. I walk in the rain from the plane to the gate, since the hydraulic gate mover is broken. But the baggage handlers are waiting anxiously to retrieve the bags from the final plane of the day. All is well with the world in Lincoln. I am an hour away from Beatrice.

I hope the Avis car rental lot is not in Omaha, which according to my map is many miles from Lincoln. I walk into the terminal. Maybe I can make it to Beatrice in forty-five minutes. Excitement runs through my veins.

A very adorable brunette woman, about thirty-five or forty, with a turned-up nose and a pouty upper lip, is holding up a sign. Next to her is a teenage girl with the reddest wildest hair I have seen since *I Love Lucy*. I read the sign. 'Loli Greene'. Oh my God, someone has come to greet me at the Lincoln airport in the middle of a deluge. The grown-up with the pouty lip approaches. 'Are you Loli Greene?'

I am so excited. And, she is … a-d-o-r-a-b-l-e. Look at that luscious upper lip, peaches and cream complexion, thick, beautiful hair. My nephew would give up the yellow race for her. She is magnificent; a little bit overweight. Who cares. Look at that sexy scar above her lip … and look at her … breasts. Beautiful. I wish Simone had breasts like that. Simone. What about Simone? Slow down, Loli. Make contact. Say something. 'Hello.'

'I'm Maggie Malone. This is my daughter Molly.'

'Nice to meet you both. What are you doing out here in the middle of such a soggy night?'

'I'm the assistant head of the Beatrice Arts Council. We wanted to welcome you to Nebraska, and make sure that you got settled in at your hotel.'

'That is so nice. I can't believe that you came out here in this monsoon to welcome me.'

'Oh, it's just a little shower.' A bolt of lightning, followed by a threatening clap of thunder, breaks a window in the terminal. The sirens roar.

'Just a shower, Ma.' Another sullen, stubborn, teenage hooligan.

'Let's get you to your car. You can follow us to the hotel. We are so excited about your coming to Beatrice. No one ever comes to Beatrice. We have so many plans for you and your troupe. Can't wait to see the play. You do know that Willa Cather was born in Nebraska?'

'I do.'

'Molly's going to be in one of your classes. They can't wait.'

'Right, Mom.'

'And you are in which class of mine?'

'Mr Willwrite's English class.'

'Is he any good?'

'I guess for an English teacher he's all right. He's a little weird.'

'Molly! Don't be rude. Apologize right now, young lady.'

'For what?'

How do parents do it? 'Not a problem. Good to know the

lay of the land before I get to class. What have you been studying this semester?'

'Willa Cather. I like the themes. I love her characters. I don't understand why those people stuck it out here. Personally, I can't wait to get the hell out; so boring.'

'Molly Malone!'

'I know, Mom. But it's true. At least in those days they were busy farming or something. And the families, they were real families. I'm sure the kids could have cared less about the farms.' Molly has touched a nerve.

Maggie is furious. 'They *had* to work the farms! Do you think those children had a choice?'

'Sure they did. They just didn't know it. They could've walked away. Whatever.'

Can't wait for class. Sexy woman. Those eyes, luminescent … I know those eyes, those hazel eyes are so familiar. My mother? No. They were brown, weren't they? It's been so long.

'Hickory, dickery, dock!

The mouse ran up the clock. Having a good time, dear?'

Here she is. Breathe, Loli. Breathe. Remember Dr Guttman. Deeper. That's better. Got to get out of here. The ceiling is spin, spin … turn, upside down …

'Here we go round the mulberry bush,

The mulberry bush, the mulberry bush.'

Maggie touches my shoulder. 'Are you … Is there something wrong?'

Molly almost acts like she cares. 'Yeah. You sick or something?'

'Hotel room for days. Airports. Airplanes. I haven't had any oxygen in my lungs for at least one solid week; got to take a few deep breaths.' Keep up the cover. 'First acting teacher taught me how to breathe like this.' Leave me alone, Ma. Leave me alone!!!

Maggie rescues me. 'You studied acting?' She cares. I breathe better.

'And singing … and … writ …'

Young Molly gets excited; an unusual event for a teenager. 'You sing?'

I nod. Enormous effort. Need to get on the road. 'My mother's name was Beatrice. It's not pronounced the same as Be-a-trice, but it's spelled the same. I've been dying to get here.'

'Me too, honey. Me too.'

I cringe. 'Oh no.'

Molly and Maggie chime in: 'What?'

'My scarf.' They are trying so hard to follow my thought process. 'I … I … stuffed … inside my knapsack. It'll be creased.'

Maggie makes it better. 'They're sure to have an iron in your room at the Holiday Inn.'

'The mulberry bush.'

Molly's still excited. 'Singing, wow! You know you've got a jacuzzi in your room. You must be someone real special.'

'That's me. Real special.'

'That's my baby … and the dish ran away with the spoon.'

I cover my ears. Groan out loud. Mom, meet me in the car! She whispers. *'Sure, baby.'*

Molly whispers to Maggie, 'She is weird.'

Maggie whispers under her breath. 'It's jet lag, sweetie. Let's get her to the hotel.'

My red bag arrives. Maggie grabs it. Molly chews gum, a sure sign of teenage inertia. Maggie hands me the keys to my hunter-green Ford Taurus.

My heart is full of Maggie Malone. My head is full of mother. I take one more deep breath. Let's swing the conversation toward the personal. 'What's your husband doing tonight?'

Molly answers. 'His bimbo girlfriend.'

'Molly Malone! Excuse us.' Maggie pulls Molly aside. They have a heated debate. On return Maggie explains: 'We're in the middle of a divorce. Molly lives with me. She's with her father on weekends.'

Bingo! 'I'm so sorry. Are you on good terms with each other?'

'Not right now.'

'That's a shame.' Good news.

'It sucks, if you ask me.'

Maggie shoots her daughter the dagger look. 'We're not asking you, honey.'

I keep things moving. 'I'll follow you. You sure you don't mind?'

'It's the Midwest. This is how we do it out here.' Mother and daughter get into Maggie's Jeep Cherokee. Maggie puts her arm around Molly. Molly fiddles with her hair. Molly turns around. Looks at me. Through the raindrops, I see her. She turns away, body stiffens. She moves away from Maggie. Mothers and daughters. I slide into my Ford Taurus, fiddle with the mirror, turn the key and off we go. We travel down Highway 77 toward Beatrice. I follow the red tail lights. The rain lets up. The wind whistles through the crack in my open window. How I love that sound. 'Don't you love that sound, Mom?'

She's divorced. Wonder why? Never thought people got divorced in the Midwest? Never thought much about the Midwest. Wonder if Midwesterners think about the east? The east coast is where the world wants to be, especially New York.

I don't want to be anywhere. Sometimes I do. Right now I want to be right here following Maggie Malone. My mother would like Maggie. 'Don't you, Ma?' Pop would want to fuck her. Dina would like her. Who's gonna move? I don't want to live in Nebraska. She's got Molly. Molly'll be graduating soon. We could live anywhere in the world. I love Italy. England's nice; no the weather sucks. I don't like the United States any more. I wonder if she's a Republican? I couldn't live with a Republican. Oh shit I'm losing them. No, there they are. Wonder what the dad is like? Probably a pig. Who wanted the divorce? Everybody wants a divorce. I don't know if I love Simone anymore. Been so long. Sex is everything. No, love is everything. I never loved anyone. Maybe I do love Simone. I loved my mother. 'I still love you, Mom. Now, don't forget your seat belt. Would hate to see anything happen to you again.'

As the ride continues, I travel my brain; left brain to right brain; cerebral cortex to cerebellum. I travel down the crowded highway of multifarious metaphors. God is my only witness.

The Holiday Inn is a Holiday Inn. The Malone girls show me to my room. There is, in fact, a jacuzzi in the living area. I am afraid to look at Maggie. I finally do … look at her. 'Thank you so much. Molly, I'll see you tomorrow.'

'If I show up.'

'Honey!'

'Maggie, do you …?'

'In Dublin's fair city.'

'Do you know what time my classes are?'

'You have an eleven a.m. Then you have a one-hour break. Your next classes are at one and two; two English one history.'

'Which class are you in, Mol?'

'Molly! I don't like nicknames … Eleven a.m. English.

'See you at eleven … Molly.'

Maggie starts to leave. 'Oh, Loli, our theater group would like to have a Q and A with you tomorrow night. We meet at seven p.m. We could have dinner after?'

I am dying. I am definitely dying. 'Sure.' Too quick a response. I am usually much cooler. I am not cool at all. Those eyes.

'Where the girls are so pretty.'

'Night, Loli. I'll see you tomorrow night. Molly will see you in the morning. Say goodnight Molly.'

'Night.'

'I first laid my eyes.'

'Night, Maggie.'

'Night, Loli.'

I run a steaming hot jacuzzi into which I pour some lavender bath oils. Perhaps the bath will calm me down.

I place my meditation beads on the night stand. I notice a small basket of daisies on the living area bureau. There is a note. I open the envelope. 'Welcome to Beatrice – Maggie Malone.'

I writhe, undulate and soak. I touch myself. My warm wet hand reaches inside. So wet … Hot … I twist. I turn. I erupt. Pounding waves … fire … heat …Oh fuck … Yes. Take it … Come on. Suck it. Harder. Harder! Oh yes. Take it! Let me come inside you. Deep ache … Hand deep inside … Feel me. Feel it … Open up … Again and again … and harder and faster and take me again, yes … Again … Feel it … Now … Maggie Malone … Ecstasy … Maggie Malone.

I realize that I am in danger. My hand is getting the better of me. My imagination's getting the best of me. I will use these feelings when I stand before that eleven a.m. English class. I will use it all. No. I have to save some of it for tomorrow evening ... for Maggie

'*On sweet ...*'

'Maggie Malone, Mom! Her name is Maggie Malone!' I dial Dina's number. It is way past her bedtime. I do not care. 'Hello.'

'I'm sleeping.'

'I'm in love.'

'I don't care.'

'I do.'

'Pop's been asking for you.'

'Night.'

'Wait! Don't hang up. I forgot to tell you. Burt died.'

'Mrs B.'s son?'

'He shot himself in the head. You should call her.'

'Poor Mrs B. ... Sorry I woke you.' Life isn't fair.

After a fitful night's sleep, I wake at eight thirty a.m. I am nervous, nauseated and giddy. I can't stop thinking about Maggie Malone. I must stop thinking about Maggie Malone. I iron my lucky scarf. Lovely. I listen to the morning silence.

'*Not a creature was stirring ...*'

Her voice punctuates most of my inner thoughts. I try to meditate. It is an impossible task. I give up the ghost (so to speak). I brew my gunpowder green tea, stir my protein drink, wrap the scarf around my neck, leave the hotel.

At school I am met by the assistant principal. He leads me into the brand new auditorium; stunning contemporary design, cool dark-blue padded seats, full light grid above stage, professional soundboard in the back of the house. It is a beauty;

a stage filled with pride, possessing the power to present any of the performing arts in all of their splendor. After the dressing room tour, he ushers me into Willwrite's room, introduces me to a fastidious man wearing a bow tie, and leaves us to hopefully enjoy each other's company.

'We've been studying Willa Cather's *O Pioneers.*'

'That's what I heard.'

'They're good kids. We only have a few problem students in the class. When it comes to manners, I am a real stickler.' He coughs as he straightens his tie. 'The Bard rules the room.' He points to a series of Shakespeare posters that grace his classroom walls. The bell rings. Molly straggles in. He whispers, 'Problems at home. Lazy. Needs special attention.' He addresses the class. 'All right, ladies and gentlemen, I want you to meet Loli Greene. She has come to Beatrice to enliven your imagination. Therefore, there will be no grammar this week.' Shouts of joy. 'But, you will be graded on your manners. Remember the three B's … Be polite … Be attentive … Behave. I will be grading term papers during the week. I will be watching every move that you make. "What shall I say, more than I have inferr'd? Remember who you are to cope withal." The king leaves you to your fate.' As he heads gallantly with ruler on shoulder toward his desk, the class applauds Mr Willwrite.

I jump on top of the nearest desk. 'What is imagination? Where does it come from? How can you inspire yourself? How will you free yourself from the complacency of your life? Creativity will set you free. All you have to do is shut off your brain. Stop thinking! Have a good time, get out of your way and get out of the box. There is no testing in my room. You can't fail in my class. If you don't like it here, for all I care, you have my permission to leave the room. Is that all right with you, Mr Willwrite?'

'As long as they read anything by Shakespeare ... In the library. I will want a written report next week. But, they *can* leave the room.'

I remain perched on top of the desk. All eyes are upon me. Not one student has fallen asleep. Miracle. 'Let's do some breath work. Stand up ... Come on, get up! Take three deep breaths ... Slow down ... Now close your eyes. Let yourself be in the wave of your fluid systems. Don't ask what that is. Whatever it is to you is fine. Now touch into the universe that lies within you ... that is you. Sit down slowly ... Now, if you haven't already, open your eyes.

'Take out a piece of paper. So, you've been reading Willa Cather's *O Pioneers*. That's right. Isn't it?' Many nods. 'Good. You are going to dialogue with your ancestors ... those that came before you. You can dialogue with a grandparent, or great-grandparent. You can even dialogue with a character from the novel. It's the past we're tapping into. Write this down. First part: what do you want this character to know about you? Second part: what advice does your character have for you? Third part: as yourself, today, what advice do you have for somebody in the next generation. So, in the third part, you're dealing with the future; future pacing. Be specific. Who are you talking to? I want names, locations, time of year, time of day ... the works. Maybe a scene will come out of it. You might even encounter all three generations simultaneously. Check out the clothes. Who's wearing what? Who are you? You can become anyone you want. You have twenty minutes for the entire exercise. That's not a lot of time. Believe me, it's all the time you need. Remember. Be specific!'

Molly looks somewhat perplexed. We acknowledge each other's presence. She begins the exercise in earnest. The entire class is writing. Not one person leaves the room. Willwrite pushes his homework aside. He too will explore the world of his ancestors. I am overjoyed. It is a great first day at Beatrice High.

After class, I pick up my lesson plan, peruse my notes. To my surprise, I have succeeded in following my own instructions. How lovely to have completed the assignment. Willwrite gives me the thumbs-up sign. Yes! I feel good about those forty-seven some odd minutes.

As I walk out the door, I see Molly engrossed in bubble gum blowing. She leans against what I presume to be her locker. The bubble bursts. Don't they all?

'Hi Molly.'

'Hi.'

'Now that's what I call good conversation.' Let's try again. 'Hi, Molly.'

'That was a great class.'

'Glad you had a good time.'

'I didn't really understand what we were doing, but I did what I thought we were supposed to do.'

More than I ever expected. 'I have an hour before my next class. What are you up to?'

She shrugs her shoulders. 'Hangin' around.'

'I see that.'

'I'm finished for the day.'

'I'm sure.'

'No! I am. Honest. I have study hall.'

'You want to take a walk?'

'I don't mind.' That means yes. 'Where you walking to?'

'Anywhere you want – the road in front of the school.'

'That's fine.' We stroll down the corridors of Beatrice High. Molly is somewhat embarrassed to be seen walking with an adult.

'What happened?'

'When?'

'In class. What happened? Who'd you talk with?'

'My grandfather.'

'And?'

'He died when I was very young. I didn't really know him. I went back to some time before I was born, but I was a grown-up, not like you, but my age grown-up. I think it was the Depression. I'm not sure ... I felt the time. Does that make any sense?'

'Definitely.'

'We spoke to each other. He was with me in this time now, and I was with him then. Time got confusing.'

'Time is confusing. What did he say?'

'Wait. Let me tell you this first.' She describes his navy blue suit, how his shirt sleeves stuck out from the end of his jacket, his little gold, square, shiny cufflinks. 'He was handsome, like my father.'

'Did he look like your father?'

'No. But something about him reminded me of my dad. It surprised me.'

'Surprises are good.'

'I was afraid of him when I was little. I liked him so much more in this whatever you call it?'

'Process. Where were you?'

'In our house here in Beatrice.'

'What room?'

'My bedroom.'

'What were you doing?'

'Brushing my hair. I kept brushing my hair.' She demonstrates. Her gestures have an other-timely feel to them.

'What was he doing?'

'Staring … at me.'

Be careful. Get back to the exercise. 'What advice did he have for you?' I stop at the driveway entrance, look both ways. A yellow school bus turns into the driveway.

She stops. 'He told me that I must never grow old; stay young forever. It made me sad.'

'Why?'

'I don't know.'

'What else?' I walk

'Asked me to forgive my father? Said he couldn't help himself.'

'What'd he mean?'

'I guess he meant the bimbo.' She doesn't move.

'You don't know that for sure. He might have been talking about something else altogether.'

'I doubt it.' We walk due east, down a little country road that leads us to a bigger country road, that leads us to the biggest country road of all. An oversized dump truck rumbles by at breakneck speed. It kicks up a life-load of dust. I cough. Molly stops in her tracks. She has something on her mind. 'Do you love what you do?'

'I do. I love a lot of things, even what I don't do.' I laugh.

'Do you make a living being a writer?'

'Sometimes yes, sometimes no.'

'Is that why you teach?'

'No. I have to teach because … I just have to teach. And … I have to write. I don't know why.'

'Are you successful?'

'Did you stay in the room?'

'Yeah.' She laughs.

'Did you discover someplace special?' She nods yes. 'Do you want to go back there?' She nods yes again ... 'Knowing that it may never be the same, that place, are you absolutely sure that you want to go there again?!'

'Oh yes.'

'I am very successful.'

'Because of me?' She doesn't understand.

'You got it.' Such sweetness. Mustn't say too much. Have to maintain some sense of grown-up rank here. We cannot be friends. Maybe we can? What if I'm trying to get to her mother through her? Keep it on the creative level. Maybe I can help her? I don't want to impose in any way. Man oh man would I love to be her age again ... It is a terrible age. Poor baby. Maggie has her hands full.

'Are you married?'

'I am not married. Enough on that subject. I want to get back to you. I want you to go deeper into that exercise. Tonight, at home, go back to the scene with your grandfather. Talk to him. Listen to what he has to say. Put it on paper. Ask him what he meant about forgiving your father. Would you do that for me?'

'I guess. If I have time. I'm having dinner with my father tonight.'

'If you have the time.' We turn around. The garbage truck rumbles by us one more time.

'I hate him.'

'Your father?' She nods a definitive teenage yes. 'I know that one. I've hated my father for years.' Too personal.

'Is he still alive?'

'He is. He's terminally ill.'

'Do you ever talk to him about how it feels?'

'No. It's a long story.' Stay under that radar of hers.

'That's terrible. Maybe you should speak to him while you still can.'

'Maybe.'

'I speak to my dad, even if I do hate him.'

'That's a good idea.' Isn't it about time that I forgave the old man?

'*That's a good girl.*'

'Even if you hate someone, it's a good idea to talk it out. That's what my mom says.'

'I agree totally.'

'Me too.'

'You're very smart, Molly Malone.'

'You think so?' She lights up from ear to ear.

'I do.'

'Did you ever want to be somebody else?' she asks.

I wonder who she wants to be. 'Yes.'

'Who did you want to be?'

'Mrs Crouse, third grade, she was the best teacher I ever had. I worshipped her.' More moist dreams about her … Always been horny. 'How 'bout you?'

'I dunno. You're pretty different, maybe you.'

'Thank you.' I am touched.

We say goodbye and return to our respective school rooms; I to a rowdy history class; she to a quiet study hall. I am enriched from our walk. I hope that she is enlivened from it.

Before history class, I remember once I had asked my mother, in a childhood conversation, if there was anyone in the world she could be, who would it be?

'You, honey. You.' She wanted to be me.

I teach the next two classes with a certain unfamiliar ease. Willwrite's class has paved the way for newly improved extemporaneous teaching methods. While the students are talking (on paper) to their ancestors, I cannot stop thinking about my father. At present I can hardly remember why I hate the old goat. I just know that it has become another all-consuming habit; much like my subscription to *Vanity Fair*. It comes in the mail once a month. I read it, and it stimulates all that I hate about myself and the world. So isn't it time to cancel the subscription? Where do I begin? Call Mary Michelin. Maybe she can help me with the evolutionary exorcism of life's nasty problem?

After school I return to my Holiday Inn home away from home. I dial Mary Michelin's number.

'Hello. This is the voice of Mary Michelin. I am on holiday until April 15th. I will be calling in for my messages. Please leave your name and number. I will get back to you as soon as possible. If it's an emergency, you may call my colleague Dr Dot at 212 …'

'Here we go round the mulberry bush,
The mulberry bush, the mulberry bush.'

Past tense meets present tense with me in the middle. There can only be one Dr Dot in the world; that Dot I knew so well. How did he end up on Mary Michelin's referral phone list? He's subbing in April?! He must be a dreadful doctor. I had my doubts about him twenty years ago.

What about her? Is she the shrink for me? After numerous psychological adventures and misadventures, my theory is why not take one more acid trip into the quagmire called memory.

The very sound of Dr Dot's name has me hankering for a neon trip to Wal-Mart: I want edibles: not egg whites and sugar. Haven't I come a long way, Dr Dot? I need sustenance. You see, I got a date tonight with Maggie Malone. How I love the sound of her name. Mommy ... I have a date tonight. Please don't ruin it.

U Turn

'84

Dina's last night in Los Angeles is almost as eventful as the Lindt chocolate caper evening. Sis retrieves a stack of letters from the bottom of her steamer trunk. They are vintage, ripped, torn, tattered letters. Some are stuffed in yellow stained envelopes. Most are barely legible. 'Read these.' She hands off the stack of relics to me. I follow her instructions. After all, I am the younger sister.

'Please come to get me. I hate everything. I hate everyone. I want to go for a ride. Could we do that soon? I promise I won't cry. Promise. I'll be good if you take me back home with you.' As I decipher the scribbles on each ancient page, I am reminded of a time from my past without road signage or map quest.

Dina hands me another letter. 'Now read this.'

'There was a little girl who had a little curl right in the middle of her forehead; When she was good, she was very, very good, and when she was bad she was horrid. Be a good girl now.

love me (she).'

'She did know nursery rhymes! I am vindicated, even if I am younger.'

Dina swears on her life that my mother never read either one of us a nursery rhyme; at least not when we were of nursery rhyme age. 'You were ten when she wrote you this ditty – a little old for an introduction to *Mother Goose*, wouldn't you say?'

'Remember, they sent you off to Camp Clydesdale: The Camp for Young Horse Lovers.'

'Wasn't that the summer I stopped eating solid foods?'

'Certainly was. You tried your best to starve yourself to death – what a lovely little girl you were. We, your mother, father and I, drove up to the Catskills, yanked you out of the infirmary. The ride back home was a veritable yell fest.'

I keep reading. 'Dr Guttman's coming back the week after next. I'll miss Dr Dot, even if he is a psychiatrist in training ... Where did you find these?'

'In the attic. She saved your letters, and made copies of hers. You should have her originals.'

'I don't.'

'Of course not. God forbid you should have any memorabilia from your past. Do you have a photo of any one of us?' I think about the question; hard. Shake my head in disgust with myself. 'It's not normal. Everyone has a scrapbook.'

'Well, I don't. Why remind yourself of something you love that's ... no longer there.'

'Anyway ... You came home, suddenly a soft-food eater. Next thing, right after you arrive, she's in some hospital for some new ailment. We weren't supposed to know.'

'I didn't know that she was hospitalized then?'

'You didn't know a lot of things. You were ten. What does a ten-year-old know about anything? Besides, you were busy having your unique food drama.' Dina continues her story. 'On the nights that Pop came home for dinner I cooked for him. He worked late ... some merger. As soon as he walked through the door, he'd change his shoes and go out again. He took endless walks around Beechwood by himself.' As she remembers Pop, her face softens, eyes smile. 'That was the summer Pop started smoking Cherry Blend … I remember, when he came back after his walks, he would sit in his easy chair, pack the tobacco into his pipe, light it up, draw the smoke down into his belly, blow out the match, and blow perfect smoke rings into the air; his nightly ritual, along with watching Jack Parr or Johnny Carson. Mrs B. cooked for you; vats of oatmeal. You were such a misery. The maid quit. The house was upside down. Keep reading.'

It was clear from the letters that my mother was versed in the language of nursery rhymes. Clear I did not want to go to Camp Clydesdale. My father had made the unilateral decision. Evidently, my mother did not want me to go, and I did not want to leave her. But we had no say in the matter.

By reading these letters, I understood what drove me into Bovar's grip in the first place. His demon lies offered me a way to bury her inside of me … forever. She and I would always be connected through a web of symbiotic symmetry.

In the entire universe, there was only one person left whom I could trust … my sister. From my auspicious beginning, Dina had been present and accountable … for all of us. She had been witness to the hospitals, the shock therapy, the numbing drugs, and the final horrendous defeat.

'I can't read anymore,' I said.

Dina replied, 'I'll take them home.'

I'm not ready to let them go. 'No, let me keep them here.'

'Loli, maybe you should get involved with something a little less drastic next time? What about meditation? Yoga? While you're working with Dr Guttman, you could do all sorts of creative things … spiritual things. When you get your life back on track, you'll be fine. You're so much better already. Aren't you?'

'I still hear her. I don't know if I want that to stop. I like hearing her voice.

'*Hush little baby.*' I shiver.

Dina sighs. 'You're so talented. You know so much about music and writing … You would make a great teacher! You're great with people.'

'I'm not bad with demons either,' I laugh.

'I'm serious. You have great people skills. You should use them.'

'I'm gonna miss you.'

'You can always come back east.'

'I'm not ready … not now anyway.'

'We're ready for you. Ralph adores you. The kids would love it!'

'Pop and I aren't ready.'

'Give it time.'

'We're talking an eternity.'

'It's been hard on him too, Loli. He loved her. He did what he could.'

I try to explain myself. 'When I hear her voice, I miss being young … very young. Back … maybe before I was born. I have always been hungry for the past … afraid of the future.'

'It'll get better,' my sister replies.

I want to believe her.

Maggie Malone

Yield

'03

The very thought of Dr Dot had impaired my ability to dress and ready myself for the much anticipated evening with Maggie Malone. Right sock, left sock, which sock, right shoe, left shoe, tie shoe, boot or …? Put on the socks and shoes already!!!

With one blue sock, one black sock, untied shoes and blithering mind, I jump into my all-American, undented, hunter-green Ford Taurus and head toward downtown Beatrice. I pass the American Chinese Cafeteria on my right, O'Brien's Chiropractic on my left. I drive by the Whopper, Wimpy, or whatever burger place on my left. There is a Cellular One store on the right with an oversized cellphone dangling from the antenna.

I locate Sixth Street, turn right, park my automobile on the south side of the one-way street that has no arrow to inform the uninformed that it is in fact a one-way street. In an empty parking lot a black cat crosses my path. I spit over my right shoulder, and shoo it away. It parks itself under my car. I look for number 5 Sixth Street. I walk a few feet due north. There, as big as a Broadway billboard, is a neon sign … EURIPIDES FOLLIES.

I am prepared for my question-and-answer evening with the local theater group. More than that, I am ready to feast my eyes on sweet Maggie Malone.

I open the yellow door, lift a torn burgundy velour entry

curtain, proceed down a narrow dimly lit hallway, enter through the rear right of The Follies Theater. It is a quaint, somewhat claustrophobic forty-five-seat house with a small proscenium stage.

Seated onstage is the Q and A cast of characters: Bill and Mike (two mild-mannered, middle-aged, Caucasian males), Claire and Debby (two, blowzy, middle-aged, Caucasian females), Jess (very young boy, approximately six years of age, also Caucasian), Peggy (very young girl, approximately the same age as young boy, Caucasian, playing with cut-outs). Seated in the front row of the audience is Maggie, her hair gleaming. My heart pounds. Out from behind the upstage scrim, with megaphone in hand, prances a handsome, light-in-the-loafers, middle-aged man (Peter Pieter). But ... the star in our cast of characters is panting on the floor downstage right ... a large black and white definitive Dalmatian, chewing on a dog bone. Its name, I am to find out later, is 'Sushi'.

Praying that no one has seen me, I step back into the shadow of the dimly lit hallway. Why don't I call in sick? I fumble for the curtain. 'Where's the fuckin' exit.' I whisper 'fuckin' exit', when from behind me I hear: 'You must be Loli Greene?' Caught, I turn around. There in front of me stands the most gorgeous man I have seen since my first viewing of Cary Grant in *The Philadelphia Story*. 'Hello.'

'I'm Maggie's brother Bill O'Brien. I saw your picture in the *Daily Cryer*. Honey, that picture doesn't do you justice. Why are you standing out here? Come on in. We're waitin' for you.' I melt like soft butta on a hot cross bun. 'We're not cannibals out here. No one bites. Sushi had her rabies shot last week ... Peter on the other hand, I can't vouch for him.' He takes my hand. I'm thinkin', this family certainly has sex appeal.

'Hey everybody … Look who's here.'

Maggie turns around. Her eyes are even more familiar than when last I saw her; the shape, the size, the color. If only, if only?

'If ifs and ands were pots and pans.'

Not now, Ma. Please.

As if in a Sheridan restoration farce, Peter Pieter claps his hands together. In a high-pitched Gracie Allen voice, he shouts into his megaphone, 'Let us have a warm welcome for Loli Greene. Move down centerstage … P-l-e-a-se! … You too, Sushi. If you are going to be in the theater you had better participate … P-a-r-t-i-c-i-p-a-t-e! I don't care if you are a dog. Pick up your bone and greet Ms Greene.' On cue, Sushi stands up on her hind legs and howls. 'That's a good dog.'

Like a well-rehearsed bunch of lemmings, the gang moves down centerstage; different sizes, shapes, genders, genera-tions, two-legged, four-legged, single, divorced, gay, straight, delightful, and certainly endearing. Sushi passes wind. After this joyful noise, the supporting cast of two-legged players shouts, 'Welcome.'

The Q and A begins. They ask me if I always wanted to be a writer. I tell them that I wanted to join the circus, travel the world. I don't tell them that my father didn't approve. 'I became a singer. I might as well have joined the circus. One thing led to another. I became a writer. I've come to realize … life is a circus.'

Molly asks, 'When did you start writing?'

I remember my wild teenage years. I pause. 'When I was much younger, a teenager, I wrote on napkins, matchbooks, receipts, anything in sight.' I fucked anything in sight, too. 'Whatever it was, I put it inside my pants pocket.' Christ, I was horny. 'My pants ended up in the washing machine. My ideas got washed away.' Drank so damn hard, hardly remember my senior year. 'I bought a spiral notebook, but I never used it.' Hated condoms. 'I liked writing on scraps.'... No commitment necessary ... 'Eventually, I wrote in that notebook.' My father was apoplectic that school night when I came home drunk at four a.m. no longer a virgin. He yelled, 'Where the hell have you been, young lady?! Your mother's been worried sick.' I replied, 'Not now,' as I ran up the stairs, 'Not now!' He chased me up the hall stairs. I slammed the bedroom door in his face. He shoved it open, came after me, was ready to slam me hard, then right before contact, he stopped. He nearly cried. I swear, there were tears in his eyes. 'What's the use?' he said. He turned around, closed the door behind him, walked back down the stairs into the den, turned on the television. I soaked for hours upon hours in a hot bath. My mother cried until the next school day. She cried ... like it was the end of the world.

They ask me, 'When did you start teaching?' I reply, 'I'm not a teacher. I'm a teaching artist. The real teacher is left with the work long after I'm gone. I can't do anything every day. It's a commitment issue.' They laugh. I am aware it's not a joke. Next question is, 'What's it like on the road?' Where the fuck is Simone? ... Speaking of commitment issues. Wonder what Maggie's husband looks like? God she is beautiful. What was the question? Oh yes ... The road. 'The road is difficult, lonely, exciting, stressful, expansive ... I visit towns that I never knew existed. I say, "Hey this town is completely different from that town." The next second I realize, this town, that town, the next town ... they have a lot in common. It's about the people.' I look at Maggie. Imagine that mouth on my ... 'I never leave any place behind. They're all in here.' Touch my heart. Heart is there, mind is racing. 'Fortunately, I deal with the creative world … wherever I go. So, I perceive a community and its schools by the creative work that we do together. The need to dream, to create, to inspire others. It is as important as food, water, or love.'

Peter chimes in, 'How many times have I told you this is serious business!?' He asks, 'What are your goals when you teach?'

I notice Maggie Malone looking my way. 'Let me see …' Drift. Return. 'I'm here to help open a door.' I think she's looking at me. 'Once in a while the door is locked. I can't do a damn thing. But, what I can do is … I can help the young adult find some way, some access into … the creative self. I don't have goals … never know what's going to happen.' I hope, I hope, I hope … 'I had some remarkable teachers. They inspired me. I'd like to do the same for others.' Can't wait to be alone with her.

In our dialogue, we agree that life and art do not lead or follow one another, but are in fact the soul of one another.

Why aren't folks in big cities friendly like these folks? Alienation, survival tactics, too busy keeping up … Simone. Isn't she sick and tired of working with rich, arrogant, assholes? To be so gifted, so committed … We haven't spoken for nearly three weeks. I should call. No. She should call. She has no idea where I am. I'll call.

The gathering ends on a jolly note. Peter has the gang gather around an old acrosonic upright piano. There it is again. The past memory of those black and white keys, only my mother is not playing them … They sing 'One' from *A Chorus Line*. After which, Peter performs the entire score. His rendition of

'Music in the Mirror' is of show-stopping quality. He has got the desperate chorus girl thing down pat. The kids run after the dog, and do that kid thing; grab tail, pull ears, pretend dog's a horse, ride, hit each other, just because they are kids.

Maggie and Bill saunter over my way. Maggie asks Bill to join us at Enzo's (the local Italian joint). I am deeply disappointed.

Enzo's is swinging, not an empty table in the joint. To my delight, Enzo has good taste in music. Frank Sinatra sings … as only Ol' Blue Eyes can …

'Fly me to the moon
And let me play among the stars
Let me know what spring is like
On Jupiter and Mars.'

Drink down a perfectly mixed martini, take in the beauty of brother and sister, listen to the lyrics of the song. Look at those open faces. He so male, chiseled face, strong hands; she so female, soft skin, smiling eyes. I would like to paint their faces and hang that work of art inside my belly. That is where it belongs. Then I too would be complete.

Though I am fond of Bill, I am thrilled when he leaves us ladies to dine alone. He, like many men in the United States, has a standing poker game on Tuesday night. I have only three more days in my mother's town, then I head east, after which I head west, after which I head east again; home to New York, my final destination. As I contemplate my travel plans, Maggie swings her hair in that Rita Hayworth heaven-sent Hollywood way.

Wonder how Pop's doing? Maybe I do care. As Dina says, 'He's your father. You only get one.' How does it happen? Do we pick them? Do we give our parents the idea to have us. And then they do … have us.

Maggie leans forward. She whispers. 'My husband's sitting in the front booth.' I turn around. 'No, don't turn around.' I turn back. 'Molly's with him.' She spills her drink on the table. 'Oh dear. Here he comes.' She wipes. He walks. She looks up, forces a smile.

He takes her napkin and cleans up the mess. 'Hi, ladies. Hi, honey. I hear you've been giving Ms Greene the Beatrice royal treatment?' He smirks.

'Loli, meet Molly's father Mike Malone.'

'My daughter has been telling me all about that exercise. Heard she talked to my old man.'

I do not like him one bit. 'She's a very creative young lady.'

'I bet the old bastard said some nasty things about his son.'

'Mike!' Maggie is clearly agitated.

'Excuse me, Ms Greene. Maggie doesn't like that kind of talk.'

'That's enough, Mike. Molly's waiting. Aren't you being rude to your daughter?'

'What do you expect from me, hon?' Hon. There's that word again.

'Mike!'

'I'm so sorry, Ms Greene. Maggie is convinced that I don't know how to behave. Right, Maggie?'

'This is not the time or the place to talk about your behavior or … about … whatever you're talking about. Please get back to Molly.' Maggie nervously plays with the wet tablecloth. Mike salutes. 'And Mike, could you try to get Molly home at a reasonable hour. She has an early day tomorrow.'

'No problem. Night, Ms Greene. Keep up the good work. Night, Maggie. Oh by the way, I have some papers for you to sign. Ms Greene, let me tell you a secret. There was nothing nice about my father.'

'Mike! If you don't have …'

'Anything nice to say, don't say anything at all.' How on earth did she ever put up with this creep? 'A pleasure meeting you. I'm sure you had a swell evening with Peter Pieter at his theater.'

'*Peter Peter…*' Mother's impeccable timing.

I shut them both up. 'I did. Beatrice is lucky to have him.'

Maggie clears her throat. 'Mike, Let's talk tomorrow. Loli and I have got to set up the reception schedule for the actors. Please get back to your daughter. Be a good father … for a change.'

'Yes, Mom.'

'Night Mike.' Maggie waves him on his way.

'Ms Greene. Hope to see you at some of the hotspots around town.'

'Nice meeting you.' He is one of the most despicable men I have met in quite some serious time: cold, condescending, arrogant asshole … like Pop. A man like that has a stone buried inside his heart. That is a lonely man, just like Pop. He must have broken her heart a gazillion times over; probably abused her, confused her. Undoubtedly a mediocre lay. Wonder if she still loves him?

Maggie whispers, 'I feel so sorry for him. He has made such a mess of his life; gambling, screwing around. The whole town knows he can't keep it in his pants. It makes me so sad.' She asks, 'Have you ever been married?'

'No.'

'Are you involved with anyone?'

'I am.' Here it comes.

'What's his name?'

'Simon.' There it goes.

'What does he do?'

'He's a photographer.' Again.

'Do you live together?'

And again and again and ... 'Yes. But, we spend a lot of time apart. I'm on the road. He travels to Europe ... We have an open relationship.' How refreshing, an honest answer.

'Mike and I were never apart. I loved it. He hated it. Then he started catting around ... and –' Maggie stops mid-sentence.

I feel her immense disappointment. 'I haven't heard that expression in such a long time. It was my mother's favorite; catting around.'

'Is she still alive?'

'No. She's long gone.' That's the biggest lie of all. 'Yours?'

'They're both gone. Daddy died during a terrible drought. He died while he was plowing his favorite cornfield. He adored that piece of land. It was the first field he ever plowed ... when he was a little boy. It was his parents' farm. His brother and his brother's sons run the place now.'

'Have you lived in Nebraska your whole life?'

'Born and raised. Went to college in Lincoln. I'd like to go back to school, study political science, foreign affairs.'

'Why don't you?'

'The year after next, God willing, Molly will be gone. Maybe then.' Maggie begins to cry. 'I'm so sorry. I don't know how I'll get along without her. She's been my rock ... what with the divorce.' She hiccups. 'Excuse me.'

I hand her my napkin. 'I had a wonderful time at the Q and A. Thank you so much for setting it up.'

'They were thrilled. You're a big hit in Beatrice. I simply can not get over that your mother's name was Beatrice. You must feel like she's here.'

'… She would love this town, even though the accent is on the wrong syllable.'

Enzo arrives with masses of food. I am unable to eat. Next to Weight Watchers or the Zone, the next best system for weight loss is limerence. Let me explain the phenomenon. During the early, pulsating stages of love falling, the self feels queasy, light-headed. This feeling impacts on the upper and lower GI tracts in the following manner. You could swear that an overly anxious flight squadron has entered your body, frantically diving into the small and large intestines. Eating becomes an impossibility. We, who are afraid to love, lose pounds during the incipient stages of love falling. For some, love brings about a sense of wholeness. For others … starvation. I could not eat a morsel on that Tuesday night at Enzo's.

Maggie, on the other hand, ate a gargantuan portion of veal parmigiana, one flying-saucer plateful of linguini with white clam sauce, an arugula salad with gorgonzola cheese, a loaf of bread, and a profiterole for dessert. 'Don't you like your dinner?'

'It's great.' Eat something. A piece of garlic bread. Shove it in your mouth … Wait! There is the possibility that you might kiss Maggie Malone before the evening's end. Do not eat the garlic bread!

Maggie smiles. 'The students have given you a nickname.'

'Don't tell me. I'm afraid.'

'I swore that I wouldn't … but …' She giggles. 'Stoner.' I have no idea what she means. 'They thought you were high … standing on top of a desk!'

Haven't smoked for three weeks. Wonder what's wrong? 'When you see Molly tonight, at home, tell her it's nerves. To get over my nerves, I give a performance. If it works, the kids enjoy themselves.'

'No!?'

'At Euripides Follies, I was seconds away from throwing up. It settled down after a few minutes. I took three deep breaths and prayed.'

'I don't believe you.'

'Performance anxiety is common amongst performers. Teaching is like performing. The students are my audience. I need their attention.' I see you Maggie Malone. Do you see me?

After dinner Maggie invites me to take a ride out into her father's favorite cornfield. She parks the car atop a frozen hilltop. We gaze at the zillions of stars in the open, early-spring, night sky. The moon is near full. I hear the moon say, 'All is well with the night. My stars know your secret.'

I wish that I could bottle the beauty of the night sky; drink it for breakfast every morning, with Maggie's head on the pillow next to mine.

Maggie reaches over. Turns on the radio. Frank Sinatra sings:
Fly me to the moon
And let me play among the stars
Let me know what spring is like
On Jupiter and Mars.'

We laugh. A shooting star falls. She gets so excited, like a little girl, giddy … silly. 'I just love shooting stars,' she says. 'Love the night sky. My father taught me all about the planets. Mostly, he taught me about the moon in relation to farming and planting.' She turns off the radio. 'Did you know that you should plant annuals, which bear above-ground crops, in the first or second quarter. Third quarter's the best time for pruning. Fourth quarter's the best phase for cultivation and harvesting.' She can't stop. 'Fourth quarter's the best phase for tilling and destroying weeds. Seems weird that the same quarter is the best for destroying and harvesting. But, when you harvest you're destroying what you grow, so you can eat it … so you can grow.' She makes her point by grabbing my hand and squeezing it. 'That makes sense. Doesn't it?' I listen as if I have never heard anyone talk before. She speaks a language that I want to learn. She talks about the rotation of the crops, the difficult life her father had, his disappointment when Molly's husband, Mike, refused to take over the farm. 'Mike just wasn't interested. He knew there was no money in farming. I think he would have been much happier if he had followed in Daddy's footsteps. But, it's too late to worry about that now.'

She is more beautiful than any woman has a right to be. 'It's never too late.'

Maggie informs me that she is a democrat. Her mother was the head of the Democratic Women's Committee of Beatrice. I am relieved. She talks about Molly, Bill, the Beatrice Arts Council, everyone but herself. Her world is in relation to those that need her most. Maggie Malone is selfless. Unfortunately, she does not have a clue about how much I need her.

It is at this moment that I resign myself to the recognition that Maggie Malone and I will never touch, never make love. No, I will not feel her tender lips on mine, never touch or be touched, never know her in that greatest of all biblical ways … through the flesh. Her elliptical love will escape my unrequited grip.

Maggie does not see the single salty tear fall from my right eye, on to my cheek, finally to land on my polar fleece jacket collar. I want her to know the truth about me. 'I'm gay.' She listens. I tell her about mother, father, sister, and finally Simone.

I cry like I haven't for years; retelling Maggie the story of the day I left my mother, when she needed me most; reminding myself of Simone's prominent place in my life since my mother's death. Maggie hugs me. 'Do you love Simone?'

'She is the sexiest, most fascinating person I have ever known, but we're never together. It's like we're avoiding something, but we can't give each other up. She's my … shadow obsession.'

'What do you mean?'

Afraid of my feelings, I pull away. Avoid her eyes. Look out my window. Imagine her tits in my mouth. 'An uncontrollable addiction … a sexual fixation … a collusive partner in crime … crime being pathological incompleteness without each other.'

'We all have that person.' I assume she is referring to her husband. 'Thank you for telling me the truth.'

'I have ulterior motives.' Maggie does not respond. I wait. Not a word. I wait. My longing paints a blush on my cheeks. Our eyes connect. A glimmer of possibility is in the air. A shooting star falls from the sky. I gasp. Make a wish, Loli.

I hear my mother say, *'There is a remedy or there is none.'*

'We'd better go. If I don't live up to my outrageous reputation tomorrow, I'll be run out of school.'

'Beautiful sky.' Maggie starts the engine.

'Beautiful. Thank you for showing me your town.'

Maggie opens up her purse, pulls out a winto-green Lifesaver, pops it in her mouth, and sucks. 'I love this town. It's my … shadow obsession.' She hugs me again. We drive down the hill, through the streets of Beatrice, without a word. We have said quite a bit tonight. She drops me off at the Holiday Inn. I do not turn around.

I open the door to my room. The message light flashes on

my phone. I'll deal with that later. For now, I'll deal with ... what I can.

Simone Duvet

Populated Area: Drive With Caution

'84

'Birds do it
Bees do it
Even educated fleas do it
Let's do it
Let's fall in love.'

Let's talk about Simone. Twenty years is a long time to be uncommitted to the same person.

My unquenchable thirst for learning life's hidden meanings led me hither, dither and beyond. I read volumes on the ascended masters, the philosophy of yoga, theosophy, the Tarot, breath work, death work, Hinduism, Buddhism, women saints, reincarnation, macrobiotic cookery, Zen meditation, astrology, herbology, psychology, Sanskrit, Edgar Cayce's writings, shamanic studies, Mayan mysteries, this book on the dead, that book on the living, other books on dying (skimmed those), the I Ching, angels (lovely departure from demons) and wounded women.

My eyes were weary from the fine print of being. Then, one day, on Melrose Avenue, while perusing the shelves at the

Bodhi Tree, I came across the title to supersede all titles *Sexual Energy And Yoga*.

At Dina's suggestion, I had already begun practicing yoga; Up Dog, Down Dog, Sun Salutation, Paschi, Pachi, Pashi ... Oh hell, seated forward fold, back bends, head stands, hand stands, but Sexual Energy!

I went to class and socialized. Met married men, single girls, jocks, babes, gays, straights. Sure, I did some deep breathing. But, mostly I was engaged in my desire mind. The LA Yoga Center became my singles bar.

Guttman, who had returned from Ol' Cape Cod, was concerned. I didn't care. After all, he had abandoned me during my August breakdown. Fuck him.

'I don't like our five-days-a-week routine. I meditate in the morning, practice yoga, read the *Times*, try to finish my writing assignments, and then there's you. It's impossible. Get here, go home ... Who's got time to work? I have to work! It's important. Sure, she left me some money, but not very much ... That's not the point. I need to work and ...'

He interrupts. 'Yes ...'

I interrupt. 'The girl on the yoga mat in front of me lost her mother when she was eleven. Suicide. I might as well have lost mine when I was ...'

He interrupts. 'Eleven is ...'

I interrupt. 'Maybe I stopped maturing during that summer at Camp Clydesdale? Certainly was the beginning of the end of life with Mrs Cleaver. You ever watch *Leave It to Beaver?*' ... I wanted to seduce. Wanted someone screaming for more, panting, legs up in the air, wanted to conquer and abandon. Wasn't interested in any long-term, for that matter, any short-term relationship. I just wanted to have sex. Lust was keeping my mind occupied. When I wasn't practicing yoga, the Kama Sutra, or meditating on my sexual chakra, I was too busy seducing everyone I met to let my mother's voice interfere with my sex life.

'Georgy Porgy pudding and pie,
Kissed the girls and made them cry.'

Snippets ... There were snippets. But, if I didn't give them energy, they would disappear.

One morning during yoga class, I looked three mats to my left and beheld a lovely, young, feminine body. She moved with rare grace and raw power, had perfect perky tits, long legs and a thrilling ass. After a few yoga classes, I introduced myself.

'Loli Greene.'

Think thick French accent ... 'Simone Duvet.'

I asked, 'Doesn't that mean cover?'

She replied, 'So, you know French?' So it began.

At that time, Simone commuted between Montreal and Los Angeles. She took care of her mother's recently widowed sister in Montreal and worked part time at a photography studio in Los Angeles. Simone was a photographer whose specialty was black and white. She felt that color photography left nothing to the imagination. Black and white demanded more from the eye. As far as Simone was concerned, the eye wasn't the only area that needed training ...

'Darlin', the tongue ... mmm ... oui ... zere ... feels sooooo goooood.' On top, on ze bottom, on ze left side, on ze right side, on ze floor, in ze shower, in ze public bathroom, under ze table ... My desire to learn about sexual energy had led me to my very own French connection.

Because Simone was absent much of the time, I had my world. She had hers. Six days out of each and every month we had our sexcapades, together in every nook and cranny of the greater and lesser Los Angeles area. Simone tuckered me out. She turned herself inside out, upside down, held her breath for what seemed like a decade, screamed 'Ahhhhhhhhhhhhh'… and then she would say, '*Une autre fois.*'

'Again?' I asked in disbelief. I was exhausted from training camp with Simone. It took one week to recover, one week to discover what I had learned, and one more week to prepare for her six-day residency in my bed. I was concerned that I might be indulging in some unhealthy sexual patterned behavior. I discussed my dilemma with Dr Guttman. 'It's all about sex. Maybe not … all. What if she's sleeping with someone else?'

He replied, 'Why don't you ask her?'

I didn't want to know the answer. I was afraid of the truth. I had fallen in love. Aside from being utterly charming, Simone was well-read, well-bred, breathtakingly beautiful, totally committed to her work, a practical aesthete transforming the ordinary into the divine. Just by her placement of flowers, she was able to make any space look and feel like a sanctuary. Simone taught me how to see. She was my eyes. On top of all that, she loved my sense of humor, even if she didn't get it. One week after my realization that I was in love, Simone informed me that she was moving to New York. She had been invited to apprentice with the world-renowned photographer Michel Varny. It was a golden opportunity. I would later find out that Simone was having a torrid affair with Michel Varny. *Quelle surprise!?* …

7:30 … Another evening chat with Dina.
'Hi … Simone is moving to New York.

'Oh … Pop's getting married. Ralph and I just came back from Beechwood.'

… And Mom recites an obtuse rhyme.

'Look to thyself,
Take care of thyself,
For nobody cares for thee.'

'What do you mean he's getting married?'

'He's getting married.'

'To whom?'

'Mrs B. They seem very happy. She was at the house when we arrived. She's so lovely. It was sweet to see them together.'

'Sweet! Excuse me. She is our mother's best friend.'

'She was our mother's best friend. Our mother is dead. He needs a companion. Having her around makes him feel good. And, they have her in common.'

'We have Ralph in common. I'm not marrying him.'

'I'm not dead yet.'

'So, that's what was happening when she was cooking those voluminous vats of oatmeal, while Mom was having her tour of duty in the nut house.'

'They're friends. People marry for different reasons at different times in their lives. You can't blame them for wanting some companionship.'

'I can see it now. The happy couple playing bridge, Scrabble, mahjong, fucking in her bed. How wonderful.'

'Mrs B. is keeping her house. She's giving it to her son Burt. Remember him? He moved to Iowa?'

'No, I do not remember Burt. Wasn't he in your class? … Aren't you six years older than yours truly? … Way before my time.'

'He's in the middle of a messy divorce.'

'I don't give a shit … Our father is deranged.'

'He's lonely. He's in mourning.'

'This isn't mourning behavior. Mourning is mourning.'

'You should call him? How's Gigi?'

'Simone! I just told you. She's moving to New York. Maybe Pop and Mrs B. would like to have a *ménage à trois* with her. Or even better, he could disinter Mom and have a four way. I gottta go.' I slam the phone down. Not Mrs B? I loved Mrs B.

'*Rock-a-bye baby.*'

'Stop it! Stop it! This is all your fault. Please go. Make your own life … Please.'

Their marriage lasted six months. Mrs B. committed the original sin. She spent too much of Pop's money. He felt used. From what I heard, she never adjusted to my mother's clothes hanging in the closet. He couldn't throw those clothes away. That pink dress was jitterbugging on the wooden hangers in the master bedroom closet. She was dancing in each and every corner of the house.

When Pop and Mrs B. were in bed, she was there. When they went to the bathroom, she was brushing her teeth. When they sat down to eat breakfast, she was reading the morning paper, which she never read when she was alive. She performed her tricks inside the seams of their psyches. Finally, Mrs B. moved into my bedroom. After three months there, she moved next door with Burt, who had come back to live with his mother.

They tried to remain friends. Things were strained. People talked. My father kept his distance. No surprise there. That was his specialty.

By the time I thought it the appropriate moment to

congratulate the newlyweds, they were separated. Timing is everything. Right?

'You are the best baby!'

'Right.'

Slippery When Wet

'03

Bathing is a soothing solution for any frustration. After my evening with Maggie, I threw myself head first into my Holiday Inn in-room jacuzzi. I felt as if I were a flaccid ancient sponge swirling at the bottom of the ocean floor. When I came up for air, I pushed the full tilt bubble button, and vibrated myself into a deep despair. How I wanted to be Maggie's lover. Here I was soaking and sulking in my mother's town. Damn!

The Midwestern moon had come and gone. There was no sleep in sight ... None. I recalled those many years long past, when my mother lost her sleep time. Night after night, she left my father alone in the master bedroom, threw her lime green housecoat over her shoulders, snuck downstairs and paced. As she paced the living-room floor, I watched her from upstairs, through the railing. She paced, lighting one cigarette after another, inhaling as if there would be no tomorrow. She already knew what we would later discover. She'd wring her hands as if she were trying to rid herself of herself. *'I just want to sleep,'* she said over and over. *'Want to feel something, anything. Can't cry. Can't feel. Can't sleep.'*

Humans are like finely tuned trucks. We need to park ourselves in a garage every now and again; let the hot rubber tires sit for awhile, shut off the engine before the radiator boils over. My mother's engine ran and ran, until one day she short-circuited the wires, threw on the ejection switch, and catapulted herself into a heavy-metal scrap pile.

I dunked my head into the jacuzzi one more time; I am in my mother's womb, this wee little bird fish, bandied about from one feeling to another. At this instant I know that my feelings have always been hers: every hurt, every fear, hers. Then I heard it: my own voice, 'Stop breathing. Stop breathing now.'

With total ease, I held my breath. Counted slowly, as if I had performed this ritual many times before, one ... and ... two ... and ... three ... and ... four ... and ... With every passing number, I slowed my count down. I felt light-headed. I reached the number eighty-three. That was the year she parked herself in the bathtub in the master bedroom and drowned out the noise.

Now, twenty years later, in her town, I was ready to follow in her footsteps. 'No!' I came up for air, gasping for breath. I saw the red numbers on the clock radio; six thirty a.m. 'Six thirty in the fuckin' morning! Shit. I have got to get ready for school. I can't do this.' Make a sound. Move. Get out of the jacuzzi, extricate yourself from the womb. 'Can you hear me? Can you fuckin' hear me!' I shouted. 'You are driving me crazy! I need to function. I am going to function. Watch me!' I splashed water everywhere. 'I'm gonna breathe you the fuck out of my mind! Out of my mind.' I dragged my soaked self from the jacuzzi, sat down on the synthetic lime green carpet, tried to breathe. Couldn't find the breath. Got up, stomped over to the dresser, pulled open the dresser drawers, heaved every article of clothing onto the bed. 'It's time to get ready for school. No! You are not invited into the classroom. Do you understand?! I am shutting you off now. And, unlike you, I am going to live. I will nurture those students from deep inside my belly. And, I will not abandon them!'

On the road to class. I am exhausted. I turn the radio on as loud as the feedback will allow. Brenda Lee sings:

'I'm sorry
So sorry
Please accept my a-pology.'

Never mind. Let's think about the lesson plan: Ancestors. Open the window, just a little bit. Listen to the sound of the air. Breathe in, breathe out, long exhale from the north-east. How I love that sound. Open the window too much, too much exhale. Has to be just right. Damn stoplights! … Destroy inhale/exhale. Press hard on the pedal when the light turns green. Sound blows right through me, touches me. That's where the inhale/exhale meet. Right there. Stretch, blink, yawn, move from side to side. Lovely feeling.

'Hush-a-bye baby on the tree top!
When the wind blows …'

'The cradle will rock. I thought I told you … Never mind. Going to school, Mom.'

'Rock-a-bye baby on the tree top!'

'Rock-a-bye or hush-a-bye? Which one, Ma? It is damn con-fusing when you keep switching the opening line.'

'Mmm mm mm mm mm on the tree top.'

'Enough! Time for class. Let's not ruin my lesson plan.' I pull into the parking lot, leave my mother in the car. She lets herself out, follows me like a shadow.

I walk into Willwrite's classroom. Molly has moved up from the back of the room. She is seated in the front row. Don't want to let her down. Remember being let down.

Rear-view Mirror

Twenty years ago … on the telephone with Dina. She informs me, 'Pop's coming to dinner. I wish you were here.'

'Family is so totally about obligation and very little else. You are the exception.'

'Is that what Dr Guttman has to say?'

'He hasn't been very insightful about much anything since his Cape Cod holiday. It's like he's bringing his own personal baggage into the room. It's annoying.'

'He's human too.'

'Not for a hundred dollars an hour. His shoes aren't shined like they were before he went away.'

'Why would you look at his shoes for a hundred dollars an hour?'

'Dick size – the wanger foot theory.'

'Don't you lie down in therapy?'

'Sometimes you do and some …'

A muffled sneeze erupts on the other end of the phone line: 'Achew. What do I take for a cold?'

'Echinacea and Goldenseal.'

'Guess what?'

'You're having good sex.'

'I have good sex. It might not be kinky like yours.'

'Where'd you get that idea? Random maybe, but not kinky.'

'You've had so much, I just figured it had to be kinky. Otherwise, why would you be having so much of it?'

Ouch.

'Guess who else is coming to dinner with Pop?'

'Who?'

'Guess. You're holding your breath again, aren't you?'

'I can not imagine who you have conjured up to replace our short-lived ex-stepmother Mrs B. at the dinner table.'

'Simone.'

The Red Flag

'And how did you come up with that brilliant coupling?'

'I didn't. Pop did. She called him. They had dinner at the house. He finds her *très charmante*.'

Later that evening I call Simone. 'You had dinner with my father and didn't tell me about it?'

'Darlin', you are so jealous. That is not like you.'

'How the fuck would you know what I'm like? You're never here. When you are, we're always running around to some black and white photo exhibition.' No response. 'Why did you move three thousand miles away? Why? Is Michel Varny more important than me?'

'Never.'

'I don't want to listen to you drone on about the poor indigent tribes of South or West or East Africa. I don't.' Still no response. 'And what were you doing with my father?!'

'He reminds me of you. Funny. So cute.'

'Have you fucked him?'

'Are you crazy?'

'What have you done with my father?!'

Unbeknownst to Molly and her fellow classmates, I am thinking about my father's broken promises to my mother, how I found out about his extramarital affairs, room-mates in college confessing to his flirtations. Blink … Blink … Blink … Close that chapter. The students are waiting. 'So, who wants to talk about yesterday's exercise? Ancestors, right?' A sea of hands: Look at that sunny, blonde, rosy-cheeked cheerleader with B on her sweater … Over there. Oh dear … sunken eyes, lip ring, striped yellow and green hair. Don't think he's slept for days. … Is that a boy or a girl? Doesn't matter. Look around the room, Loli. Without any prejudice, pick a person; random choice. Not about who catches your eye. If that were the case, Molly Malone would monopolize this forty-seven-minute period. Her mother monopolized last night. For now forget about Molly Malone. Try to forget about her mother. Impossible. Look at that tall, gangly, red-headed, freckle-faced boy. He could use some good old-fashioned schoolroom attention.

'You, you in the back, third row from the right, what's your name?'

He squirms in his seat. 'David.'

'Hi David. Refresh my memory. The first part of yesterday's process had to do with what you wanted to reveal about yourself to someone from the past? Correct?' David scans his papers. 'Isn't that right?' His papers fall like mini paper airplanes onto the floor.

'I think so. Yes.'

'Did you do the exercise?'

'Oh sure I did.'

'Good … and …'

'It's hard to talk about yourself.'

'It is. Did you?'

'I did. I never talked to a character in a book before.'

'I'm not at all surprised. Which character did you pick? More important, what did you say about yourself?'

'Alexandra, the daughter in *O Pioneers*.'

'She's a wonderful character, isn't she?'

'I like her … a lot.' He takes his time. 'When I was a child, my mother told me stories about her grandmother; my great-grandmother. She died a long time ago, before I was born. My mother said that her grandmother was the bravest woman who ever lived in Nebraska. She kept her family together. Both of her sons died when they were children: some fever. She never complained about it. She always believed in God. She loved the prairie. She never left Nebraska.'

'Did you speak to her?'

'No. I spoke to Alexandra. Maybe because she reminds me of my great-grandmother. Alexandra kept her family together just like my great-grandma.'

Like my sister. She keeps the family together. I wonder why she does that? Why keep such a screwed-up family together? Why give so much and get so little in return? 'Why don't you read us what you wrote.'

'I don't know if I did the exercise …'

'David, just read it. I'm sure that it's fine.'

'I wrote it like it was a letter. I imagined this old guy driving a mail wagon with a gray horse pulling the wagon through the prairie. I guess he was Mr Pony Express. He delivered this letter to Alexandra on the prairie. After she read it, she threw it into the fire. I think she was angry.'

'David. Please.'

He rocks back and forth like a playground swing in pants. His legs bang together as if he were dancing a new-fangled dance. His balls rattle, voice quivers, and finally, after his nerves simmer down, in spite of his fear, David reads his letter.

'Dear Alexandra. I have been reading about your life and your times in Willa Cather's *O Pioneers*. If you were living on the prairie now, you would be very unhappy. Nebraska is a dead place. I don't know how or when it died. But, there's just no life in this part of the world anymore. Hopefully, next year I will graduate from Beatrice High. I can't wait to leave this town. There's just nothing to do here. My father has a farm, but things are very bad. He's taken out so many loans to keep it going. I don't know how he's going to send me to college. Even if I get a part-time job, it will be difficult. Hopefully, I will get a partial scholarship. I'm on the varsity basketball team. Maybe that will help. None of my friends want to stay here either. I guess we're bored. There's nothing to do.' David looks up from his paper. 'I already said that, didn't I?'

'Keep reading.'

'I hate the cold dry wind, the snow in the winter; the spring is too short, and it rains so much of the time. I don't like all the dust in the summer, and I'm so busy with school and helping my father out on the farm in the fall, that I hardly even notice when the leaves have changed color. How did you survive out here? Maybe you could give me some understanding. Maybe your courage could rub off on me. Is it possible for me to like it more here? Could you explain why you thought it was beautiful? I just don't see it. Everyone I talk to wants to go anywhere but where they are, especially if they're here.

'So, I'm glad I could write you this letter. You see, I can't talk to my mom. She died last year. And like I told you before, my father's having hard times on the farm. Oh, by the way, my mother's grandmother was named Alexandra after you. She came from the old country. Just like you, she loved it here. Maybe girls like it better than boys. I guess that sounds silly, doesn't it? I'm sorry to be such a downer. But, I thought it was important for you to know how I feel about this place.' He looks up. 'I don't want to hurt anybody's feelings.'

'Don't worry about it. It's an exercise. This is what you had to say to Alexandra. You're just sharing it with all of us. And, by the way, thank you for that. Go on.'

David continues. 'There's no cute girls left in our class. All the cute ones have boyfriends.'

Willwrite gets a handle on the giggling in the room. 'All right, ladies and gentlemen, that's enough. Go on, David. You're doing a splendid job.'

'Thank you, sir.' Thrilled with Willwrite's praise, he continues his letter with a touch more confidence. 'If you want to write back to me, I'm in Mr Willwrite's class. I look forward to hearing from you. Thanks for letting me take up so much of your time. I appreciate it.

Yours truly,

David Lincoln.'

David Lincoln is in a state of shock, astonished that he was able to open up his heart and mind and talk to a character from a book. More astonishing than that, he let each and every one of his classmates in on his private feelings. Young David places his papers inside a paperback book; Willa Cather's *O Pioneers* no doubt. His next-desk neighbor slaps him affectionately on the back. David is a huge success. He is confounded by his sudden fame. After all, he is a basketball player not a writer.

Willwrite approaches David's desk. He stands next to the young man. David looks up. With great admiration, Willwrite rests his hand on David's shoulder. David Lincoln has been liberated. In but one memorable moment, he has become more than a basketball player in a hick prairie town.

'Would anyone mind if David reads Alexandra's response?' Unanimously, the class agrees to give David another turn at his imagined dialogue.

'David, do you mind?'

'Are you sure it's okay for me to go again?'

'It's fine. Go on.'

Willwrite nods his go-ahead. David unfolds a few more pieces of paper. Tentatively, he begins his second exercise.

'Go on. We're waiting for you.'

'Here goes. Dear David, I received your letter a few days ago. I read it in the beautiful moonlight. Have you ever looked up at the sky, looked up and counted the stars in the deep dark night sky?'

She whispers in my ear: '*If you tell a secret to anyone else, all of the stars will die because of the moon's disappointment. One by one their light will fade…*'

Shh not here. Not now. You promised.

'Those stars were made for you. The sky was made for you. The wind, the snow, the dust, they were created for you. It is a damn shame, forgive my language, but it is a damn shame that a young boy like yourself does not appreciate the beauty that kisses his eyes. Every moment that you are alive is a moment of unparalleled beauty.' He can't help but wonder how the word unparalleled landed on his piece of paper.

'That's beautiful, David. Keep going.'

'You may never see the likes of these stars, the dust and all of these elements anywhere else in the world. When you leave the prairie behind, you will leave every bit of its magic. Certainly there will be beauty of some other kind, but it will not be the same open, untouched, stark beauty. I bet that you have never hiked up to the mountain peaks of Nebraska, have never taken the time to watch the prairie sky as it changes color over and over again at sunset. Have you ever tasted the dirt from the ground before or after a spring or summer rain? Have you never taken a breath so deep that the air made you dizzy until you felt like you might faint dead away from its power.

'David, look around you. Don't forget to live your life as if the place you are living in is the only place on earth – no matter where that might be.

'I am so sorry to hear about your mother's passing. You are so young to have lost a parent. In my time that was a common occurrence. But, think of your great-grandmother. She survived. She lived a full rich life. She loved the prairie. Love it, David. The only way to love anything in this life is to first see it, then know it, all of it. See it, David, as if you had new eyes, as if you never saw your prairie before. Look through it. Don't look at it. Look through it and look to it. Only then will you see and understand what many of us have seen and understood before you.

'Life is never easy. The land understands the secrets of survival. Let it be your teacher. Thank you for your letter. I hope this finds you well. Love to your father. I knew his great-grandfather. We were great good friends. He too loved the prairie. That is where your father gets it from. Generation to generation, it is handed down, hopefully it will continue. I have work to do. So for now …

Goodbye.

Always Alexandra.'

Do we, any of us, appreciate the world that we inhabit? Do we? If I am in this world, what is so interesting about the world next door? If I allow myself to love this prairie, why move on to another prairie? Do we merely have this unquenchable need to step outside of one world simply because somebody, anybody, inhabits a different world, a greater world, a world with more corners than our world? But, there are only four corners. Within these four corners, there are four directions: north, south, east, west. Each direction is somehow related to the other. And the sum total of these directions represents the entirety of the traveler's geographical journey. All corners, all directions are forever in relation to one another. Look no further. This is home. This prairie, wherever that may be, is home. Wherever you are, you will take yourself with you, so that wherever you go, you will have already been there.

There are ghosts forever haunting each and every corner of me and my directions.

She is with me. No one else knows that. Take a breath. Acknowledge where we have been. David, you have forgotten the litany of no can do. Now you can travel through a land-scape of can dos ... I am so glad for you.

'Thank you, David. That is beautiful work. It relates to us all. Please make me a copy – both parts, if you don't mind? I want to take them back home with me, and show them to my education director.' Asshole. Is he sending me to Montana or not?

David is elated. 'I'll bring them in tomorrow.'

'Don't change anything.'

'My spelling's pretty lousy.'

'Don't worry about spelling. Now, we have a few minutes to get into the last exercise – the next generation. What do you say to someone you meet along the way to your future?' Five hands. Count 'em. Good response. No, Molly, I can't pick you. Why not? Hmm that chubby girl in the front row could use some noticing. Look, Molly, if I pick you, that would be a form of prejudice, special treatment. I can't do that. 'Yes. What's your name?'

'Sandy Caulfield.'

'What have you got for us?'

'I just want to tell you that I'm having a really good time.' She beams. 'I am so glad that you decided to come to Beatrice.'

Oh, Mom, they love us in your town. 'Thank you so much. I was afraid that maybe I had gone a little too far out with you. You and your town are an inspiration.'

'I don't know if you'll think that when you hear what I wrote. It's not very positive.'

'So? Who ever said the future is positive? How many of you think that the future looks positive?'

Two hands in the air; two out of twenty-eight young adults, one fourteenth of this room believe in the future as a positive probability. Kids are in sync with the rest of the conscious population of our country. 'Let's hear it.'

Sandy is brilliant; a young woman who clearly presents the future as if it were a frightening certainty. She describes the next generation; a dissociated generation that will emerge from the self-consciousness of our weary misaligned time. 'Nobody in the future is interested in anybody; no conversation. None. It's all about feeling isolated, being isolated. It's creepy.' Sandy continues: 'I can't wait to get away from it.' She runs like hell, leaves the future behind. 'Everything is theoretical, mechanical, non-feeling. Imagine a world where nobody cares about anybody but themselves!?'

Welcome to the twenty-first century. This is not tomorrow. You see it coming. But, my dear girl, what you see is *au courant*. We're not looking for a way out, but for a way in, a way to navigate within our emotional states during these hard times.

Bell rings. Class is … No. This class is never dismissed.

After class, Molly chases me down the neon corridor. 'Why didn't you call on me!? I had my hand up. You never even looked at me? Why!'

I stop. 'I thought about calling on you, but I decided it was inappropriate because we know each other. It would be a kind of bias if I called on you. As it turns out, I was biased not calling on you. Stupid.'

She mutters. 'You can say that again.'

'I figured that we would talk after class, like we're doing now … I'm sorry.'

'I wanted everyone in that class to hear what I had to say, not just you. For your information, I have never raised my hand in that class before. Mr Willwrite thinks that I'm lazy. I'm not, you know!? And, I'm not as stupid as my father thinks I am either. I'm not stupid at all. I have got a very good brain. I have ideas too. You're not the only idea person in the world. You piss me off! Grown-ups are so insensitive … All of you!'

Molly sprints down the hall.

I run after her. 'Wait a second. Come on, Molly. Damn it!' I race down the high school corridors like a prison guard chasing an inmate escaping from Alcatraz. I don't stand a chance. Oh Christ! There's the happy-go-lucky vice principal. Bang … She's out the door.

'Hello Ms Greene. How was class today?'

'Very stimulating.' That little fuck called me a grown-up. I have been called names before, but I have never been called that. No saving for the future; no sensible shoes here! I am not in the grown-up category! 'Molly Malone, get your ass back here right this minute!' The glass door slams in my face. Molly keeps going. I continue the chase. In front of the school, the Beatrice High marching band plays a John Phillips

Sousa melody. Molly takes a sharp right, marches solo down the school driveway. The trumpets are so far out of tune, I could almost swear they are playing a rag time version of 'Ave Maria'. While next to the tuba I shout, 'Molly! Young lady, don't you dare walk away from me. Who the hell do you think you are?!'

'Who do you think you are, young lady? Don't you dare turn your back on me. Don't you ever speak to your father like that. Never! You have no idea how hard he works!'

'I don't care. I hate you! When I get back home, I'm going to move in with Mrs B. You're the worst mother in the world. You're crazy.'

'Apologize right now, young lady.'

'Here we go round the mulberry bush.'

'Molly!'

'I hate you!'

'Molly, please. I made a mistake. Please forgive me.' Molly stops. The dust swirls around her body like a tornado. She turns around. There is fire in her eyes. The stare-down begins. I am losing ground here. I walk toward her with my grown-up tail between my legs.

Molly cries. I hold her. She wraps herself around me like a Christmas ribbon. I stroke her hair. She gulps that hiccup crying talk. 'I … uh … just … wanted … you … to … call … on … me.'

'Whisper, pretty baby.'

'Shh. Tell me what you wrote. Talk to me. You can tell me anything, anything at all. You are somebody very special, Molly Malone? Has anyone told you that before?'

'No.'

'That is a terrible thing. Please, please tell me. What did you write?'

'I don't want to tell you now.'

'Why?'

'You'll tell my mother.'

'No I won't.'

'You promise?'

'I promise.'

... 'My grandfather touched me. He held my breasts in his little hands. He held me in his arms and whispered. He whispered. Made me promise never to tell his secret.'

'What secret?'

'I can't tell you.'

'Did he hurt you?'

'No. It felt good. I liked it. It felt soft and sweet.'

What do I do now? There is a young life at stake. 'Did he ...'

'I can't tell you any more.'

'Were you going to share this in class?'

'No. I had another exercise. Yesterday's exercise; the homework that you gave me.'

I take her hand. 'Let's go back to school.' We stroll holding secrets in our hands. Molly leans her head against my shoulder. I almost kiss her forehead. I decide against it.

She asks, 'Do all families have secrets?'

'The whole world has secrets.'

'Why?'

'People are afraid of the truth. Truth hurts. We believe that secrets protect those we love.'

'Secrets are evil.'

'No, Molly. Secrets are what they are – a hiding place, where we bury what has hurt us the most, so the hurt won't touch our loved ones. And then one day, we can no longer hide what has trapped us inside of our shame. When I was a little girl, my mother taught me about keeping secrets. She said that if you told anyone else your secrets, all of the stars would disappear and their light would fade from the night sky.'

'That's fucked.'

'You're telling me,' I laugh.

'I love you, Loli.'

It comes out before I can stop it. 'I love you too.' I realize it's okay. 'I really do.'

'In Dublin's fair city
Where the girls are so pretty …
I first set my eyes on sweet …'

'Shh. Molly Malone.'

'What?'

'Nothing. Absolutely nothing.' It has been an afternoon of long lost-and-found secrets which have held us hostage. But for now, for each other, we have unlocked and shared our hiding spaces.

After school, I come back to my messy hotel room. Clothes strewn everywhere, soggy carpet, jacuzzi drain gurgling. The light is still flashing on the phone. I pick up my message. There is only one. It is from my father. I am taken aback. He beat me to the punch. I have no choice. I return the favor. 'Hi Pop.'

'Hello. Is that you, stranger?'

His voice has changed. It is a different color. 'I was so surprised to hear from you.'

'Your sister said you were lonely out there in the Midwest. Where are you exactly?'

'Nebraska.'

'Nebraska? Where's that? Just kidding. What the hell are you doing in Nebraska?'

'Damned if I know. Just kidding. I'm teaching.'

'Thought your sister did that?'

'She did. You still have a good memory.'

'They paying you anything?'

'Enough.' It never changes.

And so the stone
Was left alone
Fa, la, la, la, lal, de.
You are just like your father, you know?'

'Pay is fine. I'm fine.'

'Never enough! Don't you ever forget it. You're a Greene – first class.'

A compliment. 'I won't. How's the market doing? Haven't looked at a paper for days.'

He answers abruptly. 'Don't follow it. No need. Got everything in T-bills and bonds; not a gambler anymore.'

'Come on? You? T-bills?'

He avoids the topic. 'So where are you again?'

'Nebraska.'

'You know Warren Buffet lives in Omaha. Now there's a smart man for you. You couldn't pay me to live in Nebraska. Where'd you say you were? What town?'

Here goes. 'Beatrice. Bee as in honey, a as in have, trys as in tryst without the final t.' Heavy breathing on the other end of the phone … very heavy, sad breathing. 'Pop? You there?' My heart breaks. This is the man who walked over my mother's body, strolled upstairs, washed his hands, took a steam, as she lay writhing on the kitchen floor. This is the man who married my mother's best friend, who fucked half the women in Beechwood while my mother was alive. This is the man who let the men in the white coats burn her brains out in one institution after another. And my heart breaks.

'Like your mother's name.'

'Almost. You'd like it here.'

'I had a lot of business in the Midwest. Some good friends. All in Florida now …'

'How are you, Pop?'

'I been better, kid. Got the big C, so the doctors tell me. I've had a good life. Your mother and I had …' He chokes up.

'You're still having a good life. It's not over.'

'I'm having my teeth bonded next Saturday. Dr Stein thinks it's a good idea.'

I am perplexed. 'I'll be home next week.'

'Miss you, kid.'

Wish he had said that before. 'Miss you too.'

'Oh by the way, how's that friend of yours Simone?'

'She's just fine. Coming home from Europe soon.'

'Tell her to come up and visit a sick old man.'

After all is said and done, nothing has changed. 'I'll do that. How's Dina?'

'Great. Don't know what we'd do here without her. Love those kids. They call every day.'

There goes the will … again. 'How's Ralph?'

'Poor guy has shingles again. He worries too much.'

'How's the house?'

'Been busy. Got the painters painting the study. I'm not sleeping in the bedroom anymore; too much noise.'

'Great idea, you can watch television.' She's with him. I hear the piano in the background. 'I'll call you when I get back.'

'Say hi to Warren.'

'I will.'

'Night, kid.' We hang up. I sit silently with him in my heart.

Stop Signs

'84

During one of my daily sessions, I ask Dr Guttman to open a window. 'After the fourth or fifth patient, couldn't you use a little fresh air?' He gets up from his armchair, walks toward two casement windows and asks, 'Which window?' I reply, 'I don't really care.' I point to the window on my right. 'That window.' With all his might, he tries opening the window. He hits it with his hand, nudges it with his forearm, taps it with his elbow, finally he bangs it with his shoulder. 'Ouch. It won't open.' I suggest that he try opening the other window. He walks over to the window on the other beige wall in his beige office, flips the latch, opens the window, pulls a pink and white starched handkerchief from his trouser pocket, like a good little boy scout, wipes his hands clean with his little hanky, returns to his armchair.

Reminds me of a story my mother told me many years ago, when I was getting serious about boys ... many years ago. *'He starched my skirt. It was the first time a young man had ... one day you'll understand, when it happens to you.'*

That was my underwhelming birds and bees intro; her strength was not in the details. But, there was Dr Guttman, wiping his hands clean on his sanitary hanky. His every move conjured up the image of her, at the moment, when she was probably wiping her skirt clean. 'Thank you. I feel better when the windows are open.'

'Good.'

'In the last nine months, since your return from Cape Cod, my father has married and divorced my mother's best friend, has been trying to fuck or has fucked my lover, and now he has disowned me. Considering what's gone down, I should have disowned him … considering … You haven't polished your shoes for days. I discuss it with Dina every time we speak. You once had such shiny shoes. In the old days, when I walked into your office, the appearance of your shoes gave me the feeling that there was order somewhere in the world. From the looks of your shoes, neither one of us is having a particularly orderly life. You don't have to say anything; I know you won't. Dina's convinced you're overwhelmed with work. I think you're overwhelmed with life, just like the rest of us. I hope you have someone really good to talk to. Dina says all psychiatrists are crazy; that's what makes them good.' He says nothing.

That evening Dina asks me, 'Why in the name of God did you have to write him that letter? What was the point?'

'The man was or is trying to fuck my girlfriend.'

Dina won't hear it. 'They're friends.'

'He doesn't know how to be friends with a woman.'

'Why would you tell your father, at his age, that you're gay? It makes no sense to him.'

'I told him because I wanted him to know me. Besides, he's making a fool of himself. Every time he hits on one of my girlfriends, he looks like an idiot. I had hoped when she died, he would stop making an ass of himself. I was wrong.'

'His sex life is none of your business.'

'When it intersects with my sex life, it certainly is!'

'Your sex life doesn't interest him.'

'Not one solitary part of my life interests him, except of course Simone. Isn't that peculiar?'

'You are so much alike. It's frightening.'

'How is that precious marble monkey collection of his? Has he been moving the pieces from one bureau to another like the lunatic he is?'

'On Mom's bureau. In front of the mirror.'

'I haven't told you, have I? Saul Rudman's taking me to a spa called "Eros Rising", a retreat center. There's a communal nude swimming pool.'

'Do you think it's safe?'

'Is New York City safe?'

Dina asks, 'Did I tell you about Burt.'

'Mrs B.'s son?'

'He's had a nervous breakdown. His ex-wife took him for every red cent.'

'Marriage.'

'Mrs B. is taking care of him. Poor Mrs B.'

'Poor Mrs B. is right. She's a saint.'

'You should write to her.'

'You keep up with the past. I'm trying to get away from it.'

'Stop trying so hard.'

'I don't know any other way. I had no guidance from my elders.'

'You had me.'

'That's not what I call guidance … or elders. How are the kids?'

'They're odd.'

'They're yours. What do you expect?'

Dina sips her wine. 'I loved my childhood. We were a fine

family. When you were born … did I ever tell you the story…'

'Oh no not that again.' We giggle like little girls in oversized pinafores. The buzzer rings in the background.

'Ralph's home. I've got to finish cooking the brisket. The kids are starving to death. Call Mrs B. Please. Straighten things out with Pop.'

'Not ready for either assignment.'

'Loli, Pop's too old to change.'

The phone call ends.

Next day.

Once again with Dr Guttman. Both windows are wide open. Through one of the windows, a sliver of light shines on Guttman's shoes. They are polished. 'She hasn't been around lately. I miss her voice. You can close the windows. I feel much better today … I'm going to change my life.'

'Friday night's dream, on Saturday told,
Is sure to come true, be it never so old.'

'I mean it.'

'I'm sure you do.'

Pot Holes

'84

From the moment we met, Saul Rudman and I knew that we were kindred spirits. When the spring of '84 rolled around, we had only known each other for two years. In the beginning of our friendship, we had one minor hurdle to jump. We were sleeping with the same man.

Back in those days, Ben Hershey, like myself, was ambivalent about his sexuality. Saul was the only one of the three of us who knew exactly what he wanted between his legs. Ben Hershey's sweet tooth for both sexes drove Saul crazy. Saul reiterated time and time again: 'Either you are or you are not. There is no such thing as a true bisexual.' Having had not nearly enough of what he wanted and deserved, one day Saul walked away from Ben. Fortunately for both of us, he took my phone number with him.

Ben continued having his cake and eating me too. I tired of being 'the woman' in his Whitman sampler life. Eventually, I walked away from Ben Hershey, even though he was a magician between the sheets.

Saul and I forged a friendship. He had inherited a boatload of money from his father's insurance business in Wyoming. He loved to party; so did I. Most important of all, we were both in search of the great Lotus Pond in the sky, which we would later find out was right inside ourselves. Saul was my best male friend. He was at my side when my mother died. He held my hand when Simone left town. It was Saul who signed me up for the mind-altering 'Mastermind' training soon after the Lothar Bovar debacle. Saul did not like Simone; thought she was an opportunist, thought I was sexually addicted to her. Relieved when Simone left town, he knew that our tempestuous relationship was far from finished. Love is a powerful force, especially when you are the one of the two who wants it more. It damn near makes you crazy. I was crazy ... crazy for Simone.

Late spring 1984, on a sunny day in May in LA Saul pulls up in his Mercedes 260 SL convertible. He honks his horn twice. I grab my bathing suit, close the front door behind me, hop into his car, light up a joint, refuse to fasten my seat belt. For a woman heading toward her first orgy, a seat belt seems a triviality.

We drive down Laurel Canyon, turn right on Sunset, continue through Beverly Hills, Westwood, Brentwood, Pacific Palisades, hit the Pacific Coast Highway, turn right, cruise at a fast clip until we see the feed store on the right-hand corner of Topanga, hang a right, curve around winding canyon roads, turn left at an arrow marked EROS RISING > THIS WAY, right at a second arrow marked ALMOST AT EROS RISING, left and another sign with an arrow >100 yards until EROS RISING. Saul parks his car in front of an old dilapidated 1920s mansion. 'YOU HAVE ARRIVED ... WELCOME TO EROS RISING,' says a sign in the overgrown front yard. We bound up the old railroad tie steps, Saul pushes open the smoked-glass front door.

'Oh my God.' I gasp. Nudes, nudes and more nudes. Men and women of all shapes, sizes, colors. Through the bevy of nudists, is an Olympic size swimming pool. In it are hundreds and hundreds of nudists. They are fucking, sucking, splashing, screaming, kissing, groping, smoking, smacking, whacking, and Lord knows what else is going on in that sea of sexuality. 'It's like Persephone abducted by Pluto. We're in the underworld.'

Saul's eyes pop out of his head. I grab his hand, search for the undressing room, find it, lead him and me into it, and disrobe. We throw our clothes into a rusted metal locker without a lock, then proceed to the water's edge.

A beautiful, long-haired, Asian man with an enormous penis approaches us. The three of us clasp hands, hold our noses, and plunge into the pool. When we come up for air, the stranger kisses Saul. Though he never lets go of my hand, he is clearly more interested in Saul. He fondles Saul's genitals with his free hand. He kisses me. He shoves one of his lanky fingers deep inside me. Saul stands behind the young man. He fucks him in the ass. I turn around. The foreign stranger fucks me in the ass, plays with my sweet place at the same time.

On some unspoken cue, we switch positions. It is now Saul's turn to be the filling in between the cookie. He is not interested in getting it from or in the behind. His primary interest is giving it to the stranger in his behind. As I play with the stranger's nipples, I hold onto Saul's balls. Next, it is my turn. I am in the middle. The stranger fucks me from the front. Saul is about to thrust himself into my ass ... I can't do this. I do not belong here. I am disgusting, cheap, repulsive. I cry out loud. 'I do not want to be in the middle!' I want to get in a car, roll down the window, listen to the wind, go home, get into my bed, go to sleep. More than anything, I want to be with Simone, want to make love to her and no one else. I don't want to fuck guys! I especially do not want to fuck my best male friend. That's not what friends do. I gently place Sauls's cock in the stranger's hand. They hardly notice that I am leaving. I run into the undressing room, grab my clothes, and get dressed. On the wall is a sign: TEN DOLLAR DONATION REQUESTED FOR UPKEEP OF SACRED SPACE. Sacred space my ass. I hotfoot it out of the undressing area. I look around. Someone grabs my hand. I am about to kick whoever it is in the groin, when to my amazement, I see it's Tanya.

I sob until my bones fall like pickup sticks all over the floor. Tanya takes me in her arms. She strokes my hair.

'It's gonna be just fine, hon. Shh. Shh.' She walks me into the overgrown yard, sits me down on the wooden steps. 'Take a breath, hon. Now another. What the hell are you doing here?'

I can't believe it's her. She fumbles in her pocket for a joint. She lights it up. Obviously, Tanya is no longer involved with Lothar and his egg whites. 'Hon …you are too damned sensitive for all this free fornicating. You were too fragile for Lothar and no fornicating. This place is just the polar opposite of the same syndrome.'

I wipe my eyes. 'When did you leave the group?'

'When the bastard had us disinter a freshly buried corpse from Forest Lawn. He made us drag it back to Fred and Brian's house on Sunset Plaza Drive, then we sat around it and chanted the Gayatri Mantra for three days, in hopes that the soul would rise. I knew it was high time to get the hell away. You should have smelled their house. They couldn't even call in an exterminator, too embarrassed. They bought a truckload of mothballs, sprinkled them everywhere. It took months to get rid of both smells. The entire group disbanded after that fiasco.'

'What happened to Lothar?'

'He went into a deep depression when the soul didn't rise. He jumped off Fred and Brian's roof, broke his neck, died on the spot.'

'Glad it wasn't my roof. I would have gone over the edge with him.' We split our sides laughing. Like making a new acquaintance with an old best friend.

'Where's your car, hon?'

'I came in my friend Saul's car.'

'Where's Saul?'

'In the pool, fucking some oriental guy with a really big penis.'

'God knows how long he'll be. Come on. I'll take you home. You still in Laurel Canyon?'

'Do you mind telling me what you're doing here?'

'I'm the day manager,' she gloats. 'It's a fabulous job. You can't imagine the perks.'

'Oh yes, I can.' What a ride home! What a funny, forgiving ride back into each other's lives. Tanya was and still is one of the wildest madcap characters ever to have crossed my path ... The path she herself got me on in the first place. I had convinced myself that Tanya pulled the rug out from under me. She didn't. That was my doing. A breakdown is a self-imposed visit to one's own asylum.

We stop at my house. We exchange numbers. 'I had a tough time letting go of my expectations,' she says. 'I wanted to reach the highest, most enlightened plane before anyone else got there. But now that I've given up those four hours of meditating a day, started eating beef, drinking booze, doing drugs, I'm having a damn good time.'

'A radical shift in, well it's still consciousness, no matter what you call it,' I said.

She lights up a cigarette, blows the smoke my way. 'What's up with you? You in love with anybody?'

'A French woman in New York. She left me ... kind of.'

'What the hell are you doing here? Pack your bags, hon. Go get her. You got to chase after what you want or else you won't ever know if you just maybe might have gotten it right. Don't quit now. It's too soon. So what if she left you. Everybody leaves their lover at least once, usually twice. Hell, I left my first husband three times. We only just got divorced. It's that Margaret Mead thing. We're not meant to be with one person. We're not swans, you know.'

Monday a.m. – Guttman's office. Windows are closed.
  'I went to a New Age orgy yesterday, Eros Rising, hundreds of people getting it on in a huge swimming pool. You ever heard of it? I guess not. My friend Saul got it on with an oriental guy with a huge wanger. I never want to do that again. I don't like men. I miss Simone. I want to move back to New York. I ran away from New York. What I ran away from is dead. I have friends there: my sister, the kids, Simone. I want to spend time with the kids before they're all grown up … I'm tired of therapy. You've gotten me through the worst of it. Right now I need something different.'
  'It sounds like you have made some decisions.'
  'Tanya was there. Remember me telling you about her? No, that was Dr Dot. Lothar is dead. He killed himself, jumped off a roof. My gut tells me that New York is a better place for me. LA doesn't give me the emotional support that I need. The whole world runs away trying to find itself in this town. So, will you miss me?' Why the fuck doesn't he ever say anything? 'It's going to take a while to get organized, sell the car, the house, but it's a good thing, isn't it?' Hello … He'll say something soon enough. 'You excited for me? I wonder if Simone can handle it? I'm not expecting it to be easy.' A hundred

dollars an hour for this. 'You know, since my father disowned me, my mother doesn't have much to say. I miss her. I can still see her long lovely fingers dancing on the piano keys. When she played the piano, she was so beautiful, so talented.'

'You had mentioned that.' He speaks.

'I like women. They're softer than men. Simone's soft. Her skin. She's hard in other ways. I hope it works.'

'Yes.'

He needs to work on his people skills. 'I'll see you tomorrow.'

'Same time.'

'Of course.' Wish he would remember to open the window. Yawn. Leave. Beautiful day. Can't wait to call Dina. Daylight fades. I would like to paint a picture of the night sky; so many dancing shadows. Phone rings. Damn! Talk to the machine. 'Dina. Guess what? I'm coming home. Don't tell anybody.' Hang up. Dial Simone's number. 'Hello.'

'I'm moving back to New York.'

Silence

'Such wonderful news darlin'. When?'

'As soon as I get myself organized. Aren't you glad?'

'Oh yes. Very. *Je suis très heureuse.*'

'I love you.'

More silence.

'Your father will be so happy.'

'I'm moving back because I want to be with you.'

DEAFENING SILENCE

'I have to run darlin'. I love you … *à plus tard.*' For a long time, neither one of us hangs up the telephone.

In between the silence … Love is so demeaning.

Interstates /Road Construction

(Falling Rock Zone)

'03

After my conversation with Pop, sit down on bed, cry, look at mess in room, kick off shoes, take nap. I am awakened by the phone. It is Molly. She wants to thank me for the afternoon walk. As I am about to hang up, there's a knock on my door. 'Wait one second,' I say. Throw the phone on the bed, trip over some socks, open the door. It's Maggie. It's Maggie!? 'Wait one second,' I say again, close the door, try to clean up the mess, run back to the phone. 'I have to get that.' Molly wants to know who's at the door. 'The janitor,' I say. 'One second,' I scream to Maggie. 'Thanks for the call. See you tomorrow.' Hang up. Oh my God, now what do I do? Don't leave her standing in the hall. Look around room. 'Oh shit.' Beyond sprucing up. I open the door.

Maggie is carrying a cardboard box. She enters the minefield, sits down on the sofa, opens the box, places a series of reception cards on the table. 'What do you think,' she asks. 'About what?' I say. 'Reception cards for the opening-night party of *O Pioneers*,' she says. 'What about them?' I ask. 'Do you like them?' she asks. 'It's four o'clock in the afternoon. What are you doing here?' I ask. 'I don't know,' she answers. 'I was driving through town, I passed the hotel, thought you might be in, so I decided to say hi.' 'Oh,' I say. 'I'm glad you did. Sorry about the mess.' I don't know what else to say. 'It's not messy.'

She crosses her legs, folds her hands in her lap. She has beautiful hands. 'What did you mean when you said you had ulterior motives?' she asks. 'When?' I ask. 'Last night,' she replies. 'Oh that.' I don't know what else to say …

A million thoughts run through my mind: Pop is dying, Simone's hurt me, I hurt her, Molly would hurt if she knew how I wanted her mother, why do I want Maggie, my mother, this town, its name, mother is watching, Dina, poor Mrs B., mother is watching, Maggie, here … there, mess in room, mess called life, breakdowns, recoveries, fears, failure, ssssex … but, I am at a loss for words, can't speak, trapped in the fear of losing what has already been lost.

Maggie takes her hand and places it on my heart. 'Your heart is racing.' 'You should hear my mind.' 'Shh,' says she. 'Shh.' She touches my lips with her fingers. I see my mother's fingers on the black and white keys. I close my eyes. She kisses me. I kiss her back. 'I don't know what to do,' she says. I say, 'I do.' But I am not so sure … I do. Never been sure in matters that matter. Never.

We make our way through the rubble to the bed, undress ourselves, undress each other, explore. I explore Maggie Malone. She explores me. One stop at a time. Journey into each other; touch skin, smell skin, walk skin, ride skin, swallow sweet sour juices, breathe her, breathe me, taste her, taste me, devour me, devour her, mouths open, tongues deep inside, longing travelers, long, slow, wet roadways, slippery shoulders, finger fucking, sucking, blind curves, nails dig trenches, tits hard, spread wide prairies, wild rivers, mouth to mouth, mouth to nipple, mouths, tongues, clits expand, contract, open, close, hard, inside, backside, tongue up ass, roll over, easy, hold, release, coming, home, take me, home, one more stop, one more stop. Hold. Stop. Again. Once more. Don't stop. Stop! Breathe. Can't breathe! Can't … Help! Help! 'Help!' I scream. Maggie's startled. 'What's wrong? Loli! What's the matter?' She takes me in her arms; rocks me back and forth … back and forth. I barely get the words out. Gasping. 'Can't breathe. Asthma. Can't … water, please …'

Maggie runs to the bathroom, wets a wash cloth, runs back to the bed, wipes the sweat from my forehead, places wash cloth on forehead, runs her fingertips through my hair. 'Breathe,' she says. My eyes roll back inside my head, tongue goes dry. She squeezes water from rag into my mouth. 'Drink.' One drop at a time drips into my parched mouth. 'Drink,' she says again. I swallow. Maggie runs to the bathroom, brings back a glass of water, lifts my head off the pillow, places glass to my lips. I grab her wrist, wrap mouth around glass, swallow water. 'I'm sorry,' I say. 'Shh,' she says, as she strokes my hair again and again.

Three days until I leave … every morning at eleven: Molly at school. After class she says, 'I love you.' Every afternoon between four and six, Maggie in my room between the sheets says, 'I love you.' Every night she whispers in my ear, '*I love you.*' Without sleep, each and every day, start the cycle over again: Molly, Maggie, and she.

On my last night in town, Peter Pieter rounds up as many parents and children as he can fit on the Euripides Follies stage.

He thinks improvisations based loosely on my ancestral explorations will be an interesting way to bring families together.

Somnambulistic, I dress and ready myself. Maggie is on my clothes, in my hair, on my fingers, imbedded in every corner of my road map. How will I deal with seeing Molly and Maggie tonight? How will Maggie deal with me? I lie down on the kitchenette floor on my stillpoint inducer contraption trying, to no avail, to still myself. I'm late. I get up from the floor, get dressed, wrap scarf around neck in that Martha Stewart stalwart way, head out the door smelling like Maggie Malone.

Take a deep breath, enter the theater. It's packed. Stage lights on, house lights on, people milling around, chatting, waiting for me. David Lincoln's father, who looks like a basketball player himself, sits with David. Sandy Caulfield gabs with her mom, who's wearing a Lilly Pulitzer dress. Bill laughs with or at his daughter Rachel, who looks like a teenage Maggie; beautiful. Bill, Claire, Mike and Debby from the first Follies evening chat with daughters Jenny and Sharon. Maggie and Molly sit huddled up in a corner of the theater having a very serious tête-à-tête. Maggie does not look up. Peter Pieter waves.

'Loli, I'd like you to meet my "friend" Sterling Silver.'

Sterling is fair, delicate and very southern. 'Peter has been ravin' about you.' Sterling gushes. 'It is always ... fascinatin' to improvise on life.' With that Sterling and Peter take their places on stage. The rest of the group join Sterling and Peter.

Maggie and Molly pry themselves away from the corner. Molly meanders my way. She hugs me. Maggie smiles politely. But no hugs.

'Alright, folks ... Please bear with me while I set up my CD player.' As I plug in, I set the tone for the evening's exercises. 'Each parent and child ... in the same family ... will stand directly across from one another. I'm going to play music from different periods … on the prairie. When you hear the music, you will place yourself in a certain situation, as parent and child, spouses, or siblings, appropriate to that time. You can do tableaux. Does everyone know what that is?' Vacant stares. 'You have a feeling. Let the emotion rise up inside you, partner responds, then both of you freeze in place, revealing your feeling state. At any time a parent may become a child or vice versa. Of course you will have to cue each other as to when you're reversing your role. Don't think about what you're doing. Do it. Let the music become your script. Use it in a very specific way … If I see that you're stuck in a predictable moment, I will shake things up a bit.' Look at me, Maggie. 'Lord knows we all get stuck.'

Molly and Maggie steal a quick glance. Bill looks at Maggie. Maggie looks at me. I look at the floor. 'Let's begin.' I turn on the CD player. 'Can you see those wounded soldiers limping home from the bloodstained battlefield? Ladies, do you feel your crinolines crunching. I better stop those boys; fanning and curtsying … Don't go for the obvious. Relate to one another.' Peter and Sterling stare into each other's eyes. Gracefully, they move toward each other. Without touching, they look over their shoulders; flared nostrils, flushed cheeks. Finally, their shoulders meet. Locked gaze, stunning movement, deep bow. 'There you go. Much better. Next piece of music. Listen to that fiddle.' The crowd dances. It's prairie gone autistic; hands clap, heads bob, feet stomp, jump, jump … I hate to stop them but … 'Come on! Specific! Where are you? Who are you?' Maggie and Molly switch roles. Maggie pouts, mutters something about running away to the big city, defiantly blows bubbles (which I doubt they did in those pioneer days). Molly irons, pins up clothes on an imaginary clothesline. 'Good job, Maggie and Molly. Not so sure about the gum.' Maggie and Molly's role reversal inspires the rest. Soon every child in the theater attempts to imitate the parent, every parent becomes the child … How like life.

'Alright, you dancing fools … you older folks will remember this one from 1955, a year before I was born.'

'One two three o'clock four o'clock rock
Five six seven o'clock eight o'clock rock
Nine ten eleven o'clock twelve o'clock rock …'

'Do you remember Bill Haley and the Comets' "Rock Around the Clock"? Do you?' The room goes berserk. Maggie jumps so high, when she lands the floor shakes. And I love this woman. Go figure.

David Lincoln's father catches an imaginary basketball. David cheers from the bleachers. Bill combs his thick curly black hair with one hand, straightens out his bow tie with the other; a consummate multitasker. Rachel gives him a quarter. She sends him on his merry way. Looks like young Bill has got himself a hot date on prom night.

And I am … I am in the living room … again. No … no … She is here. Right there dancing between Maggie and Molly … The meanest jitterbug on two feet. She is downstage left … downstage right … centerstage … on the light grid … her shadow in the lights. She is every single person in this room: Molly, Maggie, Bill, Rachel, Peter, Sterling, Sandy, David, all of them. My mother inhabits everyone. I close my eyes, but, there she is; her energy ignites the inside of my brain. The music has set her off. She is a fandango apparition, her voice is loud and clear.

'Pat a cake, pat a cake…

Baker's man!
Pat it and prick it
And mark it with t
Put it in the oven
For Loli and me.'

Turn her off! Push click … Gone … Thank you … Next track. Everyone dances cheek to cheek … Sit down in front row. Breathe, baby, breathe. Close my eyes. Open … Look … For now I am alone. That is to say … She is no longer in the room.

I look at the parents and their children. Do they realize how fortunate they are to be in the same room, present and accounted for, in life's dance. She and I will be in the same room again but one of us will not be present and accounted for … not ever.

The evening is a smashing success. After much discussion about sound scapes, role reversal, family dynamic and life, Maggie, Molly, Bill and I head out the door. Rachel heads home. She is desperate to try out her version of tonight's games with her mother. She is even more desperate to drive her father's new Infinity SUV.

'Please?'

'Don't tell your mother.'

'I'm going to drive it home, Dad. That's kind of silly, isn't it?'

Bill mopes. 'How will I get home?'

Maggie, of course, offers, 'We'll take him.' Damn those family obligations. 'Are you sure you don't want to come with us?'

'I am so sick of Enzo's. I'd rather play with the goldfish.'

Bill is none too thrilled. 'Here, take the keys.'

'Thanks, Dad.'

'Tell your mother how good I was tonight.'

'I will, Dad.' Keys are handed off. Rachel leaves the group in the dust, we each head for our cars, before which Maggie squeezes my hand. No one notices … I do.

Enzo's is packed, but Bill had the good sense to reserve a table. To nobody's surprise but mine, Mike Malone is seated at the bar. The man is drunk … like Ray Milland, *The Lost Weekend*. Maggie and Molly march over to say hi to daddy. Enzo himself escorts Bill and me to our cozy corner booth. 'Fly Me to the Moon' is still playing.

'A tape loop,' I say.

'He sure is,' says Bill.

'I mean "Fly me to the Moon" was playing the last time I was here.'

Bill asks, 'Do you think people can change?' He doesn't give me a chance to respond. 'Mike'll never change.'

I look at Mike. 'What do you mean?'

'The man has always been a drunk. He will always be a drunk. It's a sin.'

'No, it's not. It's a shame, not a sin,' I say, 'There's no sin in a man's pain.'

'His father was a drunk. He up and left Mike and his mother. Now Mike's a drunk and … I hate it. No one cried when that man died, least of all Mike.'

Grandfather was a drunk. Mike's a drunk. Poor Maggie. Poor Mike. Molly doesn't hate him. Doesn't understand. What about the grandfather?

'If all the world were apple pie,'
She has sat down in the booth. I feel her breath on my hair.
'And all the sea were ink,'

'And all the trees were bread and cheese,
What should we have for drink?'

Bill asks me if I want a drink. 'No thanks. Sparkling water. How long ago did Mike's father die?'

'Molly was just a little girl.'

'What'd he die of?'

'Drank himself to death. Mike was the only family member who showed up at the funeral. Even Mike's mother refused to pay her respects. The townspeople hated his guts.'

'Why?'

'It's a long sordid story. I'd rather not. I don't want to ruin your impression of Beatrice.'

'You couldn't if you tried. I love this place.' He should only know.

'We love you too. Molly's crazy about you.'

'I'm crazy ...' And the girls return from their brief but sorrowful visit with Mike Malone. Maggie is agitated. Molly is pissed off.

Maggie whispers to Bill. 'I'm at my wits' end.'

'Nothing you can do, baby, absolutely nothing.'

Molly throws her napkin on the table. 'Could we please not talk about him! I want a drink!'

'You're not old enough to have a real drink,' Maggie says.

'Mom! What do you think we do at parties? Drink Diet Cola and Dr Pepper?'

'I never thought ...'

'You never thought. You never think, period. We drink, Ma. We smoke. We do exactly what you did when you were my age.'

'Molly, please don't talk to me like that. This is Loli's last night in town. Be nice.'

'Parents are so … oblivious.'

I have to agree. 'Everyone has family problems …'

Molly interrupts me. 'Not like ours. We have one fucked up family.'

Maggie shuts up Molly. 'Young lady, you are out of line.'

Bill breaks up the female wrestling match. 'Ladies, that's enough. Put a lid on it.'

Next thing I notice Mike Malone falls head first onto the floor, a thud followed by a broken glass. Maggie jumps out of her seat. Bill pulls her back down. Maggie bites her lip, wrings hers hands and sighs. Molly mutters under her breath about the idiocy of parents. Bill shakes his head in disgust. I size up the family dynamic, like I am always doing. Enzo helps Mike up from the floor, takes him outside for a bit of fresh air.

Maggie's eyes fill with tears. Those eyes. I have kissed those eyes. I know your skin. I have traveled deep down and far away with you. I know you. And you, Molly Malone, you will not be held back. Ask the right questions. You will create your future.

Look at these two women. When I glance from one to the other, east to west, left to right, for some unknown reason, I am at ease being in the middle of yet another family affair.

'I hate it here,' Molly says, 'I plan to get the hell away from this place, and every last person in it, as soon as possible.'

She sits down in between Molly and me. *'Wish I may … Wish I might …'* Her presence conjures up a teenage dinner-time when Pop had reached the point where people are no longer nice to each other. *'You're slurring your words, dear.'*

Maggie takes it personally. 'It's not that bad, is it, honey?'

'It's that bad,' replies Molly.

Bill looks my way. 'That's a shame.' I nod affirmative. Bill turns to Molly. 'Please pass the garlic bread … Molly, I said please pass the bread.'

Molly is in the midst of peeling the nail polish off her nails. 'Sorry, Uncle Bill.'

Bill stops eating. 'Maggie, you haven't touched your food.'

Maggie pushes the food around her plate. 'No, I guess I haven't.'

Oh how I hate the dinner table. I remember those dinners in Beechwood; night after night, she at one end, he at the other, me on one side, Dina on the other. We talked about the weather. After which, he'd say, 'Put your napkin in your lap, young lady.' I always asked, 'Why?' He'd say, 'Because I said so.' I'd say something like 'So' and so the decline of fine dining began. It always ended up with 'Go to your room, young lady.' I'd go. She never interfered with his disciplinary actions at the dinner table, but came to check on me after … At least no one is talking about the weather.

'Not a cloud in the sky today. I almost left the office and played nine holes. It was so beautiful outside … I remember when I didn't have one patient. I am so damn busy now.' I'm dying here.

'Mom?'

'Yes, Molly.'

'Can I ride home with Loli?' Maggie and I cop a quick glance. Guess I'll be taking Molly home. I'm ready to leave the dinner table … now. I wonder when Simone gets back? Simone. Simone would never set foot in a place like this. There are no indigent tribes to feed or photograph. Maybe there are … somewhere out there in the middle of the state.

Maggie corrects Molly. 'May I?'

'Sorry. May I?'

'I'm sure Loli has things to do.' Good girl. Molly sulks.

I give up. 'It's not a problem.' It is a problem.

'That would be wonderful.' Maggie sulks.

'Thanks, Mom.'

'Loli, what time is your plane leaving tomorrow?' asks Maggie

'Late afternoon.'

'I'll follow you to the airport. Make sure that you get off safely.'

Perfect! Where there's life there's hope.

'Mom? Can I come too?'

Oh no!

Maggie takes a moment. 'Sure, honey. As long as you don't fall behind in your school work.'

I fumble for my belly bag. 'Bill?'

'Yes, Loli.'

'I might pop in for an adjustment in the morning ... before school. My back's killing me. Lousy bed.'

'I'll be there. Ladies, what's for dessert?'

Not dessert? I'll die if I have to sit here one more second. We're all miserable. No. Bill's happy. Men are easier. Pop isn't. Families are forever. Why doesn't somebody say something?

'Loli?'

'Yes, Bill.'

'You will come back and visit us again, won't you?'

All eyes are on me. 'Absolutely.'

'Let's get the check?'

'Bill, let's check on Mike.'

'I'm sure he's fine, Maggie.'

I unzip my belly bag. 'Let me get this one.'

'Absolutely not. You're our guest.' Bill pulls out a wad of bills from his pants pocket.

'Thanks, Bill.'

'Thanks, Uncle Bill.'

'You're welcome. It was a great evening.'

It wasn't. But we did get through it.

And now ladies and gentlemen, once again, Ol' Blue Eyes 'Fly Me To The Moon' … I loved that song. I hate it now.

Rear-view Mirror /Good Visibility

'03

Gotta pack. Gotta go to school; last class in Beatrice. Does it have any meaning for Maggie? Does everything have to have meaning? At my age, absolutely! Where is my vanilla incense hiding? Last stick ... good packing job. I will never again have a jacuzzi in my living area. I know what they mean by a sunken living room. Where's my navy blue Gap sock? Maggie must have put it on by mistake. Room smells like sex. Where is Simone? What the fuck am I going to do when I get home? Class. Gotta get to class. Where's my scarf? There you are. Amazing. After all these years. When did she give you to me? When I wasn't aware that life was full of endings. You, you are still lovely. Finish packing later. Check out after class. Hope it's great! Better not set myself up for disappointment. Simone. Talented, sexy Simone. Years. Do we know each other? How will I ever find a way to get back here to see Maggie? ... Feel like crying. Leave Dina a message; tell her that I'm coming home. It's nine thirty a.m. I've got five minutes. Sick of the phone.

'Hello.' She sounds exasperated.

'What are you doing home?' A long pause.

'I took the day off.'

Try again. 'Why?' An even longer pause ...

'I was up all night with Pop. Ralph and I took him to the hospital. He's fine. He'll be fine.'

'What happened?'

'He fell, lost his balance. He fell in the downstairs bathroom. You do know that he's no longer sleeping upstairs.'

'He told me.'

'He was so happy you called. He cracked one of his bonded teeth, cut his lip, had to have a few stitches, bruised his forehead. He's very weak from the chemo. He's getting weaker. It's so sad.' She cries. My heart breaks like fine china thrown on a divorcing couple's kitchen floor. My arteries tighten. The pressure cooker inside my chest blows out steam through my ears, as she continues. 'Ralph can't handle it.'

I interrupt. 'Can you?'

'Not without you,' she admits. 'Are you coming home soon?'

'That's why I called. I'll be home late tonight.'

'Should I save you some veggies?'

'Late like one a.m.'

'I can heat them up tomorrow. You could come over then.'

'First thing in the afternoon. When is he getting out of the hospital?'

'Tomorrow.'

'I'll try to see him over the weekend.'

'That would be great. Is Simone home yet?'

'… Dina?'

'What?'

'Do you like Simone?'

'She's part of the family.'

Wrong answer. 'Do you like her?'

'Yes. I do.'

'Do you think she's good for me?'

'Does she make you happy?' I don't answer. 'Does anybody?'

'Maggie Malone.'

'You've known her four days.'

'You're right. But she makes me happy. Simone and I have broken up five times in the last three years ... and ... I don't miss her when I'm gone.'

'Do you miss anybody?'

'You! I miss you. Even when we're in the same city, I miss you. You're my only family. I don't know what I'd do ... if ... if ...' The thought of losing Dina takes my breath away.

'You're not breathing.'

'You're ...' gasp ...

'Eleven, twelve,
Here we go round the mulberry bush ...
Here's sulky Sue
What shall we do?
And when she was bad
She was horrid'

'Impossible!'

'What?'

'Now, she's mixing and matching.'

'Well, isn't she clever.'

'Thank God you still have a sense of humor.'

'I love you. Everything's fine. Go teach your class. Remember, you're the best. Those kids are lucky to have you.'

'Can't wait to see you.'

'Me too.'

'Me three. Breeeeeeeeathe. Listen to the wind. Find the crack in the window.'

'... What window?'

'If you tell a secret, all of the stars will die because of the moon's

disappointment ... The stars protect everyone's very important secrets.'

'Say hi to Pop. Tell him I'll see him when I get home.'

'That'll make him very happy. Love you again.'

'Me too.'

'Hush-a-bye baby,

Daddy is near.'

'Leave him alone, Ma. Leave the poor bastard alone. He'll be with you soon enough. When he arrives, you can even carry him over the threshold. As for now, the guy has quite enough on his plate. Remember what it was like near the end? No? You were too far gone. Natural causes ... unnatural causes; A different point of view that leads to the same inevitable outcome.

Why can't I find that sock!? Where would you be if you were a key? I will not be late. Sit down. Collect yourself. There you are. Thank you. How can I get excited? They're keys.

I drive that familiar route 77 through our town, turn left at the stop light, past the grocery store. Help Wanted sign in the window. I wonder how much they pay in Beatrice, Nebraska? 'Hey Ma. You want a job?' How fast am I driving? No police car behind me? Slow down, girl. Roll down the window. Much better. What a lovely day. Nice breeze.

This parking lot is packed. Fuck it. I'll park in the wheel-chair access space. No one will notice ... 'Hey you! Sorry.' I never saw that girl before. Must be a nightmare wheeling your-self around; in high school; good for the arms. I hope she has a loving family. The entire world is paralyzed.

Late again. Gotta run. Hey, there's the vice principal. 'Hi.' What is his name?

'Hello, Ms Greene. It won't be the same around here without you. The students have given you a rave review.'

'This is a great school.'

'We think so. Stop running. Those kids are not going anywhere. When you get there, they'll be waiting.'

'I hope so.' I run up the stairs, turn the corner, enter Willwrite's room.

The quintessential old maid, bun and all, is seated in Willwrite's chair. Where is Willwrite? I approach with trepidation. 'Hi. I'm Loli Greene, the teaching artist. Where's Mr Willwrite?'

'How do you do, Ms Greene. I'm Lydia Laws, the substitute teacher. Mr Willwrite is out sick today. Your students are present and accounted for. I sub quite a bit, and I have rarely seen them this well behaved.'

'I can't believe that Willwrite has ever missed a class.'

'He's had a difficult year. Fortunately, the Mayo Clinic has given him a clean bill of health – good news for all of us. He is Beatrice High School's best teacher.'

'I'm so sorry that I didn't thank him and say goodbye. I'll drop him a note, leave it with the vice principal.'

'You can leave it with me. I'll make sure that he gets it. He has so enjoyed having you in his classroom.'

'He has?' How would she know?

'I'm Mrs Willwrite. Laws is my maiden name, my teaching name. A pleasure to meet you, Ms Greene. If you need me, I'll be in the teacher's lounge.' She exits.

I am delighted that there is a Mrs Willwrite. The Mayo Clinic? Wonder what that's about? 'Hello, everybody. Are we ready to bend our little brains today?'

Listen to the feeble cries. 'Yes.'

'I am on my own, so be nice. It's scary up here without a real teacher.'

Molly is seated in the third row. We acknowledge each other. She is beautiful, like her mother. 'This is my last day in Mr Willwrite's room ... in your room. You have been very generous. I will never forget this class. Never.' Don't get weepy. 'So, we will do one last ancestor exercise. Wrap up the week with a final process that will hopefully bring our week's work full circle.'

Crack ... pop ... crack ...

'W-ho's chewing gum? Could you curb the cracking? I have never been able to figure out how to do that. How 'bout a lesson after class? ... Just kidding.' I perch on the edge of the desk, look around the room, take them all in, take a deep breath. They are inside my belly.

'So, the exercise is ... how do you create a sense of home? You have recently arrived from the old country. You are a man or a woman, who has traveled thousands of miles, you have arrived in this town, a town that has not yet been named. You are a homesteader. You are living during the period of Willa Cather's *O Pioneers*. You have traveled these many miles with two objects, objects that you cherish. They were given to you by ... two people ... people left behind in the old country. What are these objects? Who gave them to you? What is their meaning? Also, how did you get here? Who are you traveling with? What have you left behind?

'As you write about your journey, I want you to feel ... viscerally, in your body, your bones, your skin, your emotions, your sensations, all that you are; experience the journey; sense all that you have left in order to make a new life for yourself. Why did you leave? What have you lost? What have you gained? As you enter your new world, what does the prairie look like? After such a long and arduous journey, who have you become? What do your objects mean to you now that you are here? Any questions?' Oh shit! Who is he and what does he want? I could not have been any clearer. Could I? 'Yes.'

The gum cracker speaks. 'I don't … I …'

'What's your name?'

'Bill Carlson.'

'Nice to meet you, Bill. Could you ease up on the gum?' Bill spits out his gum, sticks it behind his ear.

'I don't get it.'

'What don't you get, Bill?'

'How can we be there when we're here?'

'Bill, have you been in my class this week?'

'No. I was in Omaha on a Christian debate club trip.'

'So, this is your first day in my class?' Never fails.

'It sure is.'

'May I make a suggestion.'

'Sure.'

'Have you read *O Pioneers*?'

'It was required reading.'

'But did you read it?' He nods yes. 'What you experience here today is required imagining … You put yourself in those pioneers' shoes, walk in their weary footsteps, travel their impossible journeys. Imagine that you have traveled from Sweden or Germany or Ireland. Wherever you choose. Imagine that you have arrived here, in your new country, with two precious items. They make you feel as if you have brought the old world with you into your new unknown world. These objects are your talisman, good luck charms. You feel safe, at home wherever you are, as long as they are in your possession.

They are as important to your survival as the water you drink and the air that you breathe. What are they? Who gave them to you? Got it?' If that isn't clear, I don't know what is.

'Does it have to be two people? What if it's one person who gave you both objects?'

What if I throw this chair at you, Bill? Be nice. He's trying. He certainly is. 'However it happens ... one, two ...'

'Buckle my shoe.'

'It doesn't matter. What matters is the exercise. Do the exercise your own unique way. Just do it.'

The exercise begins. The classroom becomes the setting for the long voyage. The students leave loved ones behind, ride the seas, ride wild horses, boil in the sun, drown in the rain, burn up with fever, lose hope time after time, until finally they arrive in the town that will one day be called 'Beatrice'. I sense their individual and unique journeys.

Molly does not come up for air. She travels and travels. When she is finished, I will call on her. It is her turn. It is her time. Finally, Molly Malone, you will be heard.

'Oh yes, one last thing. What do you want these new acquaintances to know about your past. Do you have any secrets to hide? Sorry, I didn't mean to interrupt you.'

'My name is Molly Malone. I have traveled far. The sea, the sky, the wind, the rain, the moonlight, the sunlight, the land, and all of God's infinite elements have been my guide ... my compass. I was born not that many years ago, but long enough ago to know that Dublin is no longer fair. Famine has ravaged the city. It too has ravaged my family.

'My mother Maggie is my only surviving family member. She is back home in Dublin, at least she was there when I began my long journey to this foreign land. My father, Michael, died a tragic death. Before my departure, he came down with a wicked fever. His teeth rattled inside his skull from the chill that wore him down to nothing but hot coals and wet rags. The good Lord took him from us. He was a fine bright man.

'But me, my story, let it be told now. Whoever shall find this journal, if you do so, then I will have been taken back to the soil, become one with the elements that have guided me through this, my life's journey.

'I had me a fine husband named John. After we set sail from Dublin, I gave birth to the sweetest infant son. We named him Daniel. My husband died in the bowels of the steamer called *The High Seas*. He too had a fever, just like my father. His bones came through his skin, caused him the worst kind of pain, before the Lord took him to the mighty heavens.

'My baby boy is still alive. He is lying on the ground beside me, lying on a piece of cloth that my mother gave me before I left home. She thought the cloth might come in handy. As always, she was right in her thinking. But, my little boy is ill with a blight that eats away at his skin. What is even sadder still, is that my boy has gone blind. He can no longer see the light of day, or the moonlight, or his mother's eyes.

'My breasts have dried up. There is no milk inside this hag called mother. I cannot feed my boy. Before too long, he will starve to death. Whether I live or die does not much matter anymore. All that matters is Daniel.

'I am here in some godforsaken land with no water, no ocean, no water on any side of me, only sky; the biggest sky I have ever seen. Wherever I turn, there is sky and then there is more sky painted in every color of the Lord's canvas. It has a beauty to it, like the beauty of death after a long struggle.

'My body is weary, my breath is heavy, my sleep is not what I know sleep to be, but more it is like a waking dream. I am afraid that if I sleep, the night beasts will devour Daniel and me. Maybe that would be for the best. I am not sure whether living like animals is what God had in mind for any of his human creatures. But, I still pray with all my heart to go on. I pray to God. I pray for his help and for his guidance. I pray for the safety of my mother.

'I pray for my darlin' departed father, wherever his soul might be. My father, before he passed away, gave me two buttons from his one and only woolen jacket. I promised him that I would sew them on the first dress that I made after I reached my new home in America. That way he would still be part of the fabric of our family in the new world. These buttons are buried within a sack lying on the ground. My Daniel's head rests on that sack, that sack made from an old burlap potato bag. It is filled with grain and those two buttons. It was sewn by my mother's hand. This pillow might be the final resting place for the last two generations of our family.

'I have no secrets to hide, no shameful lies. I am a young woman who has lost more than my share of family, that which matters most to me. I have no friends here. There are those who have been kindly toward me as I have traveled, but in this camp of many cultures, I do not feel safe. It is every man for himself.

'My child is not a burden to me. However, there are those who feel that he should be left behind. They say, "Let the creatures of the night take care of his suffering. His soul will be set free." That is what the foreigners say. We are all of us foreigners here. But, I will not abandon my boy. He is my responsibility until death. And I love him dearly.

'The moon is full tonight. Because of its light, I can see many tiny spring flowers popping their heads up through the tired earth. It's spring in Dublin. I wish that I were there with my dear mother Maggie. I wonder if she is still selling cockles and mussels. No matter how far away I am from her, I hope she can still feel my love. We will always be together. This I know for sure.

'As the night creatures howl, I will sleep wakefully, all the time praying for my dear father's soul, for my mother, my husband, for my sweet child, and even for myself. I do believe that God is with me somewhere here … wherever here is.

From the hand of Molly Malone.'

Molly Malone has been heard. The class is speechless.

I first set my eyes on sweet Molly Malone.
'Alive, alive oh! alive, alive oh!'
Crying. Crying.
'Alive, alive oh!

'Alive, alive oh! alive, alive oh!'
Crying. Crying.

I drive south on route 77 toward Lincoln airport. As I speed down the highway, I want to make sure that the Malone girls are close behind me. In my rear-view mirror, I catch a glimpse of two heads bobbing up and down. Molly's head is the less buoyant. But, I notice an animation in her body like I have never seen before. She must be regaling Maggie with tales of her success in English class, and expressing her disappointment at Willwrite's absence. But, Molly Malone has been accepted by her peers. She is no longer the silent lazy girl in eleventh grade English.

I turn the radio up full tilt boogie, be bop my way toward the rental car return. I am filled with sadness; the tears build up in my right eye. I so do not want to leave. After a few moments of analyzing my feelings, I glance into my side-view mirror. I see a figure sitting in between the Malone girls. There sits my mother. She reads a *Mother Goose* nursery rhyme book. I wonder which rhymes she has chosen for the girls. What I am seeing is an impossibility. Rub eyes. When I look back again, she is gone.

I am not ready to leave Beatrice behind, or is it that I am not ready to face what lies ahead.

My blue scarf is wrapped around my neck, neatly tucked inside my polar fleece jacket. I see my mother in her glory days, young and enchanting. From a 'somewhere in the Virgin Islands' straw bag, she pulls out a thin, white cardboard box wrapped with a blue ribbon. She hands me the box. My hands tremble. I can hardly wait to find out what gift she has brought me this time. As I rip and tear at the package, she slaps my hands. I stop, look up at her. What did I do wrong this time?

'Take your time, honey,' she says. *'Life is short and sweet. Children need to chew life slowly. Treat each moment as if you were eating the best candy in the world; you want each and every mouthful to last forever.'*

'Like an all day sucker?' ask I.

'Like an all day sucker.' I take my sweet time. But when I see the scarf, I forget about my new life's lesson. In a frenzy, I wrap it around my neck, like a diva making an entrance at a gala in her honor. I was not familiar with the famous dancer Isadora Duncan in those early years, but when I think about it now, that's who comes to mind.

I return the car, thank the Avis lady, drag the red relic up the out-of-order escalator. There stand the Malone girls.

Molly reprimands me. 'You drive too fast.'

'It's the music – makes me heavy on the metal. I'm just a teenage fool on a four-lane highway.'

Maggie hugs me hello. 'Molly told me about class. Sounds exciting.'

'It was.' I turn to Molly. 'She was brilliant.'

'Ma! I asked you not to bring it up.'

'I would have brought it up if your mother hadn't. It's something worth talking about.'

'I don't want to talk about it. It happened. It was fun. Mr Willwrite wasn't there, so it really doesn't matter.'

'I left Mr Willwrite a note. When he gets back to school, he'll be asking to see your paper. I hope you don't mind.'

'He's not gonna grade me on it, is he?'

'No, nothing like that. I just want him to see your work – your writing. He's never seen it before, has he?'

'No. Ma, where's the bathroom?'

'Down that hall on your left. Hurry up. Honest to goodness, Molly Malone, you have the smallest bladder in the state of Nebraska.'

'Ma!' Molly runs to the bathroom.

'She's got a gift.'

'I'm going to miss you so much.' Maggie reaches for my hand.

I pull away. 'Don't. I'll lose it. She needs your support.'

'Will you call? Willwrite doesn't like her.'

Fighting back the tears I say, 'I'll try. Why not?'

'I'll call you. When's a good time? She got caught cutting class at the beginning of the school year.'

'Depends whether Simone is home. Make sure he gets the paper. Tell her she has to participate in his class. I'll never wash my clothes. You're all over them.'

Maggie's face lights up. 'Kiss me,' she says.

'Are you crazy?!' I look around for Molly.

'Don't leave.'

'Maggie. I have to go home. I'll be back. I promise. Thank you for ...'

Once again, she places her fingers over my mouth. 'Shh.'

I kiss her fingers. 'I love you.'

Here comes Molly; eyes red with tears. Maggie pulls away. Molly runs into my arms. 'I wish you wouldn't go.'

'I wish you wouldn't cry.' One teardrop falls down my right cheek, another down my left. Soon, I am crying from both sides for both Malones.

Maggie pulls out a handkerchief, reminding me of the piece of cloth Molly wrote about in class. I see the blind child Daniel. I see Molly Malone holding on for dear life, in the middle of a town with no name. Flashback. Life is a flashback.

Maggie hugs me. I can't help but notice how buxom she is. After all, I am deeply infatuated. She whispers something in my ear, but I don't hear it. Enough crying. I have to check *the bag*, go through the inevitable inept security check, during which time they will not find my nail file, because they do not know what the fuck they are doing.

One last hug, one last tear, one more word. 'Molly ... you were astounding today. I am very proud of you. I will never forget your story.'

Molly whispers, 'Thank you for coming here and spending time with me.'

'It has been an honor. I loved every single minute.'

The wistful Nebraskans cry: 'We love you.'

And then I am off into the horizon. Torn between many lives, I peruse *The United Way* magazine. There is a longwinded article about Archer Daniels Midland. I skip it; not exactly, I squint, play a game with myself, look at the print so the ink blurs. Fun way of passing airplane time. All of the lettersruntogether. My airplane game keeps me occupied for quite some time. I smell my fingers. Maggie. Sigh. I will return to the house where Beatrice lived, still lives, might live forever, depending upon how long she is caught between these infinite planes.

Will Simone be waiting for me in my West 96th Street apartment? If she is, I wonder how our homecoming will be? Will I still love her, or will I be too full of Maggie to love anyone else?

I am anxious to unpack my feather pillow, change the pillowcase, lie my weary ass on that horsehair mattress Simone insisted upon years ago. She was right to make me spend five grand for that luxury. It is still the best night's sleep in any town, anywhere.

Can't wait to see Dina. Hope she's holding up; not to worry. She is Dina. That is what she does best. Glad that's not my role in the family tree … So many broken limbs. Do weeping willows weep for water? Or do they weep because they break so easy.

I guess Pop is sleeping downstairs full time now. Can't even sleep in his own bedroom. You ought to be ashamed of yourself.

I'm quite sure Patty the maid is feeding him dog food, pretends it's ground round, figures he won't notice the difference, pockets the change … hope it's not Alpo. I would love to know just how much silverware she's stolen? I wonder if Dina keeps inventory?

When I get back to Beechwood, I am going to check on the monkey collection, see if you know who has moved Pop's precious darlings.

I forgot to ask Dina about Mrs B. That woman has had a tough life. Burt was one strange guy. But, he was her son, family ... Right now, this second, I kind of feel like, like I belong. It's like those Robert Frost lines.

'Home is the place where, when you have to go there,

They have to take you in.'

'Have I told you about the moon and the stars?'

Look who's here! Hey Ma. Guess where I'm going? Home. First to 96th Street, then to our house in Beechwood. Maybe I'll find something incredible there. Just like I found Maggie and Molly Malone in your home town. You know what happened there, Ma? They took me in. That place, those people, they took your daughter in, and made her feel loved.

'Rock-a-bye baby on the tree top.'

I am so proud of you. If it were my choice, that's the opening line I would have picked. Bravo.

'The apple doesn't fall far from the tree, you know?'

No, it doesn't. Does it?

Merge

When I arrive home, Simone is not waiting anxiously in the apartment. I am both relieved and disappointed. My disappointment affords me the opportunity to sashay over to the freezer, open the door, grab a thinly rolled joint I had hidden from myself before my teaching escapades; Maui wowie, sound asleep in a lovely English lemon drop tin, ready to lift my spirits high.

Two hits later disappointment turns into despair. Why did I leave Maggie? Simone is never home. True, over the last double plus decades, we have had an understanding. 'If you need me, I'll be there.' I need her. I need to know that we are real. I drop my broken bag on the floor, march over to the answering machine, two messages, press play, take another hit, listen. Maggie whispers, 'Hi. Miss you so much. It's been raining non-stop since you left. Molly's locked herself in her room. I've suddenly taken up drinking Scotch. It helps. Please call soon.' And I left her standing at the airport. Second message: 'Darlin', I am so sorry I am not there. I had to stay in Zurich for business. A gallery is interested in my work. We meet tomorrow. If you are already home, please forgive me for not being there ... *Je t'adore, mon amour.*'

And where the hell are you when I need you!? For God's sake, my father's dying. I just got off the road, and you are off fucking some gallery owner in Zurich. And Maggie is in my hair. I feel her right here ... in my heart, my crotch. Conflict.

'My little maid is not at home;
Saddle my hog and bridle my dog.'

'I don't need advice right now.' I'll unpack in the morning. I fall into bed, pull the comforter up over my head, wiggle my toes, roll my head from side to side, take many deep breaths. Feel myself feeling Maggie. I cannot fall asleep. Rock and rock and rock some more. I hear a voice inside my head. A child screams. 'HELP!' I curl up into a small ball underneath the comforter.

The horsehair mattress speaks. 'Hold on, girl. Remember those open spaces. You have been there, before they were named. You are part of them always, no matter where you are. That prairie is yours. It is your home. Tomorrow will remind you of what it is you need to understand about yesterday ... Happy trails to you.'

Laundry has a rhythm. Laundry has a deeper meaning than simply being wash, especially after Maggie. Must pick and choose what goes in, what stays unclean. I sort carefully, place my favorite Maggie-scented items in my closet. The rest of the laundry is ready for Whirlpool. When you wash dirty clothes, it is a healing event. I will bet you all of the money I have made from my teaching engagement in Beatrice (not a hill of beans) that when the soaked clothing circles inside the machine, wrapping its arms and legs around itself, in one wet and wild holy experience, it forms a mandala of cleanliness. The shock comes when the wet wash is ripped away from the water, thrown haphazardly into the dryer, a vacuum where holy water is sucked out of the laundry's dripping limbs. Laundry is of vital importance, especially after one month on the road without a decent laundromat.

When I yank my favorite white jeans from the dryer, ink has

seeped through the rear right pocket; a note meant to remind me to remember an idea that is now washed away forever. I spray Zout, pour Clorox, soak the white jeans in cold water. No time to wring and towel dry. I am already late for my leftover luncheon with Dina.

The 96th Street cross-town bus speeds by. I will walk through the park. New York is beautiful in May. The park has that pre-tourist, post-winter, present-spring glint to it. The grass shimmers, birds sing, squirrels look perkier than any other time of the year. Fortunately for them, they do not suffer from allergies. They have no need for a HEPA filtration system.

Visit Pop tomorrow. Dina will advise me on 'ideal topics', so as not to agitate him. On Monday, first appointment with Mary Michelin. Can't wait to find out about Dr Dot. No time for jet lag. Got personal business needs attending.

Fred the doorman greets me. 'Hi Loli. Where you been?'

'Nebraska. How are you, Fred?'

'Nebraska? Isn't that where Warren Buffet lives?'

'Yeah. He lives in Omaha. How'd you know that Warren Buffet lives in Nebraska?'

'Everybody knows Warren Buffet lives in Omaha. At least anyone who owns any Berkshire Hathaway.'

'You own Berkshire Hathaway?'

'I do. My sister gave me one share thirty years ago.'

'Congratulations. How much is the stock worth?'

'Ninety-six thousand the last time I checked.'

Wonder how many shares his sister has? 'Don't buzz her. I've got the keys. I want to surprise her.'

'Nebraska, huh? How'd you like it there?'

'I liked it, lots of sky. People are nice. You know, Fred, people are nice everywhere. If you're nice to them, they're nice back.'

'That's not true in this building. But your sister, she's a gem. You girls are lucky to have each other. How's your old man doing?'

'Not so good. I'm going to Beechwood tomorrow.'

'Send him my love. He's a great guy, your father.'

'I'll tell him you said so.'

I open the door to 8D, throw my belly bag on the gray satin chair, stroll into the beige kitchen. Why she chose that color, I will never know. My sister walks out from the pantry.

'Oh my God! You scared me to death!'

'I'm here. Aren't you glad to see me?'

'Why didn't you call to let me know when you were coming?'

'I told you the other night.'

'I can't remember that far back.'

'Too many wine spritzers.'

'Too much stress.'

We hug. She gives me a perfunctory peck on the cheek. 'I hate when you do that.'

'Do what?'

'Never mind. I missed you.'

'Let me heat up the vegetables.'

'Please, no microwave.'

'I forgot.'

'No, you didn't. Let me do it.' I open the refrigerator to find some undercooked eggplant, overcooked zucchini, burnt cauliflower and canned pickled beets. Dina is no Alice Waters. We take out the All-Clad pots. I try to revive the vegetables, ask for some raw carrots, to save the ratatouille from further ruination. Dina grabs a bunch, rinses them, cuts the tops off with a sharp knife.

'Oh shit!' The blood drips down her index finger onto the

carrots. Nonplussed, she sits down on the kitchen stool. She looks at her finger like a baby discovering its shadow on the ceiling. The blood drips onto the cutting board. Dina does not move.

I beeline it for the guest bathroom, open the medicine cabinet, find the Band-Aids and iodine. I close the cabinet, head back to the kitchen. Dina sits staring, as the blood runs down onto each one of her fingers. I grab a dish towel, wrap it around her index finger, get some ice from the freezer, unwrap the towel, place the ice on the cut. Dina does not blink. I run back to the bathroom, find the Q-tips, race back to the kitchen, dab the iodine onto the wound. I slide the Band-Aid out of the wrapper, wind it around Dina's finger.

I turn her head toward me, stand her up. She is like a rag doll. I hug her. I stroke her hair. I dry her eyes with my index finger. I know where she has gone.

We were here, together, in this very same kitchen when she cut herself. It was raining. Nearly twenty years ago. She answered the phone. It was a brief conversation. Come to think of it, I don't even know who called that day to break the news.

From that Band-Aid to this Band-Aid. 'Dina. Dina.'

'What?'

'Let's hang out in the bedroom, read *People* magazine. Do you have the new issue?'

'*Vanity Fair*.' She points. I grab the magazine off the kitchen table.

'Fine. Just as trashy, even worse. Come on. Let's be stupid.' We get on the bed, open the magazine.

'Would she have liked it there, in Beatrice?'

'Would she have liked it anywhere? She would have loved the Malone girls. I don't know what I'm going to do. I can't stop thinking about Maggie. Let's read about Carolyn Bessette-Kennedy's final hours.'

'It feels like then,' Dina says.

'It is kind of like then … before she …' Now is the right time; tell her my secret. 'She told me she was going to kill herself.'

Dina laughs. 'She told everyone.'

'She told you?'

'She told me. She told Mrs B. She told Pop.'

'She made me promise.'

'Me too.'

'We all knew?' I kick off my shoes.

'She might have told the Good Humor man for all I know.' Dina laughs again. 'She even told Ralph.'

'I can't believe it. All these years I thought …'

'She was getting us ready. It was inevitable. You would say that it was her fate.' Dina kicks off her shoes.

'No. I would say that it was our fate to have her as our mother. It was her fate to marry Pop.' I get under the covers with magazine in hand. Dina gets under the covers. 'They were each other's shadow.' I throw off the covers. 'Didn't you say that once?' I examine the Band-Aid on her finger.

Dina pulls her hand away. 'Did I?'

I flip through the pages until a Calvin Klein underwear ad catches my eye. 'You shed your snakeskin on my kitchen floor.'

'Nothing's changed, different kitchen.'

'We have.'

'We'll never change, never.' She thinks out loud. 'Not until …'

'Don't even think that thought.' I think the thought. 'Too many perfume ads in this shit magazine – smells like a French whorehouse.'

'How's Simone?'

'Nice segue.'

'Sorry. What time are you going to Beechwood?'

'Afternoon. What should I talk about?'

Dina smirks. 'Ask him how Mom's doing?'

'Does he know I know?'

'He knows about the nursery rhymes.'

'What'd he say?'

'He doesn't say much these days. He's too busy remembering.'

'She's busy reminding him. How's Mrs B?'

'She's at Beechwood Manor.'

'The old age home?!'

'Assisted living. I visited her. It's not such a bad place. That's a lie. It's pretty depressing.'

'What isn't depressing?'

'Us. We're not depressing. We might be depressed, but we have good reason to be. We are about to become orphans.' She pulls the covers over her head.

'I never thought about it like that.' I crawl under with her. 'So Oliver Twistish.'

Dina throws the covers back. 'I'm making myself a wine spritzer.'

'I'll have one too.'

'You don't drink.' She heads for the kitchen.

'All the more reason.' I follow her ... 'Will it be over soon?'

'For those of you who believe in the hereafter, it is never over. For us, yes it will be over soon. He probably has a month ... maybe.'

'Not very long.' I watch her mix the spritzers.

'I'm sure for him, it will feel like an eternity.' She hands me my drink.

'Is he afraid?'

'No.' We toast.

'Are you afraid?'

'No. But I'll miss him.' She starts to cry. 'I will miss that old goat.'

'You will? I wonder if I'll miss him?'

'He is so wonderful with the kids. He's been a fantastic grandfather.'

'Finally got something right.'

Driving up the Saw Mill River Parkway to see Pop. Early evening. The road cuts right through a thick forest of trees. I ask myself, do trees have secrets? No. The beauty of a tree is that it's just simply there for us to love, something we cherish because of its beauty. Maggie's like that.

I park Dina's car in front of the house, climb up the front steps two at a time just like I did when I was, oh I don't know, six years old, maybe seven. Before opening the entry door, I stop, turn around, glance at the hopscotch playing field of my youth. It is intact, waiting for one more game.

From inside my jeans pocket, I dig out a temporary permanent good luck penny. Damn. I meant to give it to Molly. I throw the penny onto the flagstone walkway. I play: hop, skip, jump, balance, both feet hit ground simultaneously, and hop, skip, balance, bend forward, pick up … freeze in place … reconnect with … *the little girl who had a little curl right in the middle of her*…

I am prepared to enter his world, her world, our world, the world that none of us left behind. I flip the coin. It comes up heads. I win. I toss it across the street. It lands inside Mrs B.'s overgrown front yard. Wonder who's living there now? Patty, the maid, will tell me. Patty will tell me more than I want to know.

The front door seems smaller than it was once upon a childhood. The house, the windows, the white wooden siding, the green shutters have all shrunk.

'Glory be to God. Look who's come a callin'.' Patty has lived in the United States for more than twenty years. She has been employed and stealing from my father for almost all of those twenty years. Why does Pop keep her? He never liked the china in the first place … Doesn't want to be alone. She fusses over him. She never knew my mother, therefore she does not remind him of my mother.

Patty whispers. 'It won't be long now. He's turnin' yellow. And she's in the bedroom. He talks to her all the time. I'm afraid to clean in there. Lord knows what might happen if I run into her. I might not get out alive.'

One less room to clean. 'Where is he?'

'In the television room. He loves his new hospital bed: pushes the button, goes up and down, up and down. I swear on my dear departed uncle's life, God rest his soul, she's awaitin', whisperin', showin' him the way. She scared Mrs B. blind, killed Burt, now she's after him. The Lord is watchin'. But mercy, it ain't the Lord doin' the work here. The Devil's come a callin'.'

'Patty! The devil is not in the house.'

'Oh yes, and it is your mother's soul that the devil's got a hold of.'

'Patty! That's enough. She was my mother. You never even knew her. Don't talk about her like that. Understood?'

'I didn't know you were so sensitive about her.'

'Now you know. The TV room?'

'Probably sleepin', he is, like a baby. He'll wake up when he hears your little footsteps.'

I walk in front of the old mahogany breakfront, look at myself in the beveled mirror on the wall; no longer young, I am surprised to see this older me … in my childhood house. I gird myself, step over the dining-room line. There lies my father, looking like an under-ripe banana. He is canary yellow. It is the liver cancer. The bile has nowhere to go but into the skin. He is smaller, looks sweeter, and seems unusually lucid for a dying man. His eyes dart in my direction.

'Well, well, well, look who's come home – the prodigal child.'

'Hi Pop.' I scoot over to his bedside, kiss him on his yellow forehead, grab his bony hand. His grip is unfaltering. The son of a bitch is as strong as ever. 'Ouch.'

'Your old man's still the strongest man in Beechwood.'

'Guess so.'

'What kind of malarkey did that Irish bitch feed you? The devil's come to get me? Should have booted her Irish ass out years ago, when she was feeding me dog food, telling me it was ground round. Sure I ate it. I never let on that I knew. Thought she was trying to save me money. Now I can't get rid of her; at least she shows up. Loyal … She's good to me … You have no idea what it's like when you can't take care of yourself. Don't get old. More important, don't ever get sick. They treat you like an animal. It's despicable, demeaning, and downright demoralizing.'

'How are you, Pop?'

'Don't be a smart ass.'

His perspicacity is not diminished. He knows he's losing his grip on life, his power being stripped away. He feels it. He will go out kicking and screaming. Though he be jaundiced, incontinent and irreconcilable, he will fight for life until he is turned inside out. The bad boy from the wrong side of the tracks who got ahead has nowhere to go. He has nothing to show for making it in the world, nothing but remorse and rage; lethal combination for the final journey.

'Let me see your lip. How are your teeth?'

'Look.' He opens his mouth wide, like a racehorse having an oral exam.

'Great job.'

'The good doc fixed the chip, stitched the lip. It was nothing. He's a genius. You know it was Saturday, he took me anyway. Normally, he charges overtime on Saturday; big bucks, not me, not your old man. Didn't charge me a cent. What a great guy. Imagine not charging me … on a weekend. There's a gentleman. Tell me again? Where were you, kid? Omaha, right?'

'Here we go round the mulberry bush,
The mulberry bush, the mulberry bush …'

Good timing, Ma, right on cue. 'Beatrice, Nebraska.'

My father turns his head away. 'Oh.'

I want to cry. I'm sure that he does too. 'Daddy?' No response. 'Daddy?'

'Hmm.'

'… Is something the matter?'

'She's in the bedroom … Your mother's chased me out of the bedroom.'

'Maybe she just wanted to visit … had nowhere else to go … wanted to say …'

'She's come to get me. I know that's why she's here.' He turns toward me. 'I've given her the room. She's won.'

'Dad, it's not a contest.' I try to comfort him. 'She speaks to me, you know?'

'Your sister told me.'

'Nursery rhymes.'

'Not her. Never her.'

'That's what I said, but it's her. It is definitely her … her voice.'

'She never knew … any… how to take care of you kids … never heard a nursery rhyme from her. We hired somebody to help …' He turns away again. 'Would you check on my monkeys?'

'Be right back.' I get up, walk away. Always walk away.

He asks, 'Are you sleeping here tonight?'

Wasn't planning on it. God, I hate this house! I didn't bring a change of underwear. 'Yes. We'll have breakfast tomorrow morning. I'll make you some eggs and toast.'

'I'm not very hungry these days, but I'll sit with you.'

'That'll be wonderful. Be right back. Do you need anything?'

'The monkeys. Someone's been moving the monkeys.' Those monkeys, his good luck trophies … Whenever he closed a deal, made a killing, clobbered a hated business rival, he bought a monkey. There were jade, silver, gold, onyx, brass, glass, wood, ivory, soapstone, all kinds, types, sizes and shapes. How he loved his monkeys. The more money he amassed, the more monkeys he accumulated. His bureau top was brimming with them. Her bureau drawers were brimming with bottles; her drugs. Now she was keeping a watchful eye on *his* monkeys.

I walk into the parents' bedroom. The closet doors are unhinged, paint peeling, bed upside down, footprints on ceiling … high-heeled shoes, no less. She has been dancing on the ceiling. I want to dance with her on that cracked, aged, off-white ceiling. We have never danced upside down in her boudoir. This seems the ideal time. The room spins. I want to faint. Instead, I open a window and breathe some Beechwood air. It is toxic in that monkey master bedroom, toxic.

A ghost can hold you close, turn you inside out and upside down, but you still love it, because it is your ghost. After all these years, my father and I finally have something in common. Her. She has moved the monkeys. Each and every one of them has been turned on its side. They are lying next to each other, like a stack of dominoes in a grave.

'Peter, Peter, pumpkin-eater,
Had a wife and couldn't keep her…'

'What the hell are you doing in here?' Why talk out loud? Why ask a ghost questions? It won't answer. 'He, your husband, and I would appreciate it if you would leave his monkeys alone. He surrenders. You win. What more do you want from the poor guy?' There is no reply.

I look up at the ceiling. The footprints have disappeared. I leave the monkeys and the madhouse behind. I walk into my bedroom, close my eyes and listen. Through the walls I hear her crying: no sobs, no hysteria, just muffled cries in a pillow. It is a time long past. I am once again of hopscotch age. I listen harder. Because she cries, I cry. And I am still crying.

I stay the night. Try to fall asleep. I am fully clothed, afraid to undress, afraid that someone is watching. In my fitful slumber, I hear her feather pillow become drenched with tears. I hear my father mumble under his breath. He gets out of bed, plays with his monkeys, leaves the bedroom. Where he goes, I do not know. Where he is, well, he is downstairs. Isn't he? He too is in the master bedroom. He is in a shrinking world with no possibilities. No. He has one possibility left. But if you have but one possibility, nothing else is possible. And that is what makes life before death seem impossible.

He and I will have breakfast together in the a.m. That is a first. You see, while we are both alive, anything is possible.

When I wake up in the morning, my eyes are stuck together with sleep and nursery rhymes. I rub my eyes. The sleep falls onto my bedroom floor, floor awakens, yawns, boards creak, stretch into the new day. Still fully clothed, I walk into the upstairs hallway, once again I peek into my parents' room. The monkeys are upright, the bed on all fours, the ceiling is ceiling-white. From where I stand, in the doorway, it looks freshly painted. I take a closer look at his monkey collection. His favorite picture-jasper monkey is missing. A hidden message from the past has slipped into a disharmonious world of apparitions. She has stolen his grief and made it her own. It is no wonder that he is dying. He cannot locate a place within himself for his personal sorrow. She is his sorrow. She holds his grief in her transparency.

At breakfast I eat half a grapefruit, one poached egg and toast. He watches, does not eat a morsel. His eyes are glassy, like a still blue lake.

'Did you sleep well?'

I lie. 'I did. How 'bout you?'

'Didn't sleep. I was too worried about the monkeys.'

I lie again. 'They're fine.'

'You sure?'

'Positive.'

'She hasn't been playing with them?'

One more breakfast-time lie … 'She's not there.'

'Oh … I hope …'

'Do you want a piece of toast? Marmalade?'

'Marmalaud.'

Bless him and his phony English accent. 'Do you?'

'Not hungry. I'll watch you. You need to put on some weight.' He stops. He thinks about what he has said. 'No, you're just fine. You're fine the way you are.'

'Thank you.'

'Don't let the eggs get cold. Nothing worse than cold eggs.'

'So, that's where I get it from.'

'The apple doesn't fall far from the tree.'

'The apple doesn't fall far from the tree.'

I look. I listen. 'I know.'

'I'm glad you came home.'

'Me too.'

He yells at the top of his failing lungs. 'Patty! It's time for my medication!' He whispers. 'She's not getting a penny, not a penny. Don't you girls give her a cent. You hear me.'

'Have a piece of toast, Pop.' He leans over, nearly falls off his chair, finds his balance, nibbles at my toast.

'Needs marmalaud.'

'I'll put some on.'

'Don't bother. Just enjoy it before it gets cold.'

I am not hungry, but for you, Father, I will eat. Oh shit! I forgot to ask Patty about who's living at Mrs B.'s. 'Dad?' He is lost in space. 'Dad!'

'What?'

'Who's' … better not to ask … 'What's the best stock fund? If you were investing, who would you give your money to?'

'Warren Buffet … Berkshire Hathaway. Didn't I tell you I had business in Omaha … when I first started the firm?'

'You did.'

'How'd you like Omaha?'

Don't bother. 'I liked it. I liked it a lot.'

'Your mother would have hated it. She never liked small towns. Never.' Simultaneously, we turn toward the kitchen doorway, listen. Her voice fills the air.

'I went up one pair of stairs.'
'Just like me.'
'I went up two pairs of stairs.'
'Just like me.'
'I went into a room.'
'Just like me.'
'I looked out of a window.'
'Just like me.'
'And there I saw a monkey.'
'Just like me.'

Blow Out

I ring the outside buzzer. It rings back. Through two heavy wooden doors, I enter the brick building. I ring the office buzzer. It rings back. Push the black door open, enter Mary Michelin's anteroom. As I had imagined, the walls are beige. We will begin on a blank page. The usual magazines are on the glass table: *Vogue, Bazaar, Newsweek, Time, People, Vanity Fair*.

The door opens. There she is. Mary Michelin is no 60,000 miles guaranteed tire. She is a silver-haired beauty, wearing a black turtleneck tucked inside a long black straight skirt. Around her slim waist is a leather belt with silver buckle; and black boots underneath the fashionable skirt; not a lot of color to her outfit. But, her eyes sparkle as if she has a secret or knows the secrets that wait in her waiting room.

She opens her interior door. 'Loli Greene?'

'Yes.'

'Come in.' She closes the door. I sit in a comfortable padded armchair. She sits in a reclining easy chair. She looks so at ease in her body, in her world. I am petrified.

'Where do I begin?'

'What brought you here? Let's begin there.'

A therapist who asks questions. The jig is up. 'My father is dying – cancer. He's got about a month to live. My mother, who's been dead for at least twenty years, chased my father out of his bedroom, which was their bedroom. About a year after she died, she started talking to me in nursery rhymes during this nervous breakdown I had in LA. When she was alive, it wasn't like her to recite *Mother Goose* to anyone, especially her children. She's talking nursery rhymes again … now. My sister, I have an older sister named Dina …'

'How much older?'

'Six years. We're very close, not in age, but in other ways. She has children. I don't. I'm gay … I guess that's what I am. I've been in a … how can I say it, a … very … on-again, off-again, relationship for nearly twenty years, but now I've fallen in love with a married woman. She's getting a divorce, I think. My other relationship, Simone, the long one, has always been an open relationship.'

'Why's that?'

'We, me and Simone, wanted it that way, or she wanted it that way. I don't remember who wanted it what way… I just came back from Beatrice, Nebraska. That was my mother's first name … Beatrice. The accent is on a different syl … Never mind. It was phenomenal; see my mother's name everywhere. I fell in love with a straight woman. I already said that, didn't I? It's not important.'

'It isn't?'

'Maybe it is. Her daughter, it turns out, thinks of me as a role model. Now that's crazy.'

'Why?'

'I'm not a role model type … Hate to work. Since my mother died, hard getting up in the morning. My father and I never got along. Never. But we got along yesterday … for the first time, ever. We have my mother in common now. He sees her. I hear her. I almost liked him, loved him yesterday.'

'How lovely for you.'

'It's so sad.' Floodgates open. 'It's all … so sad. I feel so sorry for him. He's so alone, even though my mother's ghost is in the house. He has a housekeeper who takes care of him, but she doesn't care about him. She's been stealing from him for years. He pays her to stick around. He has no friends left.'

'Are you sure about that?'

'Ever since she killed herself, he hasn't had any friends, maybe one or two.'

'Ever since who killed herself?'

'Oh … my mother killed herself. Then he went and married my mother's best friend. It's been a mess for years. He tried to seduce my lover … I think. That was a while ago. My mother's best friend, my father's ex-wife, is blind. And, somehow, my mother is somewhere in this world, but she's been dead for years.' I laugh hysterically, split my sides … guts ache. 'The story is, believe it or not, it's true.' I can't stop laughing and crying. I can't … br … bre … brea … breathe … 'Help! Help!' Can't breathe! Oh my God! Suffocating … in Mary Michelin's office, first visit. She doesn't know what's happening, does she?

'Are you … Can you hear me?! Loli, are you alriii …' Fade to black.

Pounding in heart space. Pounding, pounding so hard, so heavy. Drop down through a portal onto a furry mound. Shadows surround me. Noises come toward me from all directions. Warm skin, a warm hand picks me up. I am safe. Once again I have survived.

A voice asks, 'Can you hear me?'

I open my eyes. Mary Michelin is standing over me. I am lying on her office floor. I look straight into her eyes. 'I can hear you … This is embarrassing.'

'Never be embarrassed in my office.'

'Okay. But we've only just met.' We laugh.

'I am very glad we have.'

'I'm not so sure.'

'I can see why. Would you like a glass of water?'

'No, thank you. But, I will get back in the chair. I prefer to be eye level.' We laugh again. After which there is a very, I mean, very long pause. 'How are we going to work together?'

'Quite well, I think.'

I have very little to say after the spectacle … 'So … How's Dr Dot?'

'How do you know Dr Dot?'

'He was my therapist during the California breakdown.'

'How did you know he … I left his referral number, didn't I?'

'You certainly did. Quite surprised I was.'

'I hope my professional relationship with Dr Dot and your professional relationship with him won't keep you from working with me.'

'I don't think anything could keep me from working with you.'

'When would you like to come next?'

'Tomorrow. This afternoon. This evening.'

She opens her black leather appointment book. 'I have a nine a.m. opening.'

'I … I have trouble getting … never mind. Nine a.m. I hope I didn't scare you.'

'Not at all.'

I stumble out the door. What must she think? What an opening. What happened before I hit the floor? Best not to remember. Auspicious therapeutic convergence. Mary Michelin … bet you haven't seen a lot of that on your office floor. I have Dina to thank for this. I have Dina to thank for so much of the good stuff.

I walk the Village streets; west on 10th, north on University, west again on 13th. Stop at a construction site. Can't fall through the cracks in the open sidewalk. Can fall into the bottom of sludge called personality. Shovel self into a corner of insubordinate longing. How I long for the moment when I was a bird fish, when I could swim and fly all at once, in a space with no past or future in its way. In that space is the breath, the rhythm, the endless adventure without any fragmented self, without doubt, without fear. That is where I want to be, where the bird fish spawns the present participle called life.

At Fifth Avenue I duck into the 14th Street subway, wind down deep into the city's grip, until I am standing in front of the Canarsie Line. I remember my underground motel in Iowa. That was before Beatrice, before I knew that I am not where I belong, and have never been. The train arrives.

Before too long, I arrive at West 96th Street. I do not remember switching trains, but after all that has happened, it is a miracle I am home at all.

The elevator is broken. I walk up six flights, definitely enough exercise for the day. When I enter the apartment, I feel overwhelmed with a nauseating despair. I drop down onto my knees in front of the toilet, barf, flush my grief down the bowl. There are four messages on the machine: Dina checking in on my time with Pop, as well as my time with Mary Michelin; Simone informing me that she will arrive home on Friday evening. Saul extolling the virtues of sleeping with men who scramble eggs well … And sweet Molly Malone.

Her voice is full of smiles. 'Hi Loli. You won't believe it. Willwrite thinks I have talent. He's furious at me for not having applied myself sooner. If I work hard, I might be able to get into a decent college. He wants me to submit my story to a national essay contest. Isn't that awesome? Maybe I should come east and look at schools back there. He wants me to apply to the University of Nebraska in Lincoln. He's almost positive I can get in there. That's where he went, says he'll write me a recommendation. I have to study really hard for my college boards. Who knows. Maybe I can write. Wouldn't that be something? Oh, by the way, Dad's in therapy. He asked Mom and me to come to some of his sessions. He wants to come back home.' My heart sinks. 'He's joined AA. He's dumped the bimbo. We're all going to the therapist this week.' My heart sinks again. 'Please call. I miss you a lot. So does Mom. We wish you were here.' What if she takes him back? 'Glad your message machine lets you talk for more than sixty seconds. I'm not a very good editor ... yet. I'll get better. I promise. Bye. Love you.'

Therapy. Call Maggie. If Molly picks up, I'll say I'm calling her ... Pop would love Maggie. Where's that monkey? Maybe it fell behind the radiator. I'll find it the next time I'm in Beechwood.

I pay more overdue bills than I can cope with, but I cope. I decide teaching in Montana is a bad idea. Dina's got her hands full with Pop. Do not want to feel guilty when his death is behind me. I know that feeling too well. I want to be a peaceful orphan.

I call Stuart Manly to inform him of my decision. Though I would like to be told that I am irreplaceable, instead, I am told, I will be replaced by a fledgling fellow, who is packed and ready to go, not the slightest problem. I am not pleased, but I have personal obligations that need my undivided attention. I pick up the phone and dial Maggie's number. It rings twice. I hang up. 'I need you,' I say to myself. With phone in hand,

I contemplate my mother's expertise at helping my father from this world to the next. On Tuesday morning, somehow, I manage to drag myself out of bed in time to make it to Mary Michelin's office for my nine a.m. appointment. She is wearing a new black outfit. I suppose that wearing no color whatsoever neutralizes being projected upon. She is still beautiful.

'How are you today?'

'Tired.'

'Nine is early for you, isn't it?'

'Can't think my way through my bullshit.'

'You're a night bird then?'

'Night bird fish.'

'Bird fish?'

'A bird fish, like a salmon with wings.'

'That's an interesting way to think of yourself.'

'Always felt like a bird fish. When I can't breathe, which, as you have seen, happens from time to time, I feel like I'm trying to breathe through my gills. But I don't have gills. I don't think I have gills.'

'Do you have any memory of being inside your mother's womb?'

'No.'

'As an unborn child, you are very much like a fish. The amniotic fluid is the embryo's sea.'

'Sometimes I get the feeling, when I arrived on earth, I didn't quite make the switch over from gills to lungs. Like I said, I have breathing issues. Always had them. My sister says I've had trouble breathing ever since I was an infant.'

'Why don't you ask her if she remembers when it first began. It would be helpful.'

'I will. Look, about Dr Dot.'

'I'm glad you brought it up.'

'I didn't think very much of his work. My therapist, Dr Guttman, was vacationing on Cape Cod. It was August. Dr Dot was his sub. I was out of my mind back then. It was a year after my mother's suicide. I had gotten myself involved with a cult … a crazy guru named Bovar. I left the cult, lost my mind … My mother started talking to me in nursery rhymes. I saw demons. It's hard to explain. When Guttman recommended Dot, I had no choice. Guttman was my therapist. I trusted him.'

'So you worked with Dr Guttman?'

'I did.'

Mary sighs, 'Dr Guttman was my mentor.'

'He was? What a small world.'

'The psychoanalytic world is a very small world indeed.'

'Your work is so different from his, at least so far. Guttman hardly ever spoke. I spent quite a bit of time and money looking at his shoes. His shoes were my barometer for whether I thought he was having a good day or a bad day. It was total projection. He had big feet. He must have had a huge dick. You know the foot wanger theory?' Mary Michelin seems extremely uncomfortable with where the conversation has taken us. Sensing her discomfort, I change the subject. 'And Dr Dot? Where did he come into all of this?'

'Leo had many students …' Mary reaches behind her, turns the air conditioner to low.

'Leo?' Familiar. Very familiar.

'Dr Guttman.' Mary Michelin blushes. I am not a psychic or a mind reader, but I, at the moment of blush, am certain of Mary Michelin's emotional involvement with Dr Leo Guttman. I know it's not my place to inquire about Mary's life. But … 'How is Dr Guttman?'

A wistful Mary replies, 'He died five years ago August while vacationing on Cape Cod.'

'I always imagined him playing Frisbee by the sea.'

'Yes.' … Mary Michelin spent summers on Cape Cod with Dr Leo Guttman. They were lovers for years. They made love in the dunes. They played Frisbee by the water's edge. When we patients were having our breakdowns in August, Mary and Leo were fucking their analytic minds out on Ol' Cape Cod. Mary Michelin has never loved another man. Dr Guttman was the great love of her life. I want to cry; another dead love.

'Weird that you should know both Dr Guttman and Dr Dot.'

'Quite a coincidence.'

'Quite. Would you mind opening a window? It's kind of stuffy in here.'

'I'll turn up the air conditioner.' She turns up the fan speed.

Mary, Mary quite contrary,
How does your garden grow?'

'Oh no.'

'Is that too much air then?' Mary asks.

'It's perfect. Just perfect.'

'Silver bells and cockle shells.'

I sigh, 'We can never have too much air.'

'Without it we wouldn't be here, would we?'

'Well … most of us … mere mortals … wouldn't.'

'Yes. Isn't that the truth.'

'Mortals … most of us.'

'And pretty maids all in a row.'

After the love life of Mary Michelin, I train it up to Beech-wood, to visit Mrs B. at Beechwood Manor, the old age home three blocks from the railroad station.

Walk the winding driveway, revolve into the Tudor-style building, stand in the middle of a beige florescent entry. You don't get well in a place like this, filled with that final-chapter, last-stop smell.

A lovely nurse's aide approaches. 'May I help you?'

'I'm looking for Mrs B.'

'She's in the recreation room, straight down the corridor, through the double glass doors.'

'Thank you.' I walk quite a distance, until I reach the glass doors. Behind them, I hear the sound of an out-of-tune spinet piano, playing a familiar melody. I walk through the doors, into the room. There she sits, stunning, elegant, playing and singing her heart out:

'In Dublin's fair city,
Where the girls are so pretty,
I first set my eyes on sweet Molly Malone ...'

I take a step. The floor creaks. Mrs B. stops playing, turns.

'Who's there? Who is it?' She is so beautiful, like a still life, sitting in the noonday sun. I look at her eyes. Those eyes are so familiar. She looks, but does not see me. 'Who is it? Who's there?'

'It's me, Mrs B. It's Loli.'

'Loli! What a wonderful surprise. Come here. Sit down next to me.' I sit down on the bench. She squeezes my hand. I take her right hand in mine. I kiss it, then place it back on the ivories. She looks at me. Why, I cannot imagine. She can't see me. Maybe she can ... Those eyes. Yes. Those are Maggie Malone's luminescent eyes ... Maggie and Mrs B. How remarkable.

Do you remember this song?' She begins to play.

'In Dublin's fair city,
Where the girls are so pretty ...'

We sing the next few lines together.

'I first set my eyes on sweet Molly Malone,
As she wheeled her wheelbarrow,
Through streets broad and narrow …'

And together in perfect harmony.

'Crying, "Cockles and mussels, alive, alive oh,"'

And again…

'Alive, alive, oh! alive, alive oh!'

And for the finale, she joins us adding a perfect third part harmony.

'Crying, "Cockles and mussels alive, alive oh."'

Mrs B. cries. I wipe her tears. As if she could see me, she wipes mine. I wonder if she too has heard my mother's voice; hears her voice all the time. Has she ever forgotten that day when she found my mother in the bathtub, naked, no longer out of her mind, just out of her body, and for a little while, out of this world. What are the appropriate topics of conversation during a time such as this … with my mother's best friend, my father's ex-wife, my former neighbor and stepmother Mrs B. What about Burt? What does she want to talk about? Play it by ear.

Mrs B. Takes the Wheel

'It's been a very long time. Hasn't it, Loli?'

'Very.'

'Almost twenty years?'

'At least.'

'Are you well? What a silly question.'

'I'm fine, considering.'

'Let's go back to my room. This piano bench was not made for two people.' I help her to her feet. She is shaky, but has no trouble when it comes to finding her way through the glass doors. 'I see shadows. I see light and shadows. That's how I find my way … They call them cotton wool spots. Diabetic retinopathy. That's the diagnosis. Nowadays they have a diagnosis for everything. Everything. Soon I won't see the shadows or the light.' We walk arm in arm toward Mrs B.'s room. 'How's your sister?'

'She's pretty upset about Pop.'

'I imagine she would be. He was her favorite.'

'She was his favorite.'

'Not true.'

'It seemed that way.'

'He's a good man, your father. God knows it hasn't been an easy life for him.'

'I'm so sorry about Burt.'

'Poor Burt never had a chance. When Sid and I divorced, I thought Burt was going to commit suicide.' Mrs B. opens the door. We enter her shrinking world. There is a bed, a night table, and a small porcelain lamp on the table. 'I love the light in this room.'

'It's lovely.' The room is dark. The air is heavy. Not to Mrs B. She finds beauty in the ordinary. I have always loved that about her.

'Would you mind opening the curtains?' I open the curtains. 'Open the doors too. Let some air in the room.' I open a set of French doors that lead onto a patio where Mrs B. has planted the most beautiful garden: daisies, daffodils, pansies, parsley, Johnny Jump-Ups, and violets.

'Your garden is beautiful,' I tell her.

'I love to garden. It's my meditation.'

'You always had a green thumb. I remember how envious my mother was when your flowers bloomed in late spring.'

'Your mother never had a shred of envy in her body.'

I think about my mother … 'You're right.'

'She was too kind, sensitive to ever be jealous of what someone else had.' She stares into space. 'Like Burt. Poor thing. Where was I before we started talking about your mother?'

'Burt.'

'Oh yes. So after Sid and I got divorced, Burt was never the same. We sent him to a psychiatrist. It didn't do him a bit of good. Instead, he buried himself in those books of his. He did well in school. Went to M.I.T. The pressure nearly killed him, barely got through, such a sad man. When he met Lorraine, his ex-wife, he was so happy, if you could call it that. I never understood what he saw in her. Then one day, I realized she was just as unhappy as he was. They fed off each other's misery. When he took a position at the University of Iowa, she didn't want to go. She hated Iowa. Made him pay for it, told him he'd ruined her life. Honest to God, what people do to each other.

Burt wanted kids. Lorraine didn't. The more he tried to make her happy, the less she cared. She drove him crazy.

'One day he had had it with her. He hauled off, hit her; out of frustration. Nowadays you don't hit a woman, especially a woman with a good lawyer. That was it. She took him to the cleaners. He got thrown out of the university because of the scandal ... spousal abuse. He had to sell the house. She got the bulk of the money.

'Then he came home. All he did was sulk. Of course when I started going blind, he didn't know how to deal with it. Good grief, if you can't deal with life, you might as well lay down and die. That is exactly what he did. Found a gun at some second-hand store, shot himself ... in our backyard.

'There was no point in me staying after ... I couldn't take care of myself, and being near your father for all those years, all the memories, your mother's death, finally it was time to move on. So here I am. It's not so bad. It really isn't; just another chapter in my life.' She closes the French doors, draws the curtains. 'I'm so glad you came to visit.'

'I'd like to come again, if that's all right with you?'

'That would be lovely. It's about time both Greene girls were back in my life.'

'Better late than never.'

'So true. Please give your father my love.'

'I will. After I leave you, I'm going to the house ... surprise him.'

'He was never big on surprises, your father. He must have changed.'

'I would hope so.' I say my goodbyes.

'Don't take twenty years. I can't wait that long. I probably won't be around.'

'Maybe next time, Dina and I will visit you together. The Greene girls together again for a return engagement at Mrs B.'s world of botanical enchantment.' I close the door behind me, walk down the corridor, out into the late-spring daylight. It is a gorgeous day in Beechwood.

I walk down Worth Avenue, stroll by Beechwood elementary school. I kissed Ron Johnson in the corner of the playground. Maggie is no longer in my hair, on my fingers. She is still with me, but I'm afraid to keep her too close. Simone is with me too. I can't stop swinging in the playground called mind.

The Good Humor man pulls up in his ice-cream truck right in front of school. I want to ask him if my mother told him she was going to kill herself. But it's twenty years later. For sure he's not the same Good Humor man. The kids run for the truck, much like I did when I was their age.

For some strange reason I feel hopeful about the future. My visit with Mrs B. has been an inspiration. Even though she is blind, I felt as if she saw all of me. How healing it is to be seen.

I continue my walk through town, pass the candy store, the drug store, down Post Avenue, turn right onto Bridge Court. I walk up the steps in front of the shrinking house. I have my key poised, ready for the hole. Open the door, enter the world of sick and dying.

Patty is sound asleep on the living-room sofa. I tiptoe into the television room. Pop is also fast asleep, talking his dream talk.

'Hurry up, I wanna go up. I'm here. Come on now. Hurry up. Take me up.' She is in his every sleep, every wake. She is in the bedroom. She is in whatever room he has left for her in his heart. I kiss him on his forehead. I listen for her. She has nothing to say. Where is that missing monkey? It'll turn up sooner or later.

I let myself out of the house, walk to the Beechwood train station. It is three p.m. I have had a full day.

The train arrives; the train that my father took to work every day of his life. I am on his train, going to his city, looking out his window, rediscovering the tall trees, the endless train tracks, the two-story brick buildings, the almost perfect world I took for granted as a child.

Picking Up Speed

I was relieved not to be going to Montana. Stuart Manly understood my decision to remain in close proximity to my dying father. What was not clear to Stuart was my complete and utter lack of interest in teaching altogether.

By sending my replacement to Montana, The Company was caught short. It had promised a three-day residency to Harriet Tubman High School in Harlem.

Stuart Manly assumed that I was just hanging around New York City having a la di da time. As far as he was concerned, I owed The Company a week. Three days was a deal. In theory he was right. In fact he was wrong. It requires an all-consuming focus to make peace with a dying parent, especially when you have blamed that parent for almost everything that has ever been wrong with your life.

Dina thought it a good idea for me to keep busy; best not to think … about anything. Keeping busy is another example of the older child syndrome. The oldest child chooses responsibility. The youngest child chooses to be carefree for an indiscriminate, undetermined length of time; as long as possible.

The tenth graders at Harriet Tubman High were street smart, uncontrollable, wickedly funny and enormously perceptive; white woman has arrived. What can we get away with?

The boys are slumped so low in their desk chairs that all I can see are their eyes. The black girls look bored. They gaze at themselves in tiny mirrors hidden inside their purses. The

Muslim girls wear burkhas. Can barely see their faces. Wonder how they survive during these maniacal anti-Muslim times.

Begin. 'I'm going to get right to the point here.' Three boys yawn and drop down below eye level. I had better keep it moving or else it will be a forehead-only class. 'Look, we all define ourselves by who we think we are, right?' One or two nods. Infinitely better than switchblades. 'Where we come from, who our family is, what our friends think of us … right?' Not one word.

Ms Withers, the teacher, screams. 'Come on class! Say something! … Anything!'

Screams from the teens: 'Sure. Right. What? Oh yeah, Ms Withers.'

'Thank you, Ms Withers … What if you are not who you think you are? What happens if how you define yourself is no longer your story? Your parents aren't your parents? Your sister isn't your …' Uh oh … What have I done? A young boy raises his hand. He is no longer a forehead. He is an entire face with neck attached. Things are looking up. 'Yes. What's your name?'

'Clarence Darnell The Third.'

'Clarence.'

'If you don't mind me sayin' so, miss, I don't need to do the exercise.'

'Why is that Clarence?'

'Well you see, miss, my mother lives upstairs from my father and me. She lives with my uncle, who is now married to my mother, so he's my father too. My sister lives with my uncle's son. They're living in my apartment. My sister is fourteen. She just had a baby girl. So, now I'm an uncle. My father's married my mother's sister … so I think my mother's sister is now my mother. My father and his new wife, my mother's sister, and her two kids live in our apartment. So, now my cousins are my brother and sister. You see, miss, I can't de-fine myself by who my mother, father, sister or anyone is. It's too confusin'.'

Good God! Families are so damn confusing; an organism we call home ... What do we do when parents who hold certain positions switch roles? Who do we mimic, until we are confident enough to be original without fear. Who!? It is so fucked up.

Forced to be spontaneous, I change the exercise to fit the moment. 'Let me put it another way?' They're waiting for you ... 'How well do you know yourself? What turns you on?' Music, Sunday *New York Times* Business section, sex ... 'Who turns you on?' Maggie ... Simone. The class roars. 'Seriously.' Seriously. 'How did you become who you are? ... Pick a time, a time from your past that changed your life.' I remember my mother's funeral like it was yesterday. 'Have a dialogue with the you you were then. See what your present self has to say to your past self.' Change her legacy. 'Who are you now?' Who was I then? 'How has your past influenced your present?' She never said goodbye. I never, never say ... goodbye.

After class, I hail a cab, head downtown via the parking lot doubling as the West Side Highway. On Wednesdays the traffic in New York City is nightmarish. It is matinee day; two shows instead of one. Twice as many Jersey drivers clog the city's arteries. It is an eighteen-dollar cab ride. That's no joke.

Mary is happy to see me. No, I am happy to see her. She *seems* happy to see me; projecting again.

'You wouldn't believe the class I just came from in Harlem. I feel like an absolute idiot. Stupid. I was ... I ... was ... so insensitive. I don't want to talk about it.'

'Why not?'

'I was trying to make a point about how we define ourselves. What if you weren't who you thought you were? What if your father wasn't your father or your mother wasn't … Oh fuck it's too complicated to explain!'

'Try.'

'It's not important. This one kid lives with his father who's married or living with … his mother's sister … The mother's sister has two kids … They all live together. You get it? His cousins have become his brother and sister, his mother is living with his uncle, his fourteen-year-old sister has already had her first child. For fuck's sake! Fourteen. Do you believe this story? It's not a story. It's real life. A fifteen or sixteen-year-old kid … is now an uncle with two, count them, two sets of parents. He was right. He didn't need to do the exercise. Why do people have children? Why? What about commitment? What about responsibility? Who gives a shit.'

'Do you have to have children to be committed? Aren't you committed to, excuse me, what is your partner's name?'

'Simone.'

'Are you committed to Simone? Do you feel a sense of responsibility toward her?'

'I was. I do. But, now there's Maggie … I'm not so sure.'

'How long have you known Simone?'

'Twenty years. That's not the point. If Simone weren't fucking around, I wouldn't have fucked around. I did and something happened. Shit happens in an open relationship, in any relationship. Simone made the rules a long time ago. I think she made them.'

'You went along with them.' She leans forward. 'Why? Why did you go along with those rules?'

'I don't know.'

'Off the top of your head what do you think?'

'I said, I don't know!' Mary stares right through me. 'What do you want me to say? … I don't want to lose, I don't … want to be … I'd rather be with her the way we are, than not be with her at all.'

'Her or anyone?'

'Her! Maggie just happened. Whatever we're talking about doesn't have anything to do with Maggie!'

'It probably goes back much farther than Maggie or Simone.'

'It *all* has to do with my mother, doesn't it? Is that what you're trying to say?'

'You brought up your mother.'

'I certainly did … What, if anything, does this conversation have to do with people and their lack of commitment to one another?'

'You tell me.'

'I liked it better with Dr Guttman.'

'I'm sure you did.'

My father was fading away. By Thursday, the changes in his physical appearance were staggering. He had turned a bright canary yellow. His eyes were glazed, milky, lifeless. His skin pulling away from his body. His bones piercing through his skin. There is an expression. 'The only thing that you can be sure of in life is death.' Very well put that expression is. Life, in other words, is full of surprises. Death, on the other hand, is a clear voyage.

'We all fall down.'

'Thank you for that uplifting comment.'

Dina and I suffered less than most children during my

father's final days. Saul had FedExed a two-pound care package of hallucinogenic Mexican marijuana.

During one of Pop's delirious moments, 'Hurry up I want to go up … aah … please get me out of here!' We gave him a hit of the stuff. It calmed him right down.

It was a three-ring circus. Dina and I took turns with the diapers. Some days we had the pleasure of each other's company. Patty kept herself busy stealing whatever sheets and silverware was left in the house. She made numerous trips to her car, always wearing her winter coat. It was late May.

During the death watch, I had my daily appointments with Mary. They were work. She led me so far down into my unconscious, sometimes I had no idea where I was, or if I was. She was up on all sorts of techniques: breath work, Kabbalistic symbols, dream therapy, role playing (my favorite: reminded me of my early days as an actress), chakra clearing, hypnosis. Some days we would just sit and talk.

My mother showed up every now and again. I assumed she was working overtime, trying to pry my father out of his hospital bed, out of the television room, back into the bedroom, and finally over into her world.

On Sunday night, while I am trying to call Maggie on the phone, Simone shows up at the apartment. As the lock turns, I quickly hang up the phone. Her homecoming is auspicious indeed. We do not have much to say to one another. But, Lord, do we give the word 'hot' a new meaning. We make anal love on the couch, nearly drown making love in the tub. I make love to her on top of the kitchen table. She makes love to me on top of the window bench … By late May, the radiators are turned off; we don't have to worry about burns.

Though, I did have rug burns on every inch of my exposed body parts. During our sex scenarios, I am grieving inside. I feel a revulsion for myself like I have never felt before. I can't look Simone in the eye; can have sex in any configuration imaginable, but can not, will not make eye contact. Until finally we talk.

'Do you want another joint?' She kisses my forehead.

'No.'

'I missed you.' I don't respond. 'What is wrong?'

'I'm tired.'

'It must be so difficult. Your father.'

'At least I know the outcome.'

'What?'

'I'm tired, that's all.'

'I do love you.' She pulls me into her beautiful breasts. I can't resist. 'You will adore Zurich.' She spreads her legs, grabs my hand, slides it down to her pussy. 'Here darlin'. Feel how wet I am.'

'Not now. Later maybe.' Habits, like ghosts, have a way of holding you so close that you don't dare give them up, because you don't know what your life will be like without them. How could I say goodbye to the shadow that kept me incomplete?

The day before Memorial Day weekend, Dina and I receive early-morning wake-up calls from Patty. Her rosary beads are working overtime. Pop has lapsed into a coma.

I cancel Mary Michelin, say goodbye to Simone, run down the stairs. The elevator is still out of order.

Dina picks me up. We drive in silence until I speak. 'Would you mind opening a window?'

'I have the air on.'

'Just a crack.'

'That is such a weird habit.' She opens the window.

By ten a.m. we arrive in Beechwood. We hold hands as we walk up those familiar front steps. I begin to hyperventilate.

Dina panics. 'You can't do that now!'

'I'm not doing it on purpose,' I wheeze.

'Before we walk into the house, you have to breathe normally or else I will fall apart. I will. Take some deep breaths … Now!'

'Alright.' Gasp …gasp … 'How's that?' I pray to God to make me breathe better than I breathe.

We open the front door only to hear the sound of Patty's Christ this, mercy that, Mary and Joseph, holy spirit, holy ghost, and other holy biblical phrases I am not familiar with. We walk into the TV room. My hyperventilation has now vented itself into a quiet wheeze.

My father looks exquisite; yellow like the sun, small and sweet like a newborn, and calm like he has never been in all the years since I have known him.

Patty prays. 'Oh heavenly Father! Will ya look at him, will ya.' Dina cries.

I give him a good looking over. 'Patty, are you sure he's in a coma?'

'Of course I am. I remember my dear departed uncle's coma. May he rest in peace.' Dina and I almost laugh out loud. But, this is a time for piety. I try prying open my father's closed eyes. As if a bolt of lightning has struck him in the ass, he sits upright in his hospital bed.

With eyes wide open, he speaks. 'Hurry up. I want to go up. Hurry up. Take me up.' He lies back down like a ton of skinny bricks.

'Oh Lord. She's calling his name. He can hear her. I have

been around death, I have. But never a death like his. Mary, Jesus and …'

'Patty. Would you mind leaving Dina and me alone with our father?'

'Of course not. I have so much ironing to do in the basement. I've been ironing his underwear for days.' What ironing? He's been in diapers for over a week now … Patty leaves the room. Dina and I sit, transfixed, staring at my father.

Suddenly Pop sits up again. 'Hurry up. I want to get up. Take me up.' And he's down again. And so it goes up and down, up and down, life and death, up and down. She is not only near him. She is with him, in him, all around him.

I smell her perfume. 'Do you smell that?'

'What?'

'Nothing.' I listen for her; not a word. The afternoon creeps into early evening, the spectacle continues; an outstanding final performance.

From outside, we hear the Good Humor truck pass by. Dina and I decide to have one last Good Humor. I yell down to the basement. Of course Patty is not there. She is on another silverware run to her car. I open the hall closet. Her coat is missing. I would be such a good detective.

Dina orders an orange popsicle. Boring. I have a chocolate chocolate-chip Good Humor bar. Only seconds away from asking the ageing Good Humor man if he knew my mother, a blood-curdling scream resounds throughout the neighborhood. Dina and I drop our sweets in the street. We beeline it back to our father's house.

I open the front door, race into the television room. He is nowhere to be found. From upstairs Patty screams. 'HELP! HELP! OH MY GOD! GLORY BE …'

Dina and I run upstairs. The door to the parents' room is shut. Patty stands outside the door. She is white as a sheet.

'She's in there with him. God help us all. She has come for him at last.'

I try opening the door. It's locked. Impossible! I bang, push, scream, kick, and ... mysteriously, the door opens ...

There he lies ... on the bed; dead as a dead man, with a winter-white smile, with lipstick kisses all over his face. Hail Mary is in order.

'I heard footsteps, ran into the study. The hospital bed was empty. The control box ripped out, thrown on the floor ... in the corner by his slippers. I heard a door slam upstairs.' Patty falls to her knees ... 'Oh Lord in heaven I thought ... praise Jesus ...'

I preempt her hallelujahs. 'Patty, please go downstairs. Call Ralph and the kids. Tell them it's over.'

'But.'

'Please, leave us alone. And Patty, close the door behind you.' Patty exits muttering the Lord's Prayer. Dina bursts out crying. I hold her close. After all, we are sisters and orphans. 'They're together now.'

She cries and cries. I cry only a little in comparison. But it isn't a contest.

I look down at his glorious corpse. His left hand is closed tight. I open it. There rests the missing monkey; his favorite picture jasper monkey. Before Dina notices, I slip the monkey into my pocket. I look at the pillowcase next to my father's head. I swear to whomever there is left, since Patty has used up the quota. There on my mother's old pillowcase are tears. My mother's tears no doubt. I turn the pillow over.

'What are you doing?'

'Straightening up.'

'How can you be so anal? He just died.'

I touch his forehead. 'Goodbye Pop.'

'Look at his face. That's her lipstick.' Dina can't catch her breath.

'It is.' I breathe a sigh of relief. We sit on the bed, staring at our father's corpse. I listen and listen. She is gone. He is with her. Finally. She is out of this world.

Dina whimpers. 'You know what?'

'What?'

'I won't mind being an orphan as long as I have you,' she says between hiccups.

'I love you, Dina.'

'We'd better start making phone calls,' she says anxiously.

'There's hardly anybody left to call,' I say reassuringly, as I close my father's eyes.

Dina takes a closer look at our recently deceased father. 'Where do you think we go?'

'I don't know … But neither does anyone else.'

Road Signs You Must Know

Jews bury their dead before the body is cold. Before the corpse realizes what the hell has happened, it is whisked away from its familiar surroundings. Next thing the corpse knows, it is dropped inside an extremely well-dug hole in the ground. Pop died early Thursday evening. By sundown on Friday he would have to be buried; before Sabbath.

Most of the people from Pop's past were either dead or living in Florida. Mrs B. couldn't make it to the funeral, but she did promise to pay her respects during the first evening of mourning. We of the Jewish faith call this mourning period 'sitting Shivah'.

Funerals are a black affair; everyone wears black. I wore white. Pop would have wanted me to be different, so I was; white jacket, blue silk pants, white shoes, multicolored socks, to top off the outfit, my favorite aqua scarf.

Some of my father's old cronies from Wall Street showed up in wheelchairs pushed either by nursemaids or young wives, who might as well have been nursemaids. Maggie and Molly sent flowers. Saul flew in with his new lover. Simone showed up in a black silk Yves Saint Laurent dress looking drop-dead gorgeous. And Patty was decked out in a floral dress, dabbing her eyes with one of Pop's favorite silk handkerchiefs. Ralph and Dina's kids had the best seats at the grave ... head. Dina and I stood stage left. The Rabbi stood stage right. He was world-renowned; famous for blessing ordinary ketchup, thus turning it into kosher ketchup for Passover. I was delighted to have such a prominent figure in charge of Pop's service.

We each one of us threw our handful of dirt into the grave. It was then that Dina and I lost our composure. When it was time for Dina's kids to throw their handfuls, they too cried their eyes out. They adored Pop, knew how much he loved them. He was the only grandpa they had ever known. Ralph's father had died long before they were even an idea.

Our mother's grave was right next to Pop's grave. It was the family plot on my mother's side, of course. My father's side could not have afforded such a luxury. But all sides of the family were welcome. There were plenty of plots to go around for many generations to come.

At the end of the ceremony, people complimented Dina and me on what a beautiful burial it was. They especially liked the Rabbi.

After everyone had gone, Dina and I stood side by side next to our mother's and father's graves. It was the first time I had been back to the cemetery since my mother's burial nearly twenty years ago.

Dina was hopeful. 'Maybe now that they're both here, you'll come with me on my annual outing.'

'They're not here, Dina. Their bodies are here. His body is anyway. Her body is … who knows where.'

'I feel like she lives on in you. And he'll live on in me. They won't ever die. That's why we have to visit them. So they'll live on forever. And when we're gone, people will visit us so we'll live on forever.' I did not agree with Dina.

I had not heard my mother's voice for almost a week now. It made me sad, like when you're very young, and your best friend moves away. I took one final look at Pop's freshly dug grave, one more look at my mother's old broken-in resting place. I muttered to myself. 'When it's my turn, don't pack me under ground. I want to be burned, like in India, ashes strewn wherever the bird fishes rest, wherever that place is ... maybe it isn't a place at all.'

Dina says, 'Thanksgiving.'

'What about Thanksgiving?'

'That was Pop's favorite holiday.'

'I never understood why. He wasn't a Pilgrim.'

'Cutting the turkey gave him a sense that he was part of the American Dream.' She gloats. 'Thanksgiving!'

'Yes?'

'We'll set the headstone,' she counts on her fingers: 'June, July, August, September, October, November – six months from now. That's kosher.'

'Who knows where we'll be in six months?'

'We'll be right here. It's perfect. And it's his favorite holiday.'

'We'll talk about it later.'

'I feel so much better now that we've decided on a date.'

'You decided. I haven't committed yet.'

'You will. I know you well enough and long enough.' We walk arm in arm toward the black limo. Dina stops. 'Did I ever tell you about the night you were ...'

'Please. The car is waiting.'

Dina stops. 'I'm going to cry. We're orphans.'

'Not true. According to your theory, if they live on in us forever, we're not orphans. We're possessed.'

'That's not funny.'

'I've been trying to tell you that for years.'

Back at the house, there were serious problems. Patty could

not find any tablecloths for the dining-room table. How could she? She had stolen them. The cold cuts had to be placed on top of paper doilies. Dina was furious with Patty. She endured a stress-related hot flash that lasted the entire evening.

During the evening, Saul and his new lover eyeballed and groped each other; not good grieving etiquette. Because of her dislike for Saul, based on Saul's dislike for her, Simone snubbed Saul; more bad etiquette.

The older folks talked about the good ol' days on Wall Street. They surrounded the dining-room table like vultures, ate enough cold cuts to clog their arteries for months to come, ate like there might be no tomorrow; quite possible with this crowd.

Dina and I made the rounds. Patty regaled the crowd with the story of Pop's dramatic death. I stick close to Simone. Try to keep her away from Saul. Simone insults Saul; accuses him of being a Republican. More bad grieving etiquette.

Saul storms away. 'I don't need to listen to this French crap.' He heads for the cold cuts, devours half a pound of corned beef in less than forty-five seconds.

During the climax of the Simone/Saul drama, the front door opens. The nurse's aide from Beechwood Manor leads Mrs B. into the living room. Mrs B. looks radiant. She is wearing a stunning black silk designer jacket with satin lapels, a silver silk shell, a sexy short black skirt. Wrapped around her neck is a beautiful a-q-u-a scarf; my favorite scarf around her neck! Like a child, I run for the front door, nearly knocking over Mrs B. on the way. Mrs B. asks, 'Loli, is that you?' She grabs my arm, turns to her nurse's aid. 'Theresa, I know my way around here. Why don't you sit on the couch? First get yourself something to eat. I'm sure there are plenty of cold cuts on the table over there.'

Mrs B. escorts me outside. She closes the front door behind us. We sit on the front stoop. 'I'm so sorry about your father.' I do not respond. 'How are you, Loli?' I mope. 'What is it, Loli?'

'The scarf?'

Mrs B. touches the scarf. She strokes it like you stroke your favorite stuffed animal. 'Theresa got it from my drawer.'

'Who gave it to you?' Mrs B. realizes she has walked over an irreversible line of propriety. She reaches out, touches the identical scarf wrapped around my neck. She wraps it around her fingers. She places it on her lap.

'Nassau 1967. Your father and mother … Sid and I. We took a vacation together. It was a lovely holiday. Your mother.' Mrs B. fidgets with my scarf. 'She bought two of them; one for you, one for me. There were two left in the store. She knew you'd love it, because of the color, like your eyes … and … she wanted to give me something for being such a good friend.'

'You never wore it before. In all the years I've known you. Never.'

'No, I haven't.'

'Why did you wear it tonight?'

'I forgot my promise.'

'What promise?'

'I promised your mother I wouldn't wear it in front of you … Children need to feel special.'

'It's my favorite thing.'

Mrs B. starts to talk but can't get the words out, until: 'Mine too. My good luck charm.' She cries on the front stoop of the house she lived in, lived across from, left behind, the house of secrets and promises long ago broken, but never forgotten. 'Loli.'

'Yes.'

'Please go inside, tell Theresa I want to go home.' I get up from the stoop. Mrs B. grabs my arm. 'Tell her you're going to drive me back to Beechwood Manor.'

'I don't know if it's right to leave Dina.'

'Dina will be fine. Her family's with her. Tell her I've asked you to take me home. She'll understand. You'll be back soon enough.'

I wipe off my pants. As I stand up, Mrs B. grabs hold of my pant leg.

'Bend down.' I bend. She wraps the scarf around my neck the same way I have worn it for years. 'That's how you like to wear it, isn't it?'

'Be right back. I'll bring Dina's car around. Wait here.'

'Don't worry. I'm not going anywhere.'

Dina is too busy with cold cuts and the elderly to give a hoot about my leaving. But, she makes me swear to show up for the unveiling. Damn it!

'Please keep an eye on Simone.' I kiss Simone goodbye, beg her to behave herself. She still hasn't a clue about my affair with Maggie; more secrets, more lies.

Simone informs me, 'Mauli Malone called. She has entered a contest, I forgot to tell you. Who is she?'

'Beatrice. The girl I ... not important. I wish you would have told me earlier. I'll call her tomorrow. Be nice to Saul. I'll see you later. I'm taking Mrs B. home.'

'How lovely that you have had a rapprochement with your ex-stepmother.'

On that note I leave. Glad that Molly called. What contest? Why hasn't Maggie phoned? I look at Simone. She is breath-taking. I close my eyes. Maggie appears. She whispers in my ear. I can hear her. I can smell her. Again. I taste her, feel her skin against my body. Open my eyes, wave at Theresa, tell her I'm driving Mrs B. back to Beechwood Manor. Theresa seems quite happy, at home with the elderly; sounds like a reality show. Must remember the idea.

I drive around front. Walk up the steps, escort Mrs B. down the steps. Mrs B. gets into the Mercedes. We speed down the road, turn right onto Park Road, left onto Forest Avenue, right again onto Palmer, cut through Beechwood, through the railroad station's parking lot. The 9:01 is pulling in right on time. I open my window. 'Don't you love that sound?'

'Always have.'

'Can you hear the trains from your room?'

'If I listen hard enough. Burt loved trains. Loved them. He adored looking out the window, watching the towns go by. I can see him, nose pressed against the glass, fogging up the cold window.'

'Who doesn't love to fog up a cold window? I'm sorry I never knew him.'

'You were never in the same school; like you and your sister. They were in the same class. Five grades ahead or was it six?'

'Six.'

We arrive at the Beechwood Manor. I turn the engine off, open the car door, ready to get out. Mrs B. does not budge. 'There are things I've been wanting to tell you. Why don't you roll down the windows, drive if you like. Anywhere.' I turn on the engine, step on the gas, roll down the windows, and drive through the quiet streets of Beechwood.

Mrs B. waits for some inner signal, then tells me about the once upon a time … the time before, the time of the bird fish. 'Has your sister ever told you about the night you were born?'

'A million times. She describes going into the bedroom, not

finding my mother, going into the living room where Granny was sitting … Grandma says something like "Things won't ever be the same."'

'Loli. Your sister has never told you the whole story. She doesn't know it.'

The Birth of the Bird Fish

1956

Between the time my sister and I were born, my mother had a miscarriage. It was a boy named Daniel. My father was devastated. Dina was too young to understand what had happened. When my mother became pregnant with me, she was scared to death, afraid she might miscarry again. As it turned out, mine was a difficult pregnancy. The placenta was too close to the cervix. There was bleeding. The doctors told my mother, 'Take it easy.' At six months, she was placed on total bed rest. It was hard on my father. But, it was especially hard on my sister. One day she had a normal mother, next day her mother was an invalid; rarely out of bed. Of course, Dina learned to accept the situation. My father hired a devoted housekeeper, who kept the house in order, got my sister off to school, fed her, tended to her like a mother would. Pop took care of all the details of the house. He was an adoring husband.

At seven and a half months, my mother began hemorrhaging. She was rushed to the hospital. That night, the night I was born, my grandmother came to take care of my sister.

I was a premature breech baby. They performed a C-section on my mother. When I arrived in this world, my lungs weren't fully developed; they kept me in an incubator, and I remained in hospital for many weeks.

My mother went into a terrible depression; post partum blues. She became suicidal; tried to kill herself. A nurse saved her life. Nowadays they would know what to do. But back then ... depression was ... It was different then. Most doctors didn't know the first thing about it. They gave her Valium, lithium, who knows what other drugs. The drugs made her more depressed. My father brought in the best doctors, who told him that she needed shock therapy. He didn't want to believe them. Finally, he had no choice. From the night I was born until the day my mother died, she was never the same. Neither was my father.

I stop the car, park in front of an old colonial house adjacent to the Beechwood Country Club. I close my eyes. I am in a dark room without love. I am a bird fish. Breath is external. Breath. No breath. Say hello world.

Mrs B. says, 'You and your mother were separated after a traumatic birth.'

'No wonder my grandmother was there ... that night ... But ... what happened after that?'

'Your mother went home. You stayed in the hospital.'

'I was a bird fish.'

'A what?'

'Bird fish.'

'You were a magical strange little creature. She couldn't bear leaving you at the hospital. But, the doctors felt she had a better chance of climbing out of her depression if she were home. Your father hired round-the-clock nurses. Your sister wasn't allowed to spend much time with your mother. The slightest thing got her upset. Your father didn't know what to do. I was the only one she could talk to. She babbled on and on about being a failure as a wife, a mother. Couldn't find a moment's peace. Broke my heart. Finally, they let you out of the hospital. Because you were a sick little baby, your mother didn't let you out of her sight … not for one moment. She was besotted with you. Whenever you coughed or cried, she lost her mind.' Mrs B. whispers. 'Crazy … Never paid any attention to your sister. Wouldn't let your father touch her. A mess. It was a mess. She was terrified you would die, so she never left your side.'

'It was *my* fault. It was; all those years.'

'No! It wasn't your fault. It was nobody's fault. Life undoes some people. It undid your mother. Couldn't be fixed by anybody: doctors, friends, family, we all tried. But, for some reason, your mother's spirit … broke. It just happened. The world was too much … too much for her … too much.'

'Who took care of my mother … the housekeeper?'

'Your father went to work. So, I drove your mother to the doctor's office almost every single day; some specialist for one thing or another. Of course we brought you with us. Wherever she went, you went. Your sister was in school then. As soon as Dina left the house, off we'd go, you, your mother and me, driving to famous doctors in Manhattan, New Haven, Philadelphia, wherever. We drove for hours; you crying and crying until we were at our wits' end. My guess is you cried because you couldn't breathe; drove your mother insane. When we weren't going to a doctor for her, we were going to some pediatric specialist for you. It was horrible. One day, during another endless outing, I opened my window a crack. You stopped crying. It was a miracle. You looked up at the crack, listened to the wind, smiled. It was the first smile I had seen on your face since you were born. It was as if the air coming through the window was the breath you couldn't breathe through your lungs. That sound became your sound. Whenever you cried, we opened a window, just a crack. Even your mother and I got into the sound. It soothed her. For a few hours every day, while we were driving, searching for answers, that sound was your breath and our life.'

I mourn for my mother, my father, my sister and me. I mourn for our family. Pieces of the puzzle are still missing. 'Mrs B?'

'Yes, Loli.'

'Did my mother ... when we were in the car ... when I was ... did she recite nursery rhymes?' Mrs B. does not respond. 'You see about a year after she died, right around the time you married Pop, she started reciting *Mother Goose* nursery rhymes. During the last few months, while Pop was dying, she was at it again ... nursery rhymes.'

'She was listening after all.' Mrs B. sighs. 'In the car, when-ever we drove around, I recited *Mother Goose*.'

'You?'

'When Burt was little, he adored *Mother Goose*. I should have known then he would be an odd fellow. Those stories were odd if you ask me. Only thing that made him laugh. I still don't know what was so funny. Never understood why all us mothers were reading them. Guess it was the thing to do. So, when the three of us were driving around, hour after hour, I figured why not recite *Mother Goose*. Open the window a crack, and recite. She refused to learn them, said it was good enough if I knew them. She learned them after all. Rock-a-bye baby or was it Hush-a-bye baby? ... was her favorite.' Awful lot of information on the night of my father's funeral, think I.

'Mrs B? What about my mother and father?'

'What about them?'

'Did they … love each other?'

'Very much. It was a difficult situation. Your mother didn't want to be touched, wasn't interested in sex. The doctors blamed it on hormones or some such thing.'

'Did they ever have sex?'

'Not that I know of.'

'No wonder he was fucking around.' No one speaks for quite some time.

'When your mother was in the hospital, I was having an affair with your father.' She mutters under her breath. 'On and off … we had an affair…' I don't respond. 'Your mother never knew.' Mrs B. starts to say something. 'My …' She stops. Finally, she gets it out. 'My husband suspected. I denied it. He knew.' And they went on vacations together. 'I didn't want to hurt your mother, so I ended it.' What else could she possibly say? 'It wasn't a love affair; it was about sex. I fulfilled a need for him. He fulfilled one for me. We tried to be friends, but he was uncomfortable around me. All those years later, when we got married, we were just friends, companions.'

I can't stop thinking about Pop's life. 'I feel so badly for him.'

'So did your mother. She offered to give him a divorce many times. But he wouldn't leave. He loved her so much, he found ways to live with the rejection.'

'They really loved each other?'

'They did. They broke each other's hearts, but they loved each other to death.'

'She was with him when he died.'

'She was with him every day of his life. Every day.'

I lean back, start the engine, drive. 'I better take you home. Not sure where to put my feelings.'

Mrs B. holds my hand. 'There are times when that happens.'

'I can't even find my tears tonight. They must be hiding in my heart.'

'Loli.'

'What Mrs B?'

'Your mother and I had a very special friendship.'

'I know.'

'We were there for each other during difficult times. She helped me through my marital problems, my drinking. No matter how badly she felt, she was there for me. We spent a lot of time together … almost every day. The scarf was a thank you for years of a friendship so unique, so deep, so intertwined. Your father understood.' I want to ask Mrs B. if there was anything else between them. I decide some things are private. Mrs B. reads my mind. 'Your mother didn't love me that way. We talked about it. She loved your father. I was her best friend. But you were her greatest love.'

I can hardly grasp the situation. 'And then you married him … How unbelievable is that.'

'Did she ever tell you her theory about only telling the moon your secrets in order to save the stars?'

'Mrs B., I can't hear one more truth tonight. How am I ever going to pick up all those lost stitches.'

'You will, Loli. You are your mother's daughter. You will figure it out for both of you. That's your … what do you call it … your karma.'

There are times in your life when you must let the dearest parts of yourself slip though your fingers like grains of sand. You have to let them go, or else you will turn into clay. I had been given the keys to my freedom. I felt a grief as deep as the infinite ocean called life. On the night of my father's funeral, my mother's hold on me would be lifted.

Since before the bird fish could swim or fly, since before the world was called 'world', there was a place called 'safe haven'. Now I too could live in this safe place. By understanding the elements put into play before I was born, the elements leading up to this evening's revelations, and all the elements yet to reveal themselves, I could change my life.

Sometimes it is safe in a wet womb. Sometimes it is not safe. When the womb is too close to that which separates it from being human too soon, there is no telling which way a life will or won't go.

Changing Lanes With Mary Michelin

'03

Fuck June. Every morning get up, walk to the 96th Street subway, descend into the bowels of the terra firma, hang from a subway strap, ascend from the bowels, walk the Village streets, ring the buzzer, enter Mary's office, descend into the unconscious; rearrange the past. Every single morning at nine a.m., when my guard is down below my knees, I work and work to free myself from the shackles that tie me to a life of familiar damnations …

'How do you feel?'

'Wet.'

'Good. What do you see?'

'Shadows.'

'What else?'

'Feel pressure in soft place, round like egg … many openings. Feel pressure inside a no-named place where … pain.'

'What hurts?'

'Heart space … tight. Reach toward unknown. Fluid washes over … Fly in fluid. Shh … Listen … shh.'

'What do you hear?'

'Heartbeat?'

'Whose heartbeat?'

'Mine. Hers … Our heartbeat … World beating outside of time.'

'Go inside the heartbeat.'

TIME PASSES

'Inside. Wrrrmclsh-wrrmshh-tch-tch-ka-mrrsh'

'Are you …'

'Uh huh-lllllrrrrrr mm-tch-zzz'

'Listen to me, bird fish. Listen closely; in this place where you begin and never end, skies within skies merge as you emerge into the world. Find your breath … Find your beating heart, your unique rhythm and sound. Yes. The fluid that swims within you, the fluid that surrounds you, this is your protection. Hold on to nothing. Let go of everything. Feel, know, sense the world as it awaits your transformation into life. The cycle of life outside the womb is waiting.

'Reach, stretch, glide through a waterway. The waterway opens wider and wider. The shoreline rearranges itself. You sail down the great river; the river where tides began; the river of moon and stars. You rest, for a moment, in a diamond-shaped grotto, until a mythic-sized wave carries you through the grotto's mouth into a continuation of the living sea. Good. Breathe with your gills. That's right. Now rise up to the surface. Your gills and wings in perfect working order, you breathe the salt air. Merge your fish body into your bird body. Emerge into life. Say hello to spirit. Spirit swallow human form. Human form swallow spirit and around and around it goes. Oceans upon oceans, skies into skies. Imagine you, the bird fish, are free, without limitation. The totality of that which has called you back into the universal pool of life is inside you. You are born; whole, complete, resplendent wet body.'

I reach up with gills, with wings, with hands that long for

touch, to be touched, not for an instant, but forever. The mother of all tides touches me. The mother of tomorrow, the mother of yesterday, touches me, lifts me into her arms. Lie on her belly. Let my sweet lips rest on her breast. Suck on the mother's nipple. Taste the nectar of her love. Breathe, fondle, suck, swallow and again, breathe, fondle, suck, swallow. Feel the light of the world on my body, a world where there is no separation ... from the other. Here is the holy union; elemental ... ecstatic ... in birth ... the perfect ... life. In being reborn, I am set free. Thank you, Mary Michelin. Because of you I am ...

Alive, alive oh!

The problem with 'Change History Work', as it is called in many a therapeutic circle, is while the work is taking place on the inside, the outside self falls miles and miles behind the inside self. This makes for a schism in the individual's life, causes unexpected disturbances in the status quo, leaves those close to the person going through the changes without a clue as to how to deal with the irrational behavior of the newly undone individual.

Simone and I were fucking our brains out; barely speaking, skin talking without feeling. Except for our over-stimulated erogenous zones, there wasn't much intimacy. I closed my eyes, saw Maggie's face, felt her skin. I was in two places at the same time, obviously a lesson learned from my mother. The more Simone wanted me, the more I wanted to be left alone. It was a stunning reversal of circumstances. Whenever Simone wasn't around, Maggie and I spoke on the phone. Maggie was in therapy with Mike and Molly ... Family was ... a wee bit confused. I too was ... a wee bit confused. I was mourning, at the same time, I was rewriting my past, so I could have a less tormented future. Simone was plotting our future in Zurich. We were on polar-opposite life paths. It was a mongoose/cobra moment. One night, I enter our bedroom, Simone promptly hangs up the phone. We don't talk about either her calls or my calls. To top things off, Dina was in the midst of her personal version of mourning, taking inventory of her life, counting each and every item at the Beechwood house. I'm talking towels, sheets, toilet paper, socks, shoes, canned goods, monkeys and more. Ralph suffered a sudden case of narcolepsy. When he wasn't asleep, he was deep into sleep-related hallucinations of varying peculiarity. And, of course, both kids had fallen in love with unsuitable love interests.

In mourning, Dina was more critical and hyper-vigilant than ever. 'Your nephew, Charlie, has fallen in love with a jazz singer.'

'I was a singer. What's so bad about that?'

'She's black.'

'So what?'

'A black jazz singer?! My son.'

'Is she any good?'

'You're not any help at all.'

'So what if she's black or green or pink? He's in love. What the fuck else matters? Why don't you give your kids a break!? Nothing is ever good enough for you. I'm glad you're not my mother!' Stop. 'I'm sorry I said that.' Dina cries. 'Please don't cry. I hate it when you cry.'

'Ralph thinks it's menopause.'

'Aren't you way past menopause?'

'When he's not sleeping, he watches me cry. Doesn't say a word.'

'Sounds like a marriage to me.'

'And your niece, Sara …'

'Yes?'

'I don't want to talk about it.'

'Yes you do. What about her?'

'She's fallen in love with a Rabbi she met at a Temple Emanuel Shabat service.'

'What's wrong with that?'

'He lives in Israel.'

'Long-distance relationships are great.'

'You ought to know. She wants to move to Israel.'

'It will pass.'

'They're not normal. They're never getting married. I don't understand it. Wasn't I a good mother?'

'Let them live their lives.'

Hot, hard summer. No easy answers. The world is upside down. I'm trying to change my life. Life is trying to change me. Thank the Lord for Mary Michelin, visits to Mrs B., phone calls from Maggie Malone, and Molly checks in once in a while.

Molly wins the contest. I am thrilled for her. I call her on a June morning. She is cool, but polite. 'Willwrite agrees summer school's a good idea. Have to make up for my poor grades or else I won't get into college.'

'Where are you applying?' She sounds so grown up.

'University of Iowa.'

'Great writing school.'

'And University of Nebraska. My parents want me to stay close to home.'

'How's the therapy going?'

'Fine. Mom's having a difficult time.'

'It's going around.' Why did I say that?

'What does that mean?'

'Stupid.'

'I've been to a few therapy sessions myself.'

'Oh …We're all in therapy.'

'You don't like my father, do you?'

'I don't know him.' She is so damned smart.

'He's a great guy.'

'He's your father. You only get one. Wasn't that your line?'

'Guess so. Mom wants to speak to you.'

'Wait a second. Are you angry about something?'

'No. Should I be?' Molly yells for her mother. 'Ma! It's Loli. Pick up! Bye. Speak to you soon.'

'Glad everything is going so well,' I say, as she hangs up the telephone.

Maggie picks up. In a very low voice she whispers, 'She …' yells, 'be right down!'

'I can't hear you. What'd you say?'

'Molly knows about you and me.'

'Great.'

'I talked about us in therapy. I couldn't help it. Mike cried. Molly ran out of the office. It was horrible.'

'Mike knows?'

'He does.'

'Does all of Beatrice know?'

'Of course not. Have you told Simone?'

'No.'

'What are we doing?' Maggie slams the door.

'I didn't want it to get ugly. Why does it always get ugly?' I cry out of frustration. 'I'm sorry. I better hang up.'

'I love you.'

'Love you too.' Can't do this. They're a family. 'I feel so shitty about Molly. What a disappointment I must be for her. A homewrecker.'

'He wants to come back.'

'I'm sure.'

'What should I do?'

How can I make it easier for her? 'I won't call. If you need me, call me.'

'I miss …'

'I know.' … Molly Malone. I never wanted to let you down. Please forgive me.

Re-hashing the meaning of a tawdry life is what comes of taking summers off, breaking up families, being in reconstructive therapy, having too much time on my hands. By the end of July, Simone is hobnobbing in Zurich, readying her fall show.

My moods are swinging like the old rope swing in our Beechwood backyard. Dina is still busy counting hand towels and cloth napkins. To what end, I can hardly imagine. While searching for a missing blue sock, early one morning in late July, the phone rings. I am harried, late for Mary, but some subtle inner voice yells: 'Pick up the phone, bitch!'

'Hello. Bleak House.'

'Pardon me. I must have the wrong number.'

'Maybe not. Who you looking for?'

'Ms Loli Greene, please.'

'This is Ms Greene. What can I do for you? I'm late for an appointment, so if you don't mind …'

'Ms Greene. Do you remember me, Franklin Willwrite from Beatrice High School? English, eleventh grade …'

'Mr Willwrite! Of course, of course.' Damn blue sock! …

'Thank you so much for your condolence note. That was so thoughtful of you.'

'It was the least I could do. You only have one father. I remember how it was when I lost mine.'

'Mr Willwrite I'm …'

'Call me Franklin.'

'I'll call you Franklin, if you call me Loli.'

'Loli, I need your help.'

'What can I do for you Mr … Franklin?'

'Do you know anyone who teaches the way you do?'

'Not really. Why?'

'I need someone to take over my fall classes? English literature, junior and senior years. I have been ill for quite some time now. I believe my wife told you about my recent sojourn at the Mayo Clinic?'

'She did mention it. By the way, your wife is lovely.'

'I think so. Let's not get side-tracked, Ms … Loli. I have a rare degenerative heart disease. My father died when he was forty-eight.'

'So young.'

'When he died, he looked a hundred. It was devastating. I was eighteen when it happened, I'm forty-seven now.'

'You are?'

'You probably thought I was much older?'

'No, no, not at all.' Could have sworn the guy was at least sixty-five. Poor fellow.

'The Mayo Clinic has found the perfect match for me. They want me in hospital immediately. I need time Ms … Loli. I need the fall to recuperate. Hopefully, I will be home … soon. If I follow the doctors orders, if I make it through November, I have a fifty-fifty chance of living a normal life. I could be back teaching by January. Give it some thought. If you have any suggestion, please call me.'

'Mr Willwrite ... would you consider me for the job?'

'Why, Ms Greene. I never thought ...'

'I know. I know. I might not be a teacher ...'

'Let me correct you, Ms Greene. You might not have a certificate, but you are a teacher. Ask Molly Malone.'

'Franklin. I ... I wouldn't know how...'

'Ms Greene.'

'Loli.'

'Loli, if you're serious, and I hope you are.'

'I am, Franklin. Honest.'

'It might take some doing on my part, but maybe I can make arrangements for you to receive emergency certification. What a brilliant idea! Maybe I can do that.'

'But.'

'There are no buts here, Ms Greene, only asses. Please take the job. Now my heart is set on you. Next year's seniors will be studying Mark Twain. Mark Twain ... themes, Ms Greene, fit for your inspired teaching skills; freedom, the white mans' folly called slavery, the enslavement of an entire race of people, treated like animals because of the color of their skin ... Oppression, Ms Greene. You will chew these themes up and change lives.'

'But, how do I prepare? How do I teach every day ... every single day ... day in day out?'

'Details, Ms Greene. Details. I will help you with your lesson plan, which I am sure you will throw out the window after the first day. Then, you will find your own way, I have no doubt, to inspire these young adults as they have never been inspired before. I know what I'm talking about, Ms Greene. I was in the room.'

'But ...'

'Molly Malone will be in your senior English class.'

'Molly?'

'She needs you, Ms Greene. I need you. We all need you. God knows what kind of substitute teachers they will saddle my students with. Hmm, not like me to end a sentence with a preposition.'

'What about Ms Laws?'

'My dear wife will have the difficult task of taking care of her husband; pity the poor girl.'

'Mr Willwrite, I ...'

'Don't say anything, Ms Greene. Do. Do my students and me a great service.'

'Franklin ... I'll do it.'

'Good. I will be sending you papers to peruse at your convenience. You will have to be in Beatrice for orientation by August 28th. I can't promise you a jacuzzi, but I can promise to make your stay here a most pleasant one. Maggie Malone will find you suitable housing.'

'Thank you, Franklin.' Blink ... Blink ... Change history...

When you change your life, some who love you will fall to their knees, begging you to reconsider your plans. Dina was scared I might never return.

'What about the unveiling?'

'I'll be there. I promise.' Dina knew I had to leave for my best and highest good. In spite of her imminent abandonment issues, she wished me well.

Simone was in Zurich brushing up on her philandering. It was seven a.m. Zurich time when I placed the call.

'Hello.'

'Simone?'

'*Oui*, darling. Let me take it in the other room.' Obviously, someboody's in bed with Simone. When she picks up the other phone, someone hangs up the extension.

'Simone, I have to leave New York on August 27th … for Nebraska,' I say with a lump in my throat.

'But darling, I will not be home 'til August 25th.'

'I'm going to teach high school in Beatrice. They want me.'

'Is it Maggie?'

'No. How do you know about Maggie?'

'How long have we known each other? I am not stupid. Please don't go.'

'We don't talk, Simone. We're never in the same city for more than five minutes. I feel like I'm missing something. So are you. We're just habits.'

'Please … don't leave me. Come with me to Zurich. We'll change our lives.'

'We won't change ourselves. It's time. I wish it weren't, but it is.' I begin to cry. 'I will never look at a flower without thinking about how you would look at it.' She begins to cry. 'Don't cry. Please stop crying. Listen to me … We can't do this anymore. It's not good for either one of us … Go back to bed. Whoever is with you, in your bed, enjoy them. You don't have to worry about hurting my feelings ever again. And, maybe I can find someone who won't want to be with anyone else but me.' We cry so hard, the telephone wires crackle.

'My love. I promise I never slept with your …'

I interrupt. 'It doesn't matter, Simone. It just doesn't matter anymore.' It does, but I don't want to know. 'I'll see you on the 25th … We'll always love each other. Always.'

Mrs B. was delighted with my decision to leave New York.

She talked my sister through her separation anxiety, made her understand it was time for me to try on a new life. One night, Mrs B. presents me with a gift, all wrapped and sparkling in silver paper with a blue bow. She knows her colors. Doesn't matter a bit whether she is blind. She loses her patience 'Open it.'

My hands tremble with excitement. I pull the ribbon off, tear the paper, rip the box into a zillion tiny pieces. Mrs B. waits patiently as I get to the present. I look at her, hands resting in lap. She is *the* most beautiful woman in the world. Well, Maggie Malone is the most beautiful. And my mother was more beautiful than anyone. I fold back the tissue. There it is, waiting for me ... Mrs B.'s aqua scarf ... 'I can't take this.'

'Yes you can. Give it to that girl in Beatrice. Give it to Molly Malone. She will love it.'

'She's angry with me.'

'It will pass.'

'My mother gave it to you.'

'Time for it to be passed on to some young person in the next generation. In that scarf is the best of your mother. Give it to Molly. She's your responsibility, whether she knows it or not. When you give it to her, tell her it belonged to your mother. It will mean the world to her.'

Mrs B. and I walk out onto her patio. The 9:01 arrives at the Beechwood station. She is right on time. Wonder why we think of trains as shes? Wonder why? Time to say good night. Take one last look at the house of broken ... no, mending. We're mending it now.

Dina needs me tonight. We are throwing away my mother's dancing clothes ... finally. Patty did not steal my mother's clothes. Those shoes and dresses were sacrosanct, even for Patty.

Maggie meets me at the airport … alone. We embrace. Hearts race. Hard to let go. She holds me, so tight, I can hardly breathe, so tight, I feel lost in our longing. Look into her aching eyes. When she begins to talk, I press my fingers to her mouth. I say, 'Don't talk.' We wait for my bag in silence, drive without saying a word, arrive at the Holiday Inn. She hands me the key to my room. It is my old room. I get my luggage out of the trunk, walk away from the car, wave. I do not turn around for fear of accepting the inevitable. She honks her horn, drives away. I register. Enter room, run a hot bath. Flowers on the dresser. A note. 'Welcome home. Maggie.'

Holy shit! Another sea of vacant stares, yawns, crotch-scratching teenagers. What am I doing here? How am I ever going to last? Every single day … five days a week … Lord God Almighty please give me the strength to survive. Stop fidgeting with the scarf.

What would Mary Michelin say? What would Dina say or Mrs B? Breathe. Breathe. Be present. Make them feel you are engaged with them in a dialogue; a dialogue of ideas. Acknowledge your nerves. Acknowledge the first day of their senior year, the first day of their last year of high school. Make eye contact with Molly. She is your ally, even if she doesn't know it. Do not be afraid of failure. You are here because you have been asked. So?! What are you waiting for? If you don't get to it now, they will be sound asleep in a matter of seconds.

'Welcome to the first day of your senior year, and my first day of your senior year. For those of you who did not work with me last year, my name is Loli Greene. I am delighted to report that Mr Willwrite is recuperating with flying colors. If you would like to send him a get-well card, he is at home.

He would love to hear from you. During the fall semester, I will be referring to his lesson plan.' So what if it's not entirely true. Never hurts to get their trust. 'We will be studying Mark Twain, the major themes and ideas of much of his work. I need you to feel, sense, and understand these themes, as if you were living in Huck Finn's or Pudd'nhead Wilson's time, the time of slavery. Imagine being owned by another man. Imagine you have to ask permission before you take a piss.' Quite a bit of tittering in the room. 'That is in fact what you have to imagine. Imagine your master, a white man, with platefuls of food on his table, while you go hungry. Your wife is sold down the river, your son is sold down the river. What does the river look like? How do you make peace with the loss of your loved ones? How does it feel to be without rights? No rights! None! You are a black man in a white world. You polish the master's shoes, pick cotton, sleep on a pallet, a bed made of straw, live in the barn with the livestock. Why? Why are you with the pigs in the barn? Because you are no better than they are. You are an animal! You are the property of another man! You are black! Have you ever heard of anything more absurd?!' Blank, blank stares. Mouths wide open. I have failed. I mustn't fail. I have to make them understand! 'Can you white folks imagine being black?!' I bang my fist on the desk. 'Put yourself in the black man's shoes; living your life without having the freedom to think freely, live freely, walk freely, in constant fear of losing your loved ones, your family, your self-respect. Imagine that world … Damn it!'

Molly gives me the thumbs-up sign. I am relieved. But, I have to keep it moving.

'First exercise of the day. Write a paragraph about what it feels like to be enslaved. Be specific. Know who you are. How did you get here? Let's say here is somewhere in Mississippi, near a river, in a small town. It is 1862. You have five minutes.' Christ! 'Yes?'

'I don't understand the exercise?'

'What's your name?'

'Burt.'

I should have known. 'Burt, there is nothing to understand. What you have to do is imagine yourself during a time when one man owned another. You are the man who is owned. How does that feel? Who are you? Where are you? That's the exercise. Are you with me?'

'Kind of. But …'

'Burt, there are no buts here only asses.' The class roars. Burt picks up his pencil, begins the process. He will do the exercise. He will try to think it through, but that won't work. In the end, his imagination will take over.

Instead of five minutes, I give them seven. What the hell, give the kids a break. 'Time! Let's hear from someone in the room. How 'bout you, Burt?'

'But I'm not …'

'No buts, Burt. Remember.'

He swallows hard, looks around the room for approval. He ain't getting it from me or his classmates. He has no choice. The poor guy is cornered. He stammers.

'Burt. You can't do anything wrong. I promise. Someone has to get the class going.'

He reads. 'My name is Daniel. I once was a free man. When I was free, I took my freedom for granted. I believed no one, nothing would ever own me. One day, while I was walking in the Mississippi woods, a white man captured me, tied me to his horse, dragged me away from my family, locked me up in his world of hate. He *tried* to kill my spirit, my faith. God knows, being a slave can kill the spirit of any human being. But, I will have my freedom! And when I have it, I will never take that freedom for granted … Never! I will fight until I am free. I will not be a slave forever; no matter what I am told. I will not be held down by any man who calls me nigger. In God's eyes no man can own another. Therefore, I am free. No one owns me but God. And God don't need to own me, because he knows I am his servant of my own free will.' Burt *is* a free man.

And so begins the first day of school in Beatrice, Nebraska.

Molly waits for me after class. We don't say much. As Molly and I stroll down the halls of Beatrice High, the vice principal walks out of his office. 'I had a feeling I'd be seeing you again. Welcome back, Ms Greene. Beatrice High is delighted to have you with us.'

'I'm delighted to be here.' Molly and I walk outside, into the parking lot. 'What the hell is his name?'

'William Brody. He's so cute.'

'You're a senior in high school. Anything that wears pants is cute.'

'That's not true.'

'Right.'

'I believe this is yours.' She pulls out a blue sock from her knapsack. 'My mother put it in my drawer … after you left town. I don't know why I kept it.'

'Must have missed … Look … I'm sorry.'

'Let's not talk about it, please.'

'Thank you for being so supportive in class. I was scared.'

'You seemed a little nervous, but you got over it. Why be scared? It's only high school.' We walk and talk, like people do when they're finding their way back to familiar territory. At a certain point, we laugh at ourselves, at the world at large. Molly has come to the astonishing realization that she is a Democrat. I inform her she is in the minority. I congratulate her on her choice of party.

We saunter over to her car. She beeps open her mother's Jeep Cherokee. I remember a night, late last spring, in the car with Maggie Malone. Molly gets into the car, rolls down the window.

'I've got a therapy session with my parents today.'

'How's it going?'

'Hard.'

'Therapy is an unforgiving process.'

'Even though I'm still angry at you, if I tell you something, will you promise not to tell anybody?'

'Who am I going to tell? The vice principal?'

'Remember the exercise I did last school year; the one about my grandfather? … In the bedroom?'

'I certainly do.' Do I ever.

'Remember I told you … he touched me?'

'I do. You caught me off guard … To say the least.'

'My grandfather. In the exercise, he touched my breasts.'

'So you said.'

'In real life that's not what happened.'

'What are you trying to say, Molly Malone?'

'My father was abused by his father … When he was a little boy.'

'Oh no.'

'He's so ashamed.' She cries.

'Your poor father. To live with a secret like that all these years.'

'I had to tell you.'

'I'm glad you did. I won't say a word. I promise.'

'Thanks.'

'You better get going now. Always best to be on time for a therapy session. Say hello to your parents.' She turns on the ignition, and waves.

'I love you, Molly Malone.'

'I love you too. You've changed my life.'

'And you, my dear, have certainly changed mine. Go on now! Don't be late.' Molly guns the engine. She leaves me in the dust. I scream. 'Wait! Come back!' Molly slams on the breaks, shifts, drives fifty miles an hour in reverse. 'Jesus! You could kill somebody driving like that.'

'I didn't want you running after me … at your age.'

'Very nice. I have a present for you.' I unzip my backpack, pull out an imperfectly wrapped box, hand it over to Molly. Molly rips it open just like I would. She yanks the scarf out of the box. Her mouth drops open. Her eyes fill with tears. 'You'll catch flies like that … One of my father's favorite lines.'

'It's your lucky scarf.'

'No … *I'm* wearing *my* lucky scarf. That is *your* lucky scarf. It belonged to my mother. She would have wanted you to have it.'

'It's so beautiful.'

'From one generation to another generation to another generation. It will bring you luck. It will bring us all luck.'

'Thank you! Thank you so much!' Molly wraps the scarf around her neck, much the same as I have wrapped it around mine. She opens the door, jumps out of the car, squeezes me within an inch of my middle life.

'You better be careful. People might talk.'

'They already are.' She winks. 'I'm the luckiest girl in the world.' Molly kisses me on the mouth. Then, off she goes to uncover the many hidden secrets in the attic of her family tree … Better her than I. I need a break. Oh no, I have another class to teach today … and tomorrow … and the day after … and … Dear me … a full time job. How did that happen? Look, Ma. We're free. No more secrets. No more lies. Just a life.

Alive, alive oh!

Alive, alive oh!

The bird fish is out of the bag …

Epilogue

One More Stop

Beechwood, Friday, November 28, 2003. Early morning dream.

Franklin Willwrite appears at the foot of the bed. He is naked. He holds a red object in his hand.

'Hey, Franklin! Never thought I'd see you in that getup.'

'Wonderful, Ms Greene. Very liberating.'

'Loli. Remember?'

'Sorry. Loli.'

'What you got in your hand, Frankie?'

'My old heart.'

'That's real special, quite a feat.'

'When you are in Galaxy, there is absolutely no need for this worn-out machine. Organs are obsolete.'

'I bet. So, Frankie, what's it like?'

'Indescribable, Ms Greene. I am without language on the topic.'

'Have you run into my folks?'

'Your mother is planting the most colorful garden.'

'You sure it's my mother?'

'Oh yes. There is no mistaking her. Lovely orb, she is.'

'How 'bout Pop?'

'Seeding. The man is a master seeder.'

'Nothing's changed.'

'When will you be arriving?'

'You tell me.'

'Soon enough. We'll let you know. Your sister will be first up on the docket …'

'Oh no!' I gasp.

'Dear dear Ms Greene, your heart … it appears to be breaking. I am so sorry. That heart of yours … quite a beating. One thing you can be sure of, as long as you are alive …'

Wake up! Now!

I will never again sleep in our Beechwood home. The house is on the market. Dina has hired Moshe's Moving Company. How she intends to fit one more object in her Park Avenue apartment is beyond me?

What a dream. Can't shake it. Hope I go first. Stop thinking. Pay attention. Listen to the Rabbi. Look at Ralph, Dina and the kids. Isn't that a family portrait? And Mrs B. She is luminescent. Brrr. It's fucking freezing here. Sharon Gardens Cemetery, where the Jews are buried. One more example of discrimination. Really. I bet Dina is plenty pissed off. She actually convinced herself they would be open on Thanksgiving. I told her the place was going to be closed. Christ! It's a national holiday, the great American Dream Day. No wonder Pop loved it. Oh nice. What a pretty headstone. Her stone on the other hand needs some work. Cemeteries! Obsolete if you ask me … Like Willwrite's heart. No. No heart is obsolete.

Glad that's over. Stand here for one more minute. Let the others leave first. I'm not having a good time. What was I expecting? Stand-up comedy? Dina's crying again.

She grabs my hand. 'Wasn't that a beautiful ceremony?'

'Moving. Very moving.'

'Aren't you glad you came home?'

'I am.'

'I miss you so much.' There she goes again. 'You don't know how much I love you. You're my family. You're inside here.' Dina points to her heart. 'Forever.'

Her love breaks me apart. For the first time in months, I hyperventilate. Dina is frightened.

'Breathe, Loli. Come on now. Breathe.'

'I am. I ... I had ... dream ... this ... morning ... I ... don't want ... to ... be here ... without you ... I don't.'

'You won't. You won't.'

'Everybody dies. Everybody you love ... Please don't die. Please.' I sob like Susan Hayward in *I'll Cry Tomorrow*.

'Have I told you about the night you were born? Grandma ...'

'... I am so sorry ... I ... I'm so sorry she got sick. I didn't mean for her to get sick. It just happened. And you loved me anyway. You always loved me ... always.'

Dina cradles my face in her hands. I look deep into those close-to-the-bone blue eyes of hers. 'Loli. Listen to me. I didn't always love you. I hated you. I hated you so much, that ... after you came home from the hospital ...' She can hardly speak. 'You cried and cried and cried so loud. No one knew what to do with you. She didn't know what to do. I remember her on the bed with you. Your face, the sheets. You were suffocating.' She shrieks like my mother must have done. *Dina!!! Dina!!!* I ran into the bedroom. She was rocking back and forth in the bed, like a crazy person. She had you turned upside down on your stomach, sheets over your head, on the bed; suffocating, you were suffocating, screaming at the top of your lungs. You kept screaming. She kept rocking. You wouldn't stop. I put my hand over your mouth, so you would finally shut up ... I wanted you to go away forever and ever. I kept my hand over your mouth. I knew you couldn't breathe. 'Like this, Mommy? Like this? Is this what you want?' And I pushed your face into the sheets, so you couldn't breathe, so she would be happy … again.' Dina becomes hysterical. 'She stopped rocking … saw what I was doing to you. *Dina! NO! Bad, bad, naughty girl!!! … very very naughty girl!!!* I dropped you on the rug, ran out of the room, heard her get out of bed. She picked you up. You wailed. She moaned as she sang *Rock-a-bye-baby! Hush-a-bye-baby! mm-mm-mm-mm-mm!* Over and over, again and again. It was so horrible. After that, she never let me hold you. She told Pop on me. He hired round-the-clock help to make sure you would both be taken care of.' Dina turns away. 'I'm so sorry. I'm so sorry.'

'Dina. Turn around. Hold me. You can hold me as tight as you want. I won't die. I won't scream. You are so silly; silly girl carrying a rock inside your heart. You know, a secret like that could kill you?' I whisper in her ear, 'Guess what? It's not your secret anymore. I know about it now.'

'I'm so ashamed.'

'You had a million reasons for hating me. But, look at us. We're together. We're alive. Look around you. Look at the thousands of gravestones. Generations of secrets, lies, shame, misunderstandings. If only we could forgive ourselves for being human. Wouldn't that be a relief?' We gaze at the graves of our parents, their parents, and all of their parents before. 'You know something?'

'What?'

'All these years … You have been so nice to me. Now, I understand why. Nothing like a little guilt to make a big girl feel like she's responsible for an entire family. Man oh man, it is time for someone else to take over that thankless role … Are you looking at me? Absolutely not!' … Dina hugs me, really hugs me. 'Come with me. Over there, by that footstone. Take my hand. Step on a crack, break the pattern's back. Come on now. We have no time to waste. Time enough has been wasted.'

As it turns out, my mother was, and still is the only one without a secret. Maybe she had one. She might have been jealous of Mrs B.'s garden after all. Wouldn't that be the living end?

My secret is no secret. I never wanted to say goodbye to my mother. By keeping her alive, she would always be with me. By letting her go, she would, we would, be free. Goodbye Mom. I have a lesson plan to put together for next week.

The End

Acknowledgements

Thank you: Ron Portante, Jill Robinson, Elizabeth Kendall, Laurie Liss, Jan Werner, Margot Harley, Gillian Freeman, Edward Thorpe, James Nunn, Angeline Rothermundt, Gary Pulsifer, Daniela de Groote and all at Arcadia Books.

A special thanks to the students in the classrooms across the United States.